TERRA FIRMA
A NOVEL

ANDREA DEJEAN

Terra Firma
Text copyright © 2025 Andrea Dejean
Edited by Lisa Diane Kastner

All rights reserved.
Published in North America and Europe by Running Wild Press. Visit Running Wild Press at www.runningwildpress.com. Educators, librarians, book clubs (as well as the eternally curious), go to www.runningwildpress.com.

Paperback ISBN: 978-1-960018-82-3
eBook ISBN: 978-1-960018-83-0

For Alain

... a journey is painful for the one who has to remain behind, but more beautiful than it can ever be for the traveler

Carlos Fuentes
The Old Gringo

CHAPTER ONE

The day after my cousin Treat ran away, my life took on a stillness that descended over me like a glass dome, separating me from a world I could still see but from which I felt isolated. Treat and I had always lived next door to one another. Our fathers were brothers. His family's farm and ours were literally side-by-side. We spent most of our free time together. During that summer of 1967, he'd agreed to let me hang around with him and a friend his age, Erik, if I didn't ask any All-Time Stupid Questions. Treat would turn sixteen in October and I would turn fourteen in March. He tormented me mercilessly, the way an older brother might, and I loved him like the sibling I'd never had.

When I went downstairs that morning, my parents were already busy with their usual chores. I could hear Ma scrubbing something in the bathroom, and could only deduce from the frantic rhythm coming from behind the door that she was working out her sadness and pain over Treat's disappearance on the rust-colored water stain near the drain in the tub. Just as I was sitting down at the kitchen table to try to force myself to eat a bowl of cereal, Pa came into the house to get a drink of cold water. He didn't say anything as he walked past me on his way to the kitchen sink, but tousled my hair with as much affection as I had ever known him to show. At the time, I almost wished he had hit me for not having told them about Treat's plans to run away. It was the kind of comeuppance I felt I deserved and might have even brought about a catharsis; instead, his gesture was so full of love, understanding, and forgiveness it brought tears to my eyes.

I think now that during those first few days we all still had the hope someone would soon call to tell Uncle Will, "We got your boy, here. He's a bit worn out, but he's fine."

But, as the summer came to an end, that call still hadn't come and the hope it would started to fade.

As time passed, it also became pretty clear the relationship between my family and Uncle Will's would never be the same. There were no more evening gatherings around the picnic table we shared like before Treat disappeared, talking and eating slices of watermelon, watching fireflies and looking for UFOs. After he took off, no one shouted anymore across the small space that separated the two houses asking for a hand or to borrow a tool or to see if anyone needed anything from town. Aunt Sally especially seemed to avoid us. She even went so far as to put curtains on her kitchen windows, the ones that looked out onto our house. Anything to block us out. I felt she was particularly determined to hate me. Maybe she didn't really hate me, but I was sure she blamed me for Treat's disappearance. At the very least, I was a constant, thorny reminder that Treat had chosen to leave and I, keeping what was, perhaps, a foolish promise to him, had chosen not to say anything to anyone about what he was planning.

There was still no sign of Treat when school began again in the fall, nor word from him. It was awful riding my bike alone to St. Frederick's on the first morning. When I walked into assembly, the other students became strangely quiet. Word had spread about Treat having run off. Mothers must have warned their children not to ask me about it. Because no one did. Nor did they ask me about much of anything else. My schoolmates, like Aunt Sally, avoided me. I slid past them like a magnet with the same charge: identical, yet repellent. The forbidden question in their eyes. The painful truth souring my tongue. *Yes, I could have stopped him...* I missed him more than ever then. I had never really developed any other friendships, what with Treat right there and the rest of the world at what seemed like such a distance. Like most rural districts, the farms in our community were spaced far apart. Life had taught me early that the things in that space, family and chores, were going to take up a lot of my attention. It was an important lesson to learn.

Another difference that fall was my oldest cousin Ruth Anne enrolled in the nearby community college. Between her classes and the time she spent at the library and with her newfound friends, she was hardly ever home. With Treat gone and Ruth Anne caught up in her new academic life, Katie, my youngest cousin, closed up inside herself and, according to Uncle Will, spent most of her free time in their spare room, sewing. We hardly ever saw her. In fact, Uncle Will was the only one we ever saw outside, who still talked to me and treated Ma respectfully. He even took a cup of coffee in our kitchen from time to time. Of course, he and Pa were still pretty close and, sometimes when I came home from school for lunch, I would see them talking out in our shared vegetable patch, one leaning on a hoe and the other just standing there with his hands on his hips. Blood is thicker than mud, as they say.

As the school year slowly picked up speed, I adapted to my new life the way you do when you don't have any choice. In any case, things would quickly get worse. On December 7th, Ma found a lump in her armpit. The memorial tributes to Pearl Harbor presented on the radio punctuated by replays of live wartime broadcasts, which normally would have fascinated me, seemed like a personal assault. Pa finally begged me to turn the radio off.

My folks met when my pa was in Europe serving in the Army during World War II. Ma was born and raised on a farm outside Bastogne in Belgium and must have been about 19-years old at the time. It was just after the Battle of the Bulge, a strange wartime moniker that used to make me and Treat giggle because we, of course, knew nothing about what it meant to be in a war. She had just gone out to check on the last cow the family owned, a heifer, when their house was hit by a German mortar. She lost everyone in her family. If she hadn't gone out to the barn, she would have been killed as well. Pa told us the story many times of how he pushed open the barn door and found her there, just singing softly and looking up at him, like she'd been expecting him to come and find her. Both said it was love at first sight.

Before I knew it, it was Christmas. Pa and I didn't really celebrate it although we did decorate a tree in Ma's room hoping it would make her feel better. I think it only made the two of us feel worse. It was clear my ma was dying. One might have thought such a situation would have brought the families back together. It was true Uncle Will seemed about as devastated by it as my pa, but there was only a slight, almost unnoticeable respite in Aunt Sally's attitude towards us. Loss understands loss, I guess, but is less moved by it.

Had I been paying more attention, I might have learned, as I eventually did from later reading, that a violent storm had shaken Puerto Rico that very same month. It wiped out part of the shanty town near San Juan I have come to realize must have been where the father of the family we had visited the fateful day Treat decided to run away had lived as a boy, working as a child laborer in a tannery.

I can't say I really remember much else from that winter, other than there was still no sign of Treat. I went to school and came home and hunkered down into my chores. With Ma being sick, I learned to do a million things I never would have admitted to anyone, especially Treat who surely would have teased me about it, like clean and iron and sew on buttons, although, I guess, folks must have figured. I even learned to be a pretty good cook, though it was mostly just standard, roughhouse fare like burgers and steaks and *chili con carne* with the *habichuelas* that always made me think of that traveling family, eating and dancing and playing music near their run-down camper on a sorry spit of land in the middle of nowhere. "Jurutungo" is the word the beautiful daughter, Celia, used to describe it: somewhere that is nowhere. In fact, I thought of them a fair amount that winter with the snow piling up outside, wondering if they were breathing in the balmy air of Puerto Rico – and if Treat was with them. When I finished my chores, I studied the map of Puerto Rico in the *Universal Standard Encyclopedia*, trying to keep my loneliness at bay. Pa had picked up a seasonal job at one of the nurseries near Saginaw helping to offload Christmas trees and set them up in the sales lot and they had kept him on after the holidays. We needed the money. A lot of Ma's medical bills weren't covered by our insurance and the profits from the sugar beet crop that year were not at all what Pa and Uncle Will had hoped so they were even second-guessing their decision last spring to turn all the fields over to sugar beets the following season. Ma was house-bound by then and, more often than not, in bed. I could tell being away from Ma during those working hours was killing my pa, physically and emotionally, because he raced into their bedroom as soon as he stepped through the door and I usually had to call him three times before he came out for supper.

For me, it was like we had already lost her. The wrung-out flask of spoiled skin was not the bright, energetic woman who had been my ma. That woman was gone. She died some every time I walked into her room; I died some every time I walked out. I sat with her as little as possible during those last few months. It was easier that way. Pa said she understood.

Ma's cancer took her from us on St. Valentine's Day, which in 1968 fell on a Wednesday. I remember the day of the week because I had shop class on Wednesdays. That year, we made heart-shaped key racks as Valentine's Day gifts for our mothers. The shop part included having to master using the band-saw in order to cut the curved hearts out of pieces of scrap wood. I'm certain my shop teacher didn't know as he explained the safety procedures for using the saw that, at probably that very moment, my ma was breathing in her last breath. I think I did, though. As I guided my piece of wood towards the blade, I let my fingers get dangerously close to its serrated edge. In my mind, I even imagined it cutting into my pink flesh and blood the color of crushed cranberries gushing out. The teacher marked me down a grade for being careless.

The rest of the winter seemed especially long after her death. Pa moved like a shadow around the house and I think things might not have been much different had I been living alone. Almost one month to the day after Ma's death, I got an exemption by the State of Michigan to get my driver's license a year early. Under different circumstances, such an occasion might have thrilled me. Pa had made a special appeal saying he needed me to run errands for him. And seeing how family relations were strained, there might be no one else available to drive in case of an emergency. So, on my fifteenth birthday on the Ides of March, I got a driver's license practically bestowed on me by only having to take an abbreviated written exam and doing a quick turn around the IGA Supermarket's parking lot. The IGA was probably the best proving ground for me in any case, since the grocery store was the destination I most often drove to in our sky blue Fairlane.

The spring of 1968 crept up on me in much the same way: without my much noticing it. I guess now I might recognize what I was going through then as shock, pure and simple. I moved through time and space like a sleepwalker, and probably only someone who knew me well could see I wasn't completely conscious. That person should have been Pa. Instead, he was my partner somnambulist, not any more aware of the world outside the edges of his aching heart than I was. The feeling of not being right with the world got reinforced every time I came home from somewhere like baseball practice and called out without thinking, "Ma! I'm home!" or got up in the morning expecting a pot of oatmeal to be waiting for me on the stove. Usually there was only Pa's dirty cup in the kitchen sink, instead. Pa had pretty much stopped eating altogether, stringing together his days on strong cups of coffee and an obligatory bite or two of my cooking in the evening. At supper we both remained silent. Nothing we could say would bring Ma back, so there was simply nothing to say. We orbited around each other without ever really connecting as though we were afraid any contact, rather than providing comfort, would only bruise each of us further. I probably should have tried harder to get through to Pa. But I figured if he wasn't mad at me for not having told him about Treat's plan to run away, he was probably mad at whoever took Ma away from us and the best thing I could probably do was to just let him be mad.

As a result, being at home, a place I had always taken for the most comfortable of havens, got to be pretty near unbearable. Ma was gone, but I felt her presence everywhere. Pa was there, but gone. The other farmhouse might as well have been separated from us by a wall of mortar and brick, rather than just Aunt Sally's stony wall of silence. Pa and Uncle Will were still close, but I knew Pa would never put Uncle Will into the position of having to choose between his brother and his wife. Little by little, their relationship began to flicker and fade. I hadn't set foot inside Aunt Sally and Uncle Will's house since the morning Treat's disappearance was discovered. And, finally, I didn't know where Treat was, but I did know he had gone there without me. I couldn't help but believe that he had gone off to Puerto Rico, seduced in the same way I had been by that magical, imagined place with music to its very name. Memories of our afternoon eating and dancing with Celia and her family washed over me like cooling, blue-green waters, blew salty breaths of *lomo asado* against my bare skin, chimed the word *"habichuelas"* in the sultry stillness, surprised my senses like hot pepper on fried plantains, and filled my ears with a melody that caressed my body enough to make me dizzy; in other words, those memories blew the elements of air, fire, water, and earth into the void where I had been living. And by touching me with those elements, had given me the hope that somewhere there was a place that, through the naked and pulsating rhythm of its daily life, might transform me.

I don't remember exactly how the idea of going over to the county library first came to me. I wasn't a particularly outstanding student and finding refuge in a place filled with books wasn't an idea that should have naturally occurred to me. I think it must have been because I figured, knowing folks in Millarsburg well enough, that I'd have the place pretty much to myself on a Saturday morning, especially after the weather turned nice. There'd be no one around to tell me, once again, how much Ma was missed at the sewing circle or how people used to love hearing the way she said "*Goot* morning" when she stepped into the IGA. There would be no one to ask me if we had news from Treat. Even if somebody were there, they'd have to respect the golden rule of silence the spinster librarian, Darby Millar, imposed like martial law.

Chance would have it that while I was stumbling along stupidly in the "Reference" section during my first visit, trying hard to pretend I had some pressing business at the library, I noticed *Granger's World Atlas*. By then I had become convinced my alter ego lived and flourished on the island of Puerto Rico, that my sister soul, separated from me like a twin given up for adoption at birth, was at peace with itself in the gentle climate of the Caribbean. I picked up the atlas the way I sometimes lifted Ma's hand-held mirror from her dressing table and held it to my face as though to see if, finally, the manly signs of a beard had started to reveal themselves on my chin.

I opened the atlas to the map of North America that included Alaska, Greenland, and Canada. I examined the map closely, and, for the first time, really noticed the lines that slice up the globe, the Tropics of Capricorn and Cancer, degrees of longitude and latitude, time zones. Just east of Alaska I traced the date line, the boundary dividing today from yesterday and tomorrow. If I had lived near the date line, I thought, I would have carried Ma across it to keep her alive a little longer. I would have raced across it to have had more time to decide how to stop Treat from running away.

After that first visit, whenever I had a moment or two of my own, I went back to the library to look at the atlas. By studying it, I began to realize that time and place are concepts, and how by naming things we make them real. On subsequent visits, I quickly opened to the map of the Caribbean Islands and the by-then-already familiar shape of Puerto Rico. I repeated the name *Puerto Rico, Puerto Rico* in my mind like a mantra. And, like a mantra, it had the effect of hypnotizing me.

It's a funny thing, though; while I had my nose in the atlas, the world kept turning without me. For one thing, Father Wilhelm was suddenly and quietly transferred to a parish in Ypsilanti. I learned about it only after the fact when the new priest, Father John, came around to introduce himself.

And another interesting thing happened. Treat's friend Erik, who had been with us the afternoon we visited Celia and her family, started working for The Bauer Boys at the old Sinclair station.

The Bauer Boys had always been our arch enemies even though they were bigger and tougher than we were and we mostly just practiced "hating" them from a distance. We didn't really hate them, I guess. We were just jealous of what we thought was their free-wheeling life. They weren't farm folks, but lived on a small lot in one of those shiny silver trailer homes, the kind that looks like a bullet, they and their pa had built on to and around until finally the trailer was surrounded by a house, like a yolk inside an egg. Their pa worked a lot of overtime at the Ace Tool and Die in Saginaw and their ma – well, folks said mostly she drank.

No one really knows if The Bauer Boys ever officially graduated from high school. I don't think anyone could ever really figure out what grade they were supposed to be in since they hardly ever went to school and no one forced them to since they were both quick with a knife or a fist, and the county services lady had apparently given up trying to talk to their ma about it. Mike, the elder brother, practically had a full mustache by the time he was twelve, but rumor had it for his twentieth birthday the school board awarded him enough credits to graduate after a visitor from the Michigan chapter of the NEA mistook him for a teacher. Ed, the younger brother, graduated the same year thanks to bulked up credits for shop class and extra credits for Driver's Ed.

But no one could say The Boys, as they were known around town, weren't without their talents. Their father, who basically seemed like a decent guy, must have despaired for his boys, knowing their ma had never really looked after them and they had early on learned to live by their wits. So, he threw anything at them that had a motor, used to have a motor, or could accommodate one and hoped it would grab their interest and keep them out of any real trouble. For the most part, his plan worked except for the occasional speeding ticket or noise violation. The yard in front of the Bauer trailer was full of rusted-out car parts and dismantled engines, with a lawnmower and an outboard motor or two thrown into the mix. By the time the events I have begun to relate had started changing the course of my life, The Bauer Boys had already learned their way around enough engines to take over the Sinclair gas station in Black River, the next town over, after a triple bypass had coerced the former owner into early retirement.

The hostility between Erik and his pa had always been an open secret and seemed to burn hotter than ever that spring, so no one was especially surprised to hear that Erik didn't want to work full-time with his parents at Roth's Feed and Seed after graduation. But working at the Sinclair station with The Bauer Boys was another issue altogether. I don't think anyone had ever seen Erik with so much as a screwdriver in his hand, much less anything heavier. And thin and frail as he was, you could hardly imagine him jacking up a car and changing a tire or getting his skinny fingers full of grease. In fact, he didn't seem to care a flip about cars, although he did take his ma's car out sometimes, apparently going for long drives but never telling anybody where he went.

The surprising thing was his job with The Boys seemed to work out the best for everyone. The Boys took care of the mechanics and the heavy work, and Erik pumped gas. He was clean-cut and courteous and had such a gracious way of serving people that business picked up. The Boys had hired a part-time bookkeeper who came in once a fortnight; but, otherwise, Erik kept an eye on the day-to-day accounts. Erik had also cleaned up around the station, planted some flowers in the dividers between the pumps and at the curb, and put geraniums in window boxes by the office. He even re-arranged the office and gave it a good wiping down. He cleaned the kitchenette in the back, replaced some rusted out parts on the old stove, and got it working again. He and The Boys started taking their midday meals at the station with Erik cooking for them all. Folks joked that Erik had finally found a place where he was appreciated, and The Boys finally had the mother they'd grown up without.

I saw him whenever I took our Fairlane in to fill her up. By that time, I'd more or less decided to forgive Erik for spilling the beans to Aunt Sally about our afternoon with Treat visiting Celia and her family, or at least try to forget since, as I was coming to learn, everybody has their reasons for just about everything. I even offered now and again to pick something up for him and The Boys' lunch at the supermarket. He always looked at me a long time and then thanked me slowly, but he never asked me to get him anything. He said he'd just as soon go himself. He said folks needed to see a man in a supermarket, especially in our little town. I didn't really understand what he meant at the time. Sometimes, he'd even give me an extra gallon of gas just like that, for no reason. I'd stopped "hating" The Bauer Boys, too, although I mostly "hated" them because Treat seemed to hate them. In fact, I learned to respect them since they seemed like hard workers. They asked nothing of no one. And they hung together, too. I was jealous of that. And I was also jealous of how much they seemed in their element in that sagging corner garage. Covered with grease, caught up in what they were doing, I had the impression they never even realized that there was a larger, better world out there.

I didn't know if the world out there was better or not. I had only just begun to *truly* understand there was a world out there myself, as strange as it may sound. Now that I had, though, I became nearly obsessed with studying the way it was put together.

* * *

I was sitting at the county library one Saturday morning pouring over *Granger's World Atlas* like I had taken to doing. Darby Millar actually nodded to me when I walked in. I figured she was getting pretty used to my presence there on mornings when other kids were out playing stick ball or riding bikes or meeting up on the corner of Woodbridge and Main and daring each other to smoke a cigarette right there in front of everybody. Most kids said Miss Darby had a mean streak in her a mile wide, but I'd never seen it. Mostly she ignored me and went about her business. But that day she came up to where I was sitting, staring at page twenty-seven. That was the page on which there was a detailed map of Puerto Rico. I didn't see her come up or I might have turned the page so she wouldn't see the smudges or the little tear in one corner I had put there fingering the page on previous visits. If she noticed anything, she didn't say so. To my surprise, she pulled out the chair next to me and sat down.

"If I didn't know better, I'd think you were trying to memorize that book," she said.

When she spoke quietly her voice had a trembling quality which was surprisingly touching. I didn't quite know what to say, but Pa had taught me not answering people just wasn't respectful.

"No, ma'am. I just think it's pretty," I answered. What an All-Time Stupid thing to say. Treat would have been in stitches over that one.

"Think so?" she asked.

I conceded that maybe *pretty* wasn't the right word. But it certainly was unusual.

"That's the point, I think," she said. "The point of the atlas. Mr. Granger did it to be provocative. He played around with color and scale, changing emphasis. He always said he'd done it on purpose. To make people remember they were looking at representations and not reality. At *someone else's* representation of reality. Those were his exact words, as I recall."

"You've spoken to him?" I asked. It was incredible.

"Well, yes. Many times," she said. "The first time was at a lecture he gave. Here, in fact, in this very library. An extremely long time ago."

It was too much for me to believe. The man whose book had become my constant companion had once been in the county library. Maybe he had even sat down at the very table where I was sitting.

"You know. His book wasn't very well received in '48 when it came out. It was a little too risky, I suppose. Nick bought back most of the copies and then burned them. The one you have in your hands is one of the few remaining." She smiled.

My heart pinched a little. I thought of the smudges, the fine tear.

"If it weren't for you, I might have put it up for safekeeping a long time ago."

"He never did another atlas?" I asked.

"Oh no. Never practiced the art again, as far as I know, although he was still a relatively young man. Only fifty-one when it came out. He did some sculpture and lived off of his Army pension. Pretty much a hermit these days."

Miss Darby looked off into the distance.

"You mean he's still alive?"

"Oh, yes."

"He must be pretty old."

"Not as old as all that, young man," she said, smiling again.

I'd never seen her smile quite so much. Miss Darby patted my hand. I noticed the brown spots on her paper-thin skin.

"In fact, he's the reason I came over to talk to you. Poor, dear Nick is without a reader again. You see, Mr. Granger is virtually blind. He sees only shadows. You can imagine what a terrible trial it must be for someone with as active and inquisitive a mind as his. Anyway, I've learned recently from his nephew, with whom I have remained in correspondence over the years, that the reader and caregiver he had arranged for his uncle has not, let's say, worked out. You must understand Mr. Granger is a bit of a character!" She laughed gaily. "His nephew asked me if I knew of someone who might be able to help out a bit. A few hours a day. Over the summer. Until a new situation can be arranged. He's offering a more than respectable salary." She looked at me warmly. "Of course, I immediately thought of you. The way you're always looking at this atlas. Plus, he lives over in Painted Creek. It would be just a hop and a skip."

She was right. Painted Creek was the next town over from Black River and along with Millarsburg would form the triangle of my existence over the next year. The town was named after a little sliver of a stream in whose bed were some ore deposits that gave it a coppery tone before it crashed into Black River and lost all of its color.

"There is one slight drawback, perhaps. Mr. Granger would like the person come around ten o'clock and leave sometime early in the afternoon, say about two o'clock. So, it's right in the middle of the day and not very easy for most people to fit into their schedule." She settled her faded brown eyes on me. "What do you think?"

I didn't know what to think. One thing was certain: it would get me away from the farms. But I'd never taken care of a blind person before and didn't know how, which worried me. Plus, Mr. Granger, as interesting a man as he might be, didn't sound like an easy fellow to be around.

"I think I need to talk to my pa about it."

More than two weeks passed, and I still hadn't found the right moment or screwed up enough courage to talk to Pa about Darby Millar asking me to become a reader for Mr. Granger. He was either out working in the fields or pretty much holed up in his office at the back of the house, even taking to sleeping in there, curled up all night in a faded pair of jeans and a worn, plaid shirt on an old couch which was too short for him but that he preferred to the bed in the master bedroom. I don't think he was purposely trying to ignore me or be mean or anything, I think Ma's death took just about everything out of him that used to be in there. He wafted around the house so much like a wispy ghost I didn't even try to touch him for fear my fingers would pass right through.

And I know that he and Uncle Will were worried about the farms. Little did we know when they talked about turning everything over to sugar beets in early '67 that the winter we would have later that year would be one of the earliest and hardest we'd had in a long time. I remember on October 27th, 1967, Ironwood in the Upper Peninsula got a whole 18 inches of snow. That day was Treat's 16th birthday, though, of course, we didn't celebrate it.

* * *

Then, before I knew it, school was out. After I'd cleaned out my locker and turned in my books and said goodbye to a few of the guys I didn't think I'd get to see over the summer, I took my time getting back to the farms trying to figure out just what on earth I was going to do for two whole months if I didn't read for Mr. Granger. I was just working up a way to talk to Pa when he suggested I get a ball and our mitts so we could play catch.

Knowing Pa the way I did, I knew this was a bad sign. Pa used playing catch the way some people use the bottle: to drown out other things. We used to play catch after he and Ma had had an argument, for example, or when the price of sugar beets dropped just as we got ours planted. We stood in the side yard that pretty June afternoon, and he stung fast balls into my thin mitt so hard they brought hot tears to my eyes.

"I got a job," I blurted out. "For the summer." He stopped pitching and looked at me in such a confused way I couldn't quite figure out what was going through his mind.

"What kind of job?"

"Reading. For somebody. A blind guy. Miss Millar down at the county library recommended me for it. He's kind of famous, I guess. He made an atlas and everything, before he lost his sight. I've seen it down at the library. It's a little weird." *Dang!* I thought. Maybe I'd said the wrong thing. "But Miss Millar said that for its time, it was – ." I couldn't remember the word she had used.

"Innovative?" my pa suggested.

Maybe that was it.

"It'd only be about four hours a day. Ten to two. Nearby. In

Painted Creek. I'll be back in time to help with chores. And I can ride my bike. Won't be using gas or nothing."

I didn't want him to think I was trying to get away from him or the farms, though I guess I was in a way, what with Ma gone and him so hard to reach. Or trying to shirk my duties at home, because I wasn't trying to do that, either. But every once in a while when the wind was coming out of a certain direction, I could swear I heard the crystalline notes of a double-stringed guitar like the one Celia's brother Carlos had played that day.

"And I'll be making money. I'll be able to buy my own clothes and stuff for school next year. Maybe even save a little money for – " I stopped short.

He steadied his gaze on me and the word came tumbling out.

" – someday."

"Is this something you really want?"

Funny, I'd never asked myself that question. What did I want? I wanted Ma alive. I wanted Aunt Sally not to hate me. I wanted Treat back. I wanted to circle the globe again and again, crossing back over the date line until things were like they used to be.

Miss Millar arranged for Mr. Sellers to come up from Detroit to introduce me to his uncle. We met at the county library. For some reason, Mr. Sellers looked just like I expected: balding and going to fat, wearing a crumpled gray suit, and smelling of stale tobacco. I guessed him to be in his early fifties, although it was hard to tell. He was pasty pale the way people who live in the city sometimes are and looked to me like he needed a good night's sleep. He was polite enough, but seemed to be in a hurry.

I followed him to Painted Creek in the Fairlane. There is a small liberal arts college in Painted Creek known mostly for the spring crop of hippies it turns out onto the central green every year. It was summer, so the green was relatively deserted, except for a few holdovers who probably didn't have anywhere else to go, not even to a place Celia had called *Jurutungo*, somewhere that is nowhere. Mr. Sellers pulled to a stop by the green. The neighborhood looked kind of run down. Most of the houses seemed like they could have used some fixing up. A couple of them had stereo speakers in their open, screenless windows. Rock music blared at me from several different directions. Another house had a sagging couch out in the dusty front yard. A tall, skinny fellow had slung himself into it like it was a hammock. He was drinking a beer.

Mr. Sellers stopped in front of one of the older, stone houses. It had a big front room window and I could see the living room through the open curtains. Leafy green plants showed dark against the room's clean white walls. A brightly-colored globe of some sort lit up one corner of the room.

"This is where my uncle lives," said Mr. Sellers.

Nice. Way nicer than I had expected. What I liked best about it was that it had a wide porch with a railing that wrapped all the way around the front of the house. On the porch there were two cane-bottomed rockers. I imagined myself in one of them, reading quietly to Mr. Granger who was not rocking, but tilted slightly towards me, listening with all his might. I smiled and looked back and forth between the house and Mr. Sellers. He followed my gaze.

"No, not there," he said. "Actually, that belongs to my uncle, but we rent it out to a professor from the college in order to bring in a little revenue. My uncle lives down there."

He pointed to what looked like a crawl space under the porch. There was a cavernous entrance beneath the porch stairs leading to a basement. It looked just like the kind of entranceway where you were likely to smack your head going in. The basement itself was virtually windowless except for two rectangular openings, up high. I noticed both of the small, tilting windows were closed. The room behind them was in darkness. The place was right out of a fairy tale. Mr. Sellers was reading my mind.

"My uncle is a little bit of a gnome," he said, "if that's what you're thinking. But more bark than bite. Usually, that is."

Then he shoved out his hand.

"Nice to have met you. Good luck," he said. "Let me know how it goes."

He started to take his leave.

"Hey, wait a minute. Aren't you going in with me?"

"Frankly, I think it's probably better if you go alone. Don't worry. He's expecting you. You see, my uncle and I don't get along very well. As he says himself, he can't stand the "sight" of me. Plus, he knows I don't really know you any better than he does. Darby Millar was the one who recommended you as a reader. He wouldn't accept my introducing you as anything other than what it is: a hypocrisy."

He turned to go. "By the way, be careful not to bump your head going in," he said, over his shoulder.

I went down the steps, careful to lower my head, and was about to reach for the doorbell when the door opened. I could just see the outline of a stumpy figure framed in the shadows. I squinted, trying to make out his face. A gruff voice called out to me.

"Are you coming in or are you going to stand there all day staring at me?"

I took a step forward.

"Bad enough I have to listen to you and that nephew of mine jawing to beat the band. What a racket! A fellow like me can't get any peace. I may be blind, but God – if he exists, and I doubt it! – wasn't kind enough to make me deaf, too," he said. "Come in here where I can get a look at you."

The old man turned into the obscurity of the room, leaning heavily on whatever was handy – first a stool, then a stack of old newspapers, then off to the right, a drafting table. I saw in the feeble light coming through the door that he had the curved head of a hollow aluminum cane, the dime store kind, hooked through one of the few remaining belt loops of his trousers which was not broken and sticking straight out like the others. The cane banged against him like a sword when he walked. He pointed to the door jamb.

"Go ahead. You can turn 'em on. I finally paid the blasted bill, but I think the bulb in the main room needs changing."

I slid my hand up and down the greasy wall until I found the light switch and turned it on. In fact, the naked bulb hanging in the main section of the apartment had burned out. But another bulb which lit up an alcove that served as the kitchen and worked off the same switch came on.

"But how did you know the light was burned out?"

The old man turned and made his way back to me slowly. I could have sworn he was looking at me. He raised his short arms, palms flat to the ceiling, fingers spread open.

"Have you never heard of the supreme heat wave sensitivity of the blind?" he asked me. I could tell from the way he had asked the question that he was not expecting an answer. Kind of the way Treat used to ask me questions.

Slowly, his arms still raised, he began turning in a circle.

"The organism of the visually-impaired person learns to compensate for the loss or absence of vision by developing an almost supernatural sensitivity to waves and wave particles so that anything that exists in a wave – light, sound, heat – is felt, even when it is at very low levels, in a very tactile way by the blind person."

He combed the air above his shoulder blades with an open hand, still turning ever so slowly and with much difficulty.

"Yesterday, I noticed when I was fixing myself a sandwich in the kitchen that the waves were caressing my back. But I didn't feel them a few minutes later when I came over here – " he pointed to his work table, "to sit down and eat it. So, I surmised the light bulb must have burned out."

I was dumb-struck.

"Hah-hah!" the old man shouted. He drew his aluminum cane and smacked it on the cement floor. There was no rubber tip where there should have been one, so the cane made a clanging sound. The sound seemed to please him.

"Greenhorn!" he said. "How do *you* think I knew the light was out?"

I was so embarrassed, I couldn't answer. Besides, I figured he had just told me.

"I heard it blow, you ninny. Like any other man would."

He wobbled back to his work table.

"Listen, youngster. I don't know who you are or why my old friend Darby Millar, who usually has pretty good sense, sent you around. But I can tell you that if you think because I'm blind I don't have my wits about me, then we've either got a long road ahead of us or you can just turn around and march right out of here. And don't bump your head!"

I looked around. Other than the drawing table, there wasn't much else of consequence in the room. There was a wooden, desk-style chair with a rounded back not far from the table. The only other thing to sit on was the stool, a barstool, which for some reason was in the middle of the room, positioned between the alcove and the front door. I remember thinking that, if I decided to stay, at least we'd both have a place to sit. Or, I guessed, I could sit on one of the many stacks of yellowed newspaper piled all around, for what reason, I didn't know. A single, army-issue cot in the far corner was covered with a well-used woolen blanket. Also army issue, I gathered. Rolls of what appeared to be poster board stood curling in the corners of the room or sat tucked in scrolls on the table, chair, and floor. It looked as though they were trying to hide from me. What I guessed to be drawing and surveying instruments lay on the table. I noticed a small pile of stones in the alcove near the back door.

"I hope we have a long road ahead of us, sir," I said. "I mean – I'd like to stay on."

Mr. Granger acted as though he hadn't heard me. "And don't go screaming at me, 'cause I don't like screaming. Or any kind of noise, for that matter. There's nothing wrong with my hearing."

"I'm not screaming, sir."

"I'm just tellin' ya."

I remember, in fact, how weak my voice sounded, as though it were coming from deep inside me and having trouble getting all the way out. I know now what it was: youth. Mr. Granger recognized it immediately.

"How old are you anyway?"

"Fifteen, sir."

His almost too-blue eyes seemed to scan the space around him. I don't know why, but I thought he'd be wearing dark glasses.

"Fifteen!"

"And almost four months, sir."

"Hmf! Probably get myself arrested for having you here. Probably against some kind of law."

"I don't think so, sir," I said, squaring my shoulders. "My cousin Ruth Anne started baby-sitting when she was – "

"Say what?"

I'd gone and done it, I thought. Said something stupid. In record time. He'd throw me out on my ear for sure.

"Hah! Baby-sitting!" he said. "There's a good one. Probably not too far from the truth, that said. Look here."

He walked over to the table and sat down stiffly in the chair. I got the feeling his legs didn't work right. I grabbed up the stool on my way over towards the table and set it down nearby, careful not to make any noise. There was a copy of a map, the *City of Painted Creek*, on the wall facing the table.

"Look at this map here."

I got back up and stepped closer.

"Find the corner of Elm and Baron Streets. Should be around here, someplace."

The old man stood up and took a step. He walked right into the stool, sending it clattering over.

"Confound it!" he yelled, rubbing his left knee. "Who put that stupid thing there?"

I picked up the stool and held it. I noticed he had the habit of asking questions which didn't necessarily need to be answered.

"Look, son," he said. "This place may look like a mess to you, but I know where everything is. Best you leave it all where it is or at least you let me know when you've moved something. Is that clear?"

"Yes, sir," I said.

"Is that thing out of my way?"

"Yes, sir."

I was still holding it.

"Why don't you put it back where it belongs? You'll find two Xs made from electrician's tape on the floor where the legs go."

I put the stool back in its place while the old man made his way over to the map.

"Now come back over here and find the corner of Elm and Baron Streets." He fingered the edge of the map halfway down the left side and then slid his forefinger across about six inches. "Should be about here."

I peeked at the map. Elm and Baron. Exactly.

"Yes, sir," I said. "Got it."

"What do you see?"

"Where, sir?"

"Where? There! At the corner of Elm and Baron!"

I looked again. Nothing.

"There's nothing there, sir."

"Nothing? Are you sure?"

"Yes, sir. There isn't anything. It's just white."

"Ah! Then, there *is* something."

"Sir?"

"You just said it. There is something there."

"The white, sir?"

"Um-hum."

"But white is nothing, sir."

"Nothing?"

"A blank," I said, searching.

"And, how would you define a blank, young man?"

His eyes tick-tocked skyward, like some crazy spring had banged loose behind them. Time passed while I looked for a good answer.

"It's an emptiness, sir. An absence."

"And you're sure there's nothing at the corner of Elm and Baron Streets – really?"

"Well," I hesitated. "I guess there probably is something there in real life like maybe a mailbox or a fire hydrant or something."

The old man nodded his head.

"In cartography, some of us tend to refer to these "blanks," as you call them, as "silences." You know, since I've become blind, I've been much more interested in speech, in words, in oral communication – and in silences. Because there's always something behind a silence. A map is like speech. It has its own symbols and signals. And it has its own silences."

He made his way back to his wooden chair and sat down again slowly.

"I happen to know," he said, "that on the corner of Elm and Baron is an old, disenfranchised Armenian Jew who sells roasted cashews from a broken-down wooden cart most afternoons. How do I know? Because he has for the past thirty years. Best roasted cashews around. As you might guess, it's not on the map."

I didn't know whether to laugh or not. I decided not to.

"I also know," he said, "because I helped to develop that map, and they wouldn't let me put him on there."

"*They* sir?"

"The powers that be."

I didn't know who that was.

"Maybe they didn't think it was important, sir."

"Precisely. What do you think is important enough to be put on a map?"

I thought of the framed map of Millarsburg in the main post office. "Schools. Churches. Railroads."

The old man tilted back the wooden chair and remained that way, leaving his legs dangling in the air.

"Well," he seemed to think for a minute. "I haven't been to school in many years. Don't have any children. Don't believe in God, so I don't go to church. And I haven't been out of this apartment – other than in my own backyard – for nearly seven years, when I started losing my sight. So, I don't need to know where the train station is because I never go anywhere."

Seven years. Nearly half of my lifetime. I could hardly imagine.

"Wait a minute," I said. "If you haven't been out of the apartment for almost seven years, how do you know that guy still sells cashews on the corner of Elm and Baron?"

The old man smiled.

"That's what I was hoping you would tell me."

He pulled a dollar out of his shirt pocket and handed it to me along with a key to the front door. "It's not far from here. Look on the map."

I thought I heard the old guy laugh when I ran out of the apartment, banging my head on the underside of the steps leading to the porch. But I'm not sure.

* * *

By the time I got back, Mr. Granger seemed to have lost interest in me. I found him at his work table hunched over a piece of black, molded plastic about a yard square. It had little mounds on it and small indentations. It looked like it had been dipped or coated so that the entire piece was lacquered into a hard, unbroken surface. He trailed his crabbed fingers over it lightly. Watching him touch the piece made me uncomfortable, almost as though I were watching him touch a woman's naked body. I left the paper sack of cashews on a corner of the table and turned to go.

"The cashews, boy."

"On your left, sir. At the edge of the table," I said.

"I know," he answered. "I can smell 'em."

I couldn't figure him. He either asked me questions he already knew the answer to or ones he didn't need answered at all. I wondered if I'd know it if he ever asked me a real question. He hadn't even asked me anything about myself. We hadn't talked about anything very important. I didn't know any more of my hours or pay than what Miss Millar had hinted at. I didn't even know, really, what was expected of me. Maybe it was just this: to run out and get his cashews and listen to his funny ideas about what should and what shouldn't be on a map. I wondered if I had made a mistake. Here I was going to spend the sunniest hours of my summer vacation in a dark cave with a blind and maybe even crazy old man. In any case, I decided I wouldn't go back the next day. It was the Fourth of July. A holiday is a holiday. I didn't owe Nicolas Granger every waking hour of my life, even if his map was about the only thing I really had other than the *Universal Encyclopedia* and my own memories of a hot afternoon to tie me to a magical place called Puerto Rico.

I stopped by to visit Erik at the Sinclair station on my way home in the same way I started doing a lot of things at that time in my life: without thinking about it beforehand. So, when Erik invited me to sit down and have an RC Cola with him, I couldn't find a reason to refuse. Sitting there with him like that allowed me to experience my own little bit of *Jurutungo* by being somewhere without being anywhere, even though I wasn't sure it was exactly where I wanted to be, either. That's how I've always pictured Purgatory. Whenever Father Wilhelm used to talk about Purgatory when I was a kid, I always figured it was up in the sky close to heaven, rather than down under the ground near hell, for some reason. In the middle of the sky someplace. That day, the gas station was for me like a white-washed little Purgatory between heaven and hell. Erik seemed happy enough to have my company. We talked a little bit about a lot of things. Baseball. Millarsburg High School. Superman. Even The Bauer Boys. Neither one of us mentioned Treat. A taboo subject even in such a middle-sky place. Mostly we sat outside on folding chairs and watched people pass. I actually enjoyed myself.

It didn't hit me until I got back to the farms: I had left the light on in Mr. Granger's place.

CHAPTER TWO

I found Pa sitting at the kitchen table looking grim-faced as he scratched numbers onto a pad of paper. From the doorway, the columns of figures reminded me of the way sugar beets are planted in wide-spaced rows. I didn't dare mention this to Pa because I could see he was working on a balance sheet and I don't think the balance was quite coming out the way he wanted. Line item. Cost. Return. Difference. Loss.

"Hey, Pa. I'm back."

I guess he didn't hear me.

The decision to turn the summer fallow over to sugar beets in the spring of 1968 was Uncle Will's and I knew Pa had been uncomfortable with it from the start. It was a risk and a big one. Sugar beets could bring in a lot of money, but they were expensive to grow and, if you couldn't afford all the machines needed to plant, weed and harvest them, the work had to be done by hand. Uncle Will and Pa had invested over fifteen hundred dollars each in a specialized 12-row planter the fateful summer Celia and her family came into our lives, figuring seeding the beets was the hardest part and that, among the eight of us, we should be able to weed and harvest without having to buy any special machines, especially since the harvester cost twice as much as the planter! They already had fertilizer stored and decided to take a chance on leaf spot rather than spend a bunch of money on chemicals Ma had argued would just "poison" the land.

Then cancer poisoned Ma and Treat running away poisoned what was left of our family life. It didn't help the mood around the farms any when my cousin Ruth Anne announced she wouldn't be returning to community college in the fall. She had joined up with a missionary group and was going off to a place in Africa Pa said was called The Congo. I looked it up in *Granger's World Atlas*. I worried maybe Ruth Anne's joining up with a missionary group was another way of running off and Pa just didn't want to tell me. What with folks running off all of the time, maybe he was afraid I'd gotten it into my head to run off, too. Maybe running off was like an epidemic of the flu. You caught it no matter how hard you tried to avoid it. Then again, maybe folks didn't necessarily run *from* something, but *to* something, to someone, to somewhere. To Celia. To Puerto Rico. The awful truth was Pa was right. I thought about going off to Puerto Rico all of the time.

* * *

For the first time in years, we didn't have anything planned for the Fourth of July holiday. Nobody had the heart for it, I guess. As far as I knew, the only one who had anything planned for the day was Ruth Anne who was going to see the fireworks in Painted Creek with her missionary group in the evening.

When I got up in the morning, the house was strangely quiet. Pa had cleared his work things from the kitchen table, but I found a broken pencil on the floor with teeth marks on the end. I nearly scolded Reilly, our Irish Setter, for chewing on it, mistakenly thinking he was lying under the table. But Pa had chained him up to the big maple tree in the side yard and, knowing Reilly, he probably would have swallowed the thing whole had he found it, not just gnawed on one end. The teeth marks were Pa's.

I took a quick peek into the garage and saw the car was there, so Pa was either out in the fields or holed up in his office where he had taken to sleeping when Ma first got sick. Far as I knew, he had never moved back into their bedroom. Instead, he slept on the couch in what was supposed to be a combination family room/office/guestroom but, as time went by, had gotten cluttered up with Pa's clothes and other things he had retrieved from their bedroom but had never had the courage to take back so when he had to do the books, like he did the day before, he did them at the kitchen table.

I nearly went over to Painted Creek first to see Mr. Granger. I figured it's no fun being alone on a holiday. In the end, I didn't go though. I couldn't face the old guy. The truth was he kind of scared me. And I knew I'd get a queasy feeling in the pit of my stomach if I pulled up and the light in his main room was still burning.

I decided to go over and see if the Sinclair station was open. I didn't need gas. I just needed some company. Erik was at the station. Alone. The Bauer Boys weren't there. They'd decided to take a real holiday, which I guessed meant they were working on an engine at home. I wasn't surprised to find Erik there, though. The station had become like a second home for him. He sat on his folding chair in front of the office the way other folks sit on their front door stoop. When I pulled in, he didn't even get up. Just sat there and smiled. Like he knew I was coming. And why. It made me think of the time when Eugene Becker told my folks how it was crazy what you knew about people just by driving the same routes, delivering milk every day. Said you knew who was home, who was out or away, who was sick and who was having family trouble just by clinking bottles of milk into metal boxes on folks' porches and picking up empty ones or full ones whose milk had gone sour. I think Erik was starting to feel the same way, at least about me. I slid into the empty chair next to him.

"Hey, Erik."

"Hello, Bass."

He put down the *Superman* comic book he was reading and went to the vending machine where he pulled out a couple of celebratory bottles of RC Cola, saying, "It *is* the Fourth of July, after all." We sat there sipping and fanning ourselves. I was thinking about how hot it had been the day the three of us had ridden over to the place where Celia and her family had camped. I had been wishing for a bottle of RC Cola then.

Another thing was reminding me of that day. Erik. He was grinning a wet kind of grin. Like Treat was grinning that August afternoon. Made me think I didn't know what to talk about. It wasn't like I was hurting for subjects. After all, Ruth Anne was going off to Africa and I had been to see Mr. Granger, although I hadn't told anyone other than my pa what I was going to do with my "free" time that summer.

Erik picked up his comic book and flipped through it absent-mindedly.

"You know one of the things I like the most about Superman?" he asked.

I waited. By then, I was used to people asking questions they didn't really want answered. But when Erik looked at me for an answer, I had to admit I didn't know.

"That he's not what he seems to be. Or that he's not *only* what he seems to be. The people of Metropolis are happy enough to have him as –" he lowered his voice, "mild-mannered

Clark Kent. Because mild-mannered Clark Kent is a type they know and understand. Even Superman is a type they know and understand. The rub is that they are one and the same guy, which is something the people of Metropolis can't truly understand. Which is what makes the whole thing so interesting, right?"

"I guess," I shrugged. "But I think leading a double life would be hard."

"Of course. Any kind of double life is hard," Erik assured me. "Father Wilhelm and I talk about that a lot," he added.

"About Superman?"

Erik laughed.

"The Biblical equivalent: Christ. How He was God, but had to live on Earth as a man. How He had to die on the cross when He had the power to save Himself."

I wanted to know what all that had to do with Superman.

"Well," Erik began, "Father Wilhelm has this theory. He believes the Bible story has led Christians to have a kind of split personality. Where it's a virtue to seem like something you're not. Or rather, *not* to seem like something you are. Like Superman."

I had to admit it was the first time in my life I heard someone compare Christ and Superman and, of all people, Father Wilhelm.

Erik's use of the present tense slowly registered.

"What do you mean you and Father Wilhelm *talk* about this a lot?" I asked.

Erik looked puzzled.

"Don't you mean you *talked* about this a lot?"

"No," Erik answered. "We still do."

"You still see him?"

"When I can."

"Here?"

"No. At his new parish."

"Does your pa know?"

A bright red Ford pick-up pulled in for gas. I found myself strangling my cola bottle, wondering if it was Uncle Will. He'd bought a similar pick-up right before Treat ran away and all Treat ever talked about was getting his hands on it. Pa had told me a few days earlier that Uncle Will was thinking of selling the Ford. He'd explained it by saying they didn't really need two cars, seeing as how Katie was still a couple of years away from driving, and the farms weren't doing so well and they could use the money. I knew part of the reason was the Ford pick-up reminded us all a little too much of Treat.

If the person in the cab turned out to be Uncle Will, I'd be ashamed of being caught sitting with my feet up at the Sinclair station with the "peculiar" Roth boy, my co-conspirator in Treat's running away, drinking ice-cold RC Cola. But it wasn't Uncle Will. A middle-aged fellow who didn't look at all familiar was at the wheel. Erik got up, waited on him, then came back and sat down.

"Well?" I asked.

"Well what?"

"Does your pa know you're still seeing Father Wilhelm?"

Erik shrugged. "I haven't exactly been announcing it on a loud speaker at home. But I think he probably knows deep down inside. Just like he probably knows about a lot of other things he doesn't want to admit to himself."

"What kind of things?"

Erik looked at me a long time. "Like what kind of man his son has turned out to be."

I couldn't hold Erik's stare. I figured he meant working at the gas station rather than with his folks or not being a good enough student to go off to college. Or maybe even being so religious.

"How is Father Wilhelm doing in his new parish?" I asked just to change the subject.

"He's fine. I drove down to Ypsi yesterday in Granny Stein's clunker. With the old bird's permission, of course. The thing hadn't been run on the highway in a coon's age. Question of blowing the gunk out of it. At least that's what Ed said."

If I didn't understand him when he talked about religion, at least I understood him when he talked about cars.

"Must not get much use," I said.

"Just back and forth to the supermarket," Erik said. He looked at me and we both laughed.

"At least I go more than twenty miles an hour!" I protested.

"At least you can see over the steering wheel!"

We fell into an uncomfortable silence. Or maybe I was the only one who was uncomfortable, which was how being around Erik was starting to make me feel. I chugged the rest of the cola so fast, it burned my throat and nearly came back out my nose.

"Whoa," Erik said. "What's your hurry?"

"I need to get back to the farms. We're going to have a cookout and I need to get the fire started so it can burn down."

I don't know why I said that. It was obviously a whopper, probably the biggest one I'd told since I lied about Treat. I knew it. And I knew Erik knew it. But he just shrugged.

"Thanks for the cola," I said, "and happy Fourth of July."

As I was getting into the Fairlane, Erik called out, "Hey, Bass! You really should read *Superman*."

* * *

Back at the farms I sat out by the picnic table trying not to think about the times we all sat out there, all eight of us, on holidays like this one, laughing and eating and sometimes even singing songs. Now, I sat out there alone, not wanting to go into the house and not really knowing what to do. I was just about ready to walk out to the back lot to see if Pa was out there, when Katie came out and sat with me. She was stitching up the hem on a pleated skirt. She was quiet as always, and I wondered how someone as young and seemingly self-sufficient as Katie could sense when I needed for her to keep me company.

We'd been sitting there for a while when I heard shouting. It was coming from Treat's house, and the voice sounded a lot like Aunt Sally's. I thought for a minute she and Uncle Will were having a fight when he came walking out of the house rubbing his face before sticking both of his hands deep into his pockets, but Aunt Sally just kept right on shouting so I figured she was either making sure to get the last word in or she was shouting at someone else.

"Happy Independence Day," he said.

"Happy Fourth," I answered.

Then I heard Ruth Anne's voice and she wasn't shouting exactly, but you could tell from the way she was saying whatever it was that well – she was *really* saying it. Pa came out of our house a couple of minutes later and I realized Aunt Sally and Ruth Anne were probably having their quarrel in Uncle Will's office, which, of course, was just across the space separating our two houses from Pa's office even though they probably had no idea he was in there, hearing every word they said to one another. It had embarrassed him enough to make him get up and come outside.

Pa looked strangely pale and sickly and the skin beneath the stubble on his jaw had such a bluish-grey tinge to it, it made my stomach flip. Pa had always been as thin as a rail, but it seemed to me, studying him in the bright sunlight for probably the first time in months, that he had lost even more weight. It was true that I hardly bothered calling him for supper anymore, he ate so little. And I'd mostly taken to eating cereal at night, so what was the point?

Uncle Will was standing there running his tongue around the inside of his mouth as though he was looking for something he lost in there, when he finally blurted out to my Pa. "Wouldn't happen to have any beer, would ya, Thomas?"

My pa thought for a minute and then looked down at me. Of course, I'd been doing almost all of the shopping since Ma died and I wasn't old enough to buy beer. He looked back at his brother and shucked his shoulders. "I don't think so," he said. "Don't you?"

"Sure do," Uncle Will replied, and then tossed his head towards his house, "but I'll be durned if I'm going back in there to get it." He smiled and pulled his wallet out of the back pocket of his pants. We all waited while he counted the bills. "If you're in the mood for a beer and a bratwurst, my treat. We ought to be just in time for the parade. What'ya say?"

I swear it looked like my pa was going to cry, but he kept it all in and nodded his head once or twice. "Sounds good."

"You two coming with us?" Uncle Will asked.

I was up and on my feet so fast, I banged the top of my right thigh against the edge of the picnic table hard enough to bring tears to my eyes. Katie hunkered down over her sewing just as a volley of sharp syllables came flying out of the farmhouse. She straightened up a little, but didn't release her grasp on the hem. "Can I bring this?"

Uncle Will just wagged his head in disbelief.

* * *

That bratwurst was maybe one of the best I'd ever had in my life – in fact, I had two, though I was right at the limit of being polite by accepting when Uncle Will offered to buy me a second one. But Pa didn't say anything, seeing as how his own mouth was full and judging from the look Uncle Will gave him. I think we all understood that if this wasn't exactly a "regular" family outing, it was about as normal an outing as we were going to get anytime soon, and so the usual rules didn't apply. I was so happy, I just couldn't contain myself, and screamed and laughed and applauded at every group in the parade, even the Shriners. Pa did tell me once to "settle down" and I heard Uncle Will say, "He's just havin' fun, Tom. Let the boy be." The phrase "Let the boy be" froze me up for a second because it was exactly what he said to Aunt Sally the morning they discovered Treat had run off and she wanted to drag me in front of judge and jury. But I decided I wasn't going to let anything stop me from enjoying myself, so I just kept on acting up and clowning around and when Katie looked up at me from where she was sitting on the edge of the curb with her sewing still in her lap and rolled her eyes, it made me smile because, hey – it was just about the most normal thing she could do.

After the parade, we were making our way back to Uncle Will's pickup when a lady called to Katie from across the street. Katie excused herself and went to talk to her. The woman was youngish and pretty in an athletic kind of way. Her shiny, brown hair was cut into a bob that curled under her chin and she was dressed in a smartly tailored pair of Bermuda shorts and matching top and was wearing cream-colored, rope-soled sandals all of which made her stand out from a crowd mostly dressed in cut-off jeans, tank-tops and flip-flops. Maybe two men out of three were sporting baseball caps with either "International Harvester" or "John Deere" stenciled on them and a few women who were probably old enough to be my grandmother had even left the house still wearing their aprons. The hippie movement had mostly by-passed Millarsburg and my personal opinion on the matter was most people were just too busy trying to keep their farms and businesses afloat to worry too much about peace and love, and so there was only the occasional tie-dyed T-shirt, Indian-style dress or string upon string of sandalwood beads around someone's neck or wrist.

Katie and the woman talked for a few minutes with Katie so ram-rod straight she seemed to be standing at attention. The woman smiled a lot and bent down a little to talk to my cousin as though they were discussing something private and she didn't really want any of the people who were milling around near them to hear it. Of course, we were all straining our ears to try and figure out what in the heck they could be talking about, but we were too far away and finally Uncle Will spoke for all of us when he suggested we wait for Katie at the truck. She arrived looking a bit flushed and I couldn't tell if it was because she had walked fast or what. Katie smiled her winningiest smile, but didn't say anything while she waited for Pa to open the door to the passenger side of the cab so she could slide in between him and Uncle Will. I climbed glumly into the back of the truck, sure I was going to miss out on something and Pa must have sensed it because he slid open the window separating the cab from the bed of the truck so I could hear what they were saying in there.

"Who was that?" Uncle Will asked. "Or is it none of my business?" There was a slight edge to his voice it usually didn't have, but Katie was either too happy to hear it or decided to ignore it because, all things considered lately, it was pretty understandable that he had an edge to his voice.

"Miss Jansen."

"And who's Miss Jansen?"

"She was my home economics teacher last year."

"Home economics teacher!" Uncle Will slapped his forehead so hard he knocked his cap off. "Well, I'll be durned," he said. "I don't remember them looking like that when we were in school. Do you, Thomas? Remember Mrs. Mueller? She was as lumpy as a dumpling."

Pa laughed and looked over his left shoulder at me and winked. "Miss Jansen looks more like a phys ed teacher," he said.

"She's the girls' volleyball coach."

Uncle Will snugged his cap back onto his head. "Well, I'll be *durned*," he muttered again. "Those two things don't hardly seem to go together. What did she want to talk to you about?"

"My sewing." Katie grinned. "Did you see her outfit?" Nobody bothered to answer since I think we all had noticed the outfit mostly for the pair of shapely legs sticking out of the shorts. "I'm sure she sewed that up in no time. She's a very professional seamstress and has such good taste. She grew up in the East somewhere – Philadelphia, I think. She's a really good teacher, too, though I think it's kind of hard for her having her first teaching assignment out here in the middle of nowhere."

"Nowhere!" Uncle Will shouted. "Millarsburg isn't nowhere. It's somewhere. It's right there on the map with – "

Jurutungo, I thought. Somewhere that is nowhere.

"With where?" Pa teased.

"Painted Creek!" Uncle Will answered, and we all laughed. I can't remember the last time we all laughed so much. And Katie was more talkative than maybe I'd seen her since before Treat ran away. "So what did she say about your sewing?"

"It's a surprise. I'll tell you all about it back at home."

* * *

Things were strangely quiet back at the farms and I noticed right away Aunt Sally's station wagon wasn't in their garage because when she left she hadn't bothered to close the door, and we all knew that wasn't a good sign because she *always* closed the garage door so the raccoons wouldn't get into the garbage can. We all migrated to the picnic table, a little bit sheepishly, as though we had every right to be ashamed of the fun and the food we'd just had in town. And I felt especially bad for Katie because I think she wished she had told us her good news on the ride home.

Ruth Anne came outside and asked where we'd all been and we all looked at each other trying to decide who was going to be the one to tell her we'd been at the Fourth of July parade while she and Aunt Sally were screaming at each other.

"In town," Uncle Will said quickly. "Where's your ma?"

Ruth Anne made a face. "I don't know. She just slammed out. She didn't say where she was going."

"How mad was she?"

"Pretty mad." Ruth Anne sat down at the picnic table as though someone had knocked her feet out from beneath her. "We had words."

"So we heard." Uncle Will picked at his teeth. "Should I go looking for her?"

I don't know why, but I had the feeling that this wasn't the first time Aunt Sally had taken off like that.

"I don't know. Maybe give her some time." Ruth Anne shifted so that she could cross her legs under the picnic table. "Did you know she smokes?" she asked no one in particular.

Uncle Will tugged on his baseball cap the way he did whenever he was nervous or embarrassed. "Well, I kind of figured she did. I can smell it on her, especially when she comes in from outside. How'd you find out? Did she tell you?"

"I borrowed her car this morning and the ashtray was overflowing with cigarette butts. They were all ringed with her lipstick, so I figured it had to be her."

"Is that what you had the fight about?"

Ruth Anne made a face. "About her smoking or about me borrowing her car?"

"Either or both."

"That's about it."

Uncle Will yanked off his baseball cap and scratched his head. "I'm not followin'."

"We had a fight about either of those things or both of them, if you want. We had a fight about letting people be what they want to be and do what they want to do. Ma seems to think the rule applies to everyone around here but her."

Uncle Will tossed his cap onto the picnic table and ran his hands over his face. "Well, it may pretty well be close to the truth, if you think about it."

Just then Aunt Sally pulled into the drive and their garage. I think we all expected her to slink off into their house and slam the door when she saw all of us standing around the picnic table and Ruth Anne sitting at one end of it, but, I had to hand it to her, instead she came over to us and sat down. It was true she smelled of smoke and I wondered how I hadn't noticed it before. Then again, Aunt Sally had been avoiding me for so long I wouldn't have noticed if she'd shaved off her eyebrows and grown a mustache because I just simply hadn't seen much of her. She sat at the opposite end of the picnic table from Ruth Anne, but didn't make a big deal about it so it seemed like most of her anger had passed.

Uncle Will went over and stood behind her and put his hands on her shoulders. "You're just in time, Sal. Katie has been wanting to tell us something special, but we wanted to wait for you." He looked over at Katie with his eyes as big as saucers and I could tell he was just hoping whatever she had to tell us was really good news.

"I'd like for all of you to call me 'Kate' from now on," she said in a voice that seemed very grown up. "I don't want to be called 'Katie' anymore."

We all agreed. If that was all it took to start gluing this family back together, then that was easy enough.

"And I want to invite you all to my show at Black River High a week Saturday."

"Your show?" Aunt Sally asked.

"Yep," Kate said. "The Area Chamber of Commerce is putting on a 'Young Talents' show and Miss Jansen, my old home economics teacher, asked me early last spring if I would show some of my clothes."

"Do you have enough for a show?" Ruth Anne asked.

Kate smiled, "Miss Jansen said so. Seven different outfits. Some of the cheerleaders from school are going to model them. Butterby's Shoes over at the mall in Millarsburg is going to lend shoes and Steinberg's agreed to lend some costume jewelry. The only thing we haven't worked out yet is who is going to be the emcee. Miss Jansen said it's not right for me to announce my own show. And, traditionally, it's supposed to be a man."

Kate turned to me. "I suggested you, Bass, but Miss Jansen said it wouldn't look good if it were someone from my own family."

I was touched. Not only had Kate thought of me, she had called me "family." But I was just as glad not to have to do it. I didn't like speaking in front of people.

"So she suggested Erik Roth."

"Erik Roth!" Aunt Sally shouted.

The devil incarnate. I screamed in my mind, too. Why Erik? I looked over at Aunt Sally. She stared back at me. Regardless of what had happened before or since, Erik and I would forever be linked in her mind. For our treason.

"Miss Jansen says Erik has a proper way about him and a good voice. He's one of her old students, I guess."

"What was Erik doing taking Home Economics?" Uncle Will asked, shaking his head. "Good Lord, that boy truly is peculiar."

Kate rolled her eyes. "Miss Jansen also teaches Public Speaking," she explained. "He took *that* to get out of taking shop class, I guess. Funny how he ended up working in a gas station. But, anyway, a lot of folks know him from the Sinclair station. He's like a celebrity."

Aunt Sally blanched at the word "celebrity."

"The thing is," Kate continued, "I don't really know him."

"Maybe someone who does can introduce you," Ruth Anne suggested. "Or ask him on your behalf." She turned to me. "You know him, don't you, Sebastian?"

I looked at my pa.

"That would be a fine gesture on your part," he said.

"Oh, Bass! Would you?" Kate asked.

If someone had just promised her the world, she wouldn't have looked happier. How could I refuse?

"Sure, I'll go see him tomorrow," I said. After I go to see Mr. Granger, I thought.

"That's great news, Katie." Ruth Anne said. *"Kate."*

"Sure is," Uncle Will added.

Kate beamed at them. "Thanks."

Aunt Sally cleared her throat. "Well, I guess since this is the day of announcements, I have one to make, too." She looked over at my uncle. "Will already knows, of course, and approves."

Uncle Will nodded.

"I've decided to go back to school in the fall," she said.

"Wow," was all Kate managed to say.

"What are you going to study?" Ruth Anne asked.

"Business management."

"Where?" I asked.

"Ann Arbor."

Ann Arbor was a good drive away and the students there were in the news more often than not those days for the parties, sit-ins and peace rallies they organized than for what was going on in the classrooms. I looked over at Uncle Will. He held my look.

"Night school?" Ruth Anne asked.

"No," Aunt Sally answered. "I don't want to be driving around too much at night, especially in the winter when it's snowing. So, I'm registered like any other daytime student, but will only carry a partial load. I'll still be around to clean up everybody's mess and take care of the cooking and shopping."

Ruth Anne uncrossed her legs and let her forearms drop onto the table. "That's not what I was implying."

I think the rest of us had almost forgotten the two of them were fighting, but I guess they hadn't.

"Not that it should make much difference to you. You're not going to be around anyway!"

Ruth Anne stood up and looked like she was going to head for the house in a hurry, but Uncle Will grabbed her arm.

He looked from her to Aunt Sally and back again. "Let's get back to how it's a wonderful thing for all three of my women to have these projects and how this whole family should be behind them one-hundred percent and durned proud of them." He let go of his grip on Ruth Anne and stepped over to Kate, bent down and kissed the top of her head. "And I also think we shouldn't forget how today is an important holiday in the history of this country, because people gave their lives so we could live in freedom and if that freedom means the right to strike out on one's own for whatever reason, then it's a glorious right and one that belongs to each and every one of us – Sal, Ruth Anne, Kate, Thomas, Sebastian, me and Treat – wherever he may be and God keep him safe."

The fireworks exploding over Millarsburg that evening had the same effect on me as gunshots going off. It made me wonder how people lived through war.

*   *   *

I must have slept all of ten minutes that night, if that much. When daylight finally came, I got up. I was at the Sinclair station before it was even open. Erik was in the office, reading *The Millarsburg Eagle*.

"My, my," Erik said. "To what do I owe these daily visits?" He put on an exaggerated look of surprise. "RC Cola?" he asked, laughing.

I think he knew neither Treat nor I were allowed any at home. Pa complained it was expensive and Ma used to say it was bad for my teeth. And Aunt Sally was known for her homemade lemonade.

"C'mon, Erik," I said.

I was in no mood for joking. In fact, I was in a pretty rotten mood. I pulled up a chair.

"Better be careful about coming around too often," he laughed, "or folks will start talking."

I figured folks had already talked enough about the little incident at the Feed and Seed when Erik had told everyone Treat had been all riled up since he met Celia and especially about the afternoon we spent with her family after I had said I hadn't noticed anything different about him and didn't know anything about his plans to run away. As far as I could tell, there were only two people who still suffered from Treat's departure on a daily basis: Aunt Sally and me. Uncle Will seemed to have accepted Treat's absence. I figured maybe that's how it is when you lose somebody you really love – one extreme or the other. Pure pain or the complete inability to feel anything. I knew if I let myself think too much about my ma, I was courting disaster. So I tried to think about her as little as possible. She was gone, and there was nothing I could do about it. Something told me Treat was still alive. And something also told me he was trying, like I was, to make sense of things, trying to figure out what the world really looked like, and to find his place in it. Trying to become a man. If he had stayed around long enough, maybe we would have tried to figure it out together. As things were, there were days when I rode my bike over to Black River hoping there would be a bottle with a message in it from Treat to help me find my way.

"I've got to ask you something," I said.

Erik put the newspaper down, interested.

I took a deep breath. "What do you think it means to be a man?"

He thought for a moment. "'Man' with a big 'm' or a little one?"

I gave him a funny look.

"You know," he said, "'Man' like 'Mankind' or 'man' like 'Me, Tarzan; you, Jane.'"

"Erik, why can't you ever be serious?"

"I *am* being serious."

"What difference does it make?"

"Ask Katie, your cousin."

"*Kate*," I explained. "She wants to be called 'Kate' from now on."

Erik made a face. "So, ask your cousin, *Kate*."

"What's she got to do with this?" Actually, she had plenty to do with my being there, but I wasn't ready to talk about it yet.

"Never mind, Tarzan," he said. He rolled his eyes.

"What's *that* supposed to mean?"

"Look. Kate's a girl, right?"

"Right."

"If you mean, 'Man' with a big 'm' or 'Mankind,' then she's a part of it because regardless of whether someone is a boy or a girl, they're still a human being. Right?"

"Right," I said again.

"But if you mean 'man' as in 'Me, Tarzan; you, Jane.' then you leave her and half of the population out. In fact," he said, smiling, "we're probably dealing with more than half of the population here."

I figured he was dodging me to be smart. "So, are you going to answer my question?"

He shook his head. "So to answer your question…how should I know?"

"Well, that's just great," I grumbled. I was disappointed. Not even Erik could tell me. And here he was working and nearly on his own.

"What are you askin' *me* for, anyway? Why don't you ask your pa?"

I didn't quite know what to say to that. I was embarrassed to ask my pa in case it was something he thought he had already taught me and that I should've known. Or worse, after all of this time, he didn't really know, either.

"Do you think Treat figured it out?" I asked.

"Treat? If he did, he took the news with him."

Erik picked up the *Eagle* again. He looked angry.

"Maybe that's why he went," I said hesitantly.

Erik shrugged his shoulders, but didn't take his eyes off the page. "Beats me."

I sat there and watched him read the paper for a little while. I needed to ask him about the fashion show, although I didn't reckon I should anymore.

"Erik?"

"What!"

"I need to ask you something else," I said.

"What now?" He set down the newspaper and stood up. "Maybe you want to know what it means to be a *woman*?"

"Cut it out, Erik."

"I think it's time for you to go," he said, sitting down again.

I was going to have to explain to Kate. She would be heartbroken. Worse, she'd hate me, and Aunt Sally would hate me even more than she already did. I slammed out of the station. Who needed Erik Roth anyway? He'd already ruined my life once.

CHAPTER THREE

I was relieved to see his light was off. I don't know how he knew I had left it on, but the important thing was it was off when I went back on Monday after the Fourth of July weekend. And he wouldn't get me believing any of his old wave particle theory or whatever it was. Knowing him even as little as I did, I wouldn't have been surprised to learn he had called someone in from the street just to turn it off. I had to laugh. Maybe he had even badgered that person into going to buy cashews for him. Who knows? All I knew then was I had decided to take on the job, and I wasn't going to be turned back. I don't even know why I was being so stubborn about it. It might have had something to do with the *World Atlas*. If Mr. Granger had all the markings of a mad hermit, his atlas had become my feeble link to Puerto Rico and to a world I was just beginning to realize existed. I was counting on him to help me to see that world.

I knocked.

"Come in!" he growled.

I had the key, but it didn't matter. The front door was

unlocked. When I stepped in, I saw the back door was wide open. The sunlight streaming through it actually lit up the basement apartment pretty well. I found him hunched over his table, trailing his fingers over the black plastic piece. Although I'm sure he had heard me come in, he continued what he was doing, ignoring me.

"Don't you think that's dangerous?" I asked.

"What? This?" He indicated the black molded plastic.

"No," I said. When would I learn to ask the *right* question? "Leaving the front door unlocked. And the back door is wide open."

"What do you mean, 'dangerous'?"

"Well, ugh – " I stammered. It seemed obvious.

He swiveled around, facing me but his pupils looked past me, somewhere off to my left. I felt an impulse to take a step that way, to walk into his blinded line of vision.

"Whatsa matter? Afraid someone might come in? Steal everything I own? Bash me over the head and render me blind?" He guffawed. "They'd do me a lot more harm by coming in and then going out and leaving the light on!"

He swiveled back around. I hung my head and only lifted it when I remembered he couldn't see me.

"I'm sorry, sir," I said.

"Sorry, smorry," he answered. "You'd do better to pay attention to what's important and worry a little less about what's not."

"Yes, sir," I said. Well, we were off to a great start, I thought.

"In fact," he continued, touching the black plastic piece, "this probably *is* a lot more dangerous. At least in certain circles."

"What is it, sir?"

He slid the piece off of the table and onto the floor.

"You'll know when I'm ready to tell ya. But there's nothing

guaranteeing you'll understand." He swiveled back around to face me. "What are you doing here, boy?"

His question caught me short. "What am I doing here?" I repeated. "Er – well, I came to read to you, sir."

"Hah – hah!"

He drew his aluminum cane and smacked it on the ground. Even though I watched him do it, the noise it made surprised me and made me jump.

"Hah – hah! Hah – hah!" he laughed. "Read to me? And it ain't even beddy-bye time yet."

"I mean – "

"Maybe you can read me a fairy tale? Something with ghosts and goblins and some poor little tyke who trots off into the woods to get eaten up by a wicked witch! Hah! I love that stuff!" he said.

He reached up and wiped a tear from his eye. He'd laughed so hard, it'd made him cry.

"That wasn't exactly what I meant, sir."

He laid the cane along the edge of the table.

"A reader! Hah! This must be another one of my nephew's harebrained schemes. Or maybe that old biddy down at the library. What's 'er name..."

"Old biddy" is exactly what some of the kids at school called her. I remembered how highly she had spoken of Mr. Granger. And hadn't he called her, "My old friend, Darby Millar" during our first meeting? What was this?

"Miss Millar, sir."

"Right. Derby."

"Darby, sir."

"Whatever."

"I thought you had asked for – "

"Me? Ask for someone to come around to read to me? Do I look like someone who would do that? No, this is my nephew again, sneaking around behind my back, making arrangements for me, spending money needlessly. And the old gal – what's 'er name again?"

"Miss Millar, sir."

"Right. Been trying to run my life for the past forty years."

"Forty years, sir?"

He waved a hand in the air. "More or less."

"You don't want a reader then, sir?"

"Well, it looks like I've got one now, doesn't it?"

"I mean, you didn't ask for one, sir?"

"Arg!" He stood up and threw both hands into the air. "Stop calling me 'sir'! I feel like I'm in the flippin' Army again."

"You were in the Army, s – ?"

"Sir!"

"Sir!" I repeated. "No, sir. I mean – I didn't mean to say 'sir,' sir."

Mr. Granger shook his head. "Been trained like *you* were in the Army. Who did that to you? Your pa? Your ma?"

I was suddenly glad Mr. Granger couldn't see me. "My ma's dead."

"Ah? I see," he nodded. "Didn't know." He sat down like his legs would no longer hold him. "Well, then, enough of that," he said, waving a hand. "Truth be told, I'm none too interested in 'family' things. Your friend down at the county library has probably told you that."

I wondered what Miss Millar had to do with this.

"Did you leave home early?" I asked.

"Not early enough."

"Why'd you want to leave your family so badly? If you don't mind me askin', that is."

Mr. Granger waved a hand at me again.

"Who knows? Who understands anything at that age? I guess I thought it had something to do with being a man."

With being a man! "Is that why you ran away?" I asked.

"Ran away? You might say that. Ran straight into the Army. I joined up in '17 just as the Yanks were seeing action. I was only nineteen."

He stopped and tilted his chin towards me. I would learn after time that it was his way of looking at me.

"My twin brother did the same thing in his turn, six months later. Never saw him again. Left behind a young wife who, it turns out, was pregnant. She remarried a few years after, though, and the new man was correct enough to adopt the boy. Ah, right. You know him. That confounded nephew of mine."

Mr. Sellers, I thought.

"Why'd you join the Army?" I asked. "I mean, instead of just getting work?"

"There was little work to be had for someone with no skills and no education. Plus, I figured I was going to get called up sooner or later, so I might as well get it over with. It seemed like the most sensible thing to do. Three squares and a bed, as they say. Things were pretty tough at home. The family farm was going under. We were a big family and I – we – were the eldest. Three girls after us two boys. Wasn't always enough to go around. I'd already contracted rickets as a youngster and was still in pretty bad shape when I signed up. Probably the thing that saved my life, strangely enough. Kept me from seeing any real action. How do you think I got to be a chart jockey in the first place?"

"I thought maybe it was something you wanted to do."

"Wanted? Hah! Why would I have wanted to do something like that?"

I pictured the map of Puerto Rico in the *Atlas*. The lines marking its roads were like the life lines in the palms of my hands.

"I just thought that," I said.

"Well you can unthink it."

"You don't want me to be your reader, then, sir?"

"I thought I told you to stop calling me that."

First Katie wanted to be called "Kate." Now Mr. Granger didn't want me calling him "sir." What did it matter if I called him "sir"? *Geez.* My rotten mood was getting worse. I wondered what the old guy wanted from me.

"I didn't say that. I just said I didn't know that's what you were coming around for. How often did they say you were supposed to come around?"

"Every day."

"Every day!"

"During the week, I mean."

"From when to when?"

"From about ten to two."

"Hmpf!"

"Those are the hours they said you wanted."

"What do they know about what I want?"

"What do you want, Mr. Granger?" Pa's question echoed in my ears.

"I told that nephew of mine that I needed someone to come about once a week, buy me some grub, see that the rats haven't taken over the place. Make sure I'm not laid out flat with little green worms crawling out of my eyes!"

Suddenly, I imagined my ma lying in her coffin, dressed in her favorite blue dress, her head pressed into the pillow and her eye sockets filled with wriggling masses of small, green worms. I must have screamed as I ran out of the cellar apartment, because somewhere behind me I heard Mr. Granger ask me, "What is it, boy?" I didn't answer him. I don't even remember if I bumped my head. All I know is that once I hit the street, I just kept running and almost ran right past my car, which wasn't parked all that far away. Once I got to the car, though, I didn't quite know which way to turn. I didn't want to go back to the farms, *couldn't* go back to the Sinclair station in Millarsburg. I threw the Ford into gear and did the only thing that made much sense to me at that point. I drove to the site where Celia and her family had camped which was located somewhere in between.

* * *

I hadn't been there since Erik and I went the morning Treat's disappearance was discovered and we had been hoping to find him, Celia and her family there but they had all vanished. To my surprise, I found the road to the camp easily enough. Like something had guided me there. I turned at the blue spruce. Without stopping. The lot didn't look all that much different than it had then. In fact, I had expected it to be much more overgrown. I got out of the car and walked around a bit, as though it would help me to try to figure out where Treat was and if he was coming back. Maybe Celia and her family camped there every August and, if that were the case, then he'd be coming back with them. Then again, what made me so sure that he was with them? Or what if he was with them and they had taken him back to Puerto Rico? Then again, maybe Celia had never even *been* to Puerto Rico. Maybe she was from someplace like Saginaw or Detroit. I'd heard there were a lot of people from Puerto Rico in Detroit. Maybe her pa was really an autoworker. He just pretended they were a family of happy-go-lucky vagabonds because it was easier than accepting the truth: that he'd left a hard life working in a San Juan tannery for a life-stealing existence doing double shifts on an assembly line. He'd gotten away from the *barrio*, but hadn't entirely escaped his destiny. I was beginning to suspect that some things have a way of following you across borders. So, every August the family headed north for a week or two, squatting on wooded State lands seeking relief from the heat and violence of the city. Like hundreds of other downstate folks. If that were the case, it also meant they might be back again that August – which was only another month away.

My mind was reeling. I sat down for a while, as if I might just as well wait for them. But, finally, I had to admit there was nothing for me at the camp. If it held clues to where Treat had gone to and if he had gone there with Celia and her family, I wasn't able to decipher them. Not any more than I had been able to the morning we rode there after Treat disappeared when Erik had snatched up a broken guitar string and put it in his pocket the way one does a memento. I drove slowly back to the farms.

* * *

I found Ruth Anne and Uncle Will out at the picnic table. They had glasses of lemonade in front of them and both turned to look at me as I walked up. I remember thinking how happy they seemed. I didn't ask where my pa was. I knew he was probably in his office, worrying over the books. The light-heartedness of our afternoon together at the Fourth of July parade hadn't lasted. Aunt Sally wasn't home because her car wasn't in their garage. And I just figured Kate was in her usual place in the spare room in front of her sewing machine. I couldn't face her, so I sat down at the picnic table.

"Ruth Anne and I are going over the list of things she needs to take to Africa," Uncle Will said, "especially that 'girl stuff' she might not be able to find and the mission headquarters not able to send."

"Pa!"

"Well, we *are*," he insisted.

Ruth Anne blushed.

"Nothing to be ashamed of. He knows about the stuff women need. Bass is a grown man, now."

It was my turn to blush. It was true that I knew about "girl stuff" because Pa had explained the facts of life to me when I was just 12 years old, saying it was a time when me and a lot of my friends would be starting to go through changes and I needed to know what was what. But I didn't feel like a grown man. I was still trying to figure out what being a grown man meant! Plus, I didn't like thinking about Ruth Anne as a grown woman, though I knew she was. She was nearly a sister to me and the less I thought about the "girl stuff" she needed, the better.

One thing did strike me, though. Why was she talking about "girl stuff" with Uncle Will? Shouldn't she be working out the list of things she needed, especially the "girl stuff," with Aunt Sally? Best I could figure, Ruth Anne was talking to Uncle Will about that stuff because she was hoping he would talk to Aunt Sally about it. Aunt Sally managed the household affairs and worked out the family's monthly budget with a tight fist, just like a lot of women in the community. My ma had been an exception. I don't remember hearing her talk about money or worrying much over it, but, then again, there were only the three of us. Plus, Ma had a lot more of what I would call "old world ways" compared to Aunt Sally. She sewed most of our clothes and pretty much everything we ate she made from scratch. She cooked and canned and even made her own ham and sausage, but didn't shy away from modern conveniences that made her life easier.

"What have you been up to, son?" Uncle Will asked.

Son.

Uncle Will called me "son" the way men his age called boys my age "son." The way Sherriff Walker had the day we discovered Treat had run away. I don't think he even realized he'd said it. I could tell from the look on her face that Ruth Anne had heard it, though. And so had I.

I knew Uncle Will was just being the kind man he was by showing interest in what I had been doing, but it didn't make answering his question any easier. I sucked in a deep breath. Just like Ruth Ann had probably figured it would be easier to bring up the subject of her needing supplies with Uncle Will, I reasoned it would probably be easier to tell Uncle Will that I hadn't been able to ask Erik to be Kate's emcee than it would be to tell Aunt Sally. But before I could exhale, we heard a car pull into our shared driveway, its tires crunching beneath the gravel. None of us spoke as we followed its slow progression. My heart fluttered when I heard the car turn left. Aunt Sally.

She walked over to us in the kind of headlong rush she had adopted recently, skirt flying and hair-sprayed hair blown stiff and skyward on her left side by the wind coming in through the car window. She hadn't even taken the trouble to smooth it back down. It was starting to bother me, this new way of dashing about as though to show us *she* had important things to do and we were just a bunch of slackers. She sat down between Uncle Will and me with a thud and a sigh. She seemed tired and smelled of cigarette smoke.

"Well?" Uncle Will asked.

"Okay. Things went okay. We took measurements of the tables that are going to act as the runway so Katie can make skirts for them and found out how to turn on and off the lights since Katie wants to start her show in complete darkness."

I noticed how we often still referred to her as "Katie."

"The Theater Club is going to lend some wooden and cloth screens they have so the girls can have a little dressing room on stage in order to be able to change quickly. There are only three of them, so they'll have to move fast. The prettiest one will show three outfits."

"Sounds like a lot of work," Ruth Anne said.

"It is. But we still have more than a week. I left Katie at the school. Maybe you could go and pick her up when she calls, Ruth Anne. I'm tired of racing around in this heat. By the way, Bass, what did Erik say?"

I felt everyone turn and look at me.

"Ugh – I didn't get a chance to ask him."

"What do you mean you didn't get a chance to ask him?" Aunt Sally repeated. She shook her head.

I looked at my watch. It was nearly four o'clock. I must have spent a lot more time at the camp then I realized. I needed to think of something, quickly.

"The thing is..." I began, "...the thing is that he was in a pretty bad mood. I was afraid that if I asked him, he would just refuse because he was in a bad mood. I didn't want to risk it."

"Oh?" Aunt Sally asked. "That was good thinking."

Whew. Sure was, I thought. I didn't tell her I was the one who had gotten him into that bad mood.

She got up and brushed a lock of hair out of her eyes. "This heat," she said. "Looks like it might just be egg salad sandwiches for dinner tonight, unless someone else feels like doing the cooking."

She picked up her keys and her purse and headed toward the house.

"Ma, may I use your car?" Ruth Anne called out after her.

"You sure can. To pick up your sister."

Ruth Anne rolled her eyes, and then got up and followed her mother.

* * *

Uncle Will and I were left alone at the picnic table.

"I'd caught him at it once before, you know."

Caught who at what? I wondered.

"I've been meaning to tell you for almost a year now. Just never seemed like the right time and what with everything else that has happened in the past year." Uncle Will scratched the stubble on his chin. "Guess I was a little embarrassed, too. Felt like I had failed him as a father. It took me nearly a week to tell your pa. He just shrugged it off and said a lot of boys think about running away. Wasn't nothing too unusual. I hadn't though. I'd never thought about it. Don't think your pa ever did, either. Maybe it's kind of like what folks say about having twins," he said with a wry smile. "Skips a generation."

He looked at me. For the first time, I saw the pain in his eyes.

"You ever think about running away, son?"

I hardly knew what to say. I traced the outline of the island of Puerto Rico along the faded wood of the picnic table.

"Oh, he might not even have realized what he was doing was running away. He was only ten. Caught him packing up his pillowcase. Wanted to take off on an 'adventure,' he said. Didn't want to be stuck in 'dumb ol' Millarsburg', as he put it, for the rest of his life. Said he was going to the Amazon or the South Pacific. He wanted to explore the African jungle. I talked him out of leaving by telling him he could do it later, when he was older. I didn't fully understand at the time what was going through his mind. Thought it was just a boy's fantasy. I thought it would pass. I figured he'd been reading too many adventure stories. Huck Finn. Tarzan. Jules Verne. That kind of thing. Your aunt understood what was happening before I did. Not too surprising, I guess."

"Probably mothers understand that kind of stuff," I said, not really sure if it was what he meant.

"Well, your aunt sure does."

"Then why is she always telling folks that he was kidnapped or something like – "

"Your aunt," he said, cutting me off, "needs to think that."

"But it might be true." My bottom lip trembled as I said it.

Uncle Will leveled his gaze at me. "You and I both know full well that Treat ran off of his own free will. If you ask me, it was because – even after all of this time – he didn't want to be stuck in 'dumb ol' Millarsburg' for the rest of his life. And that's all right."

"You really think it's all right, Uncle Will?"

"What I mean to say, son, is that if my boy has gone off because he thinks that's the only way he can be free – well, I'd rather be without him than watch him die a slow death tilling a soil for which he has no love."

"Do you think he's okay?"

"Yeah, I think so. If not, we probably would have heard by now. Folks might take Jackson Walker for a red-necked hillbilly, but he knows what he's doing. He's plugged into networks all over the country, and he's kept a bead on this case. He would have told us if he'd found something out."

* * *

I was at the county library the next morning when it opened. I sat at my favorite table and divided my attention between Granger's map of Puerto Rico and a book Miss Millar brought to me which told the history of the island. On the map, I sought out place names that begged to be formed in the mouth like *Mayagüez* or *Playa de Guayanilla*. In the process, I stumbled onto other unimaginable places: *El Yunque*, the rain forest, or the *Bahia Fosforescente*, the Phosphorescent Bay. Then there were places with names like *Carolina* or *Florida* or *Rio Grande*

– names which were familiar in a place that wasn't. And for all I knew, names that existed in a hundred other places around the globe.

From the book on Puerto Rico, I learned that the Taínos, the Indians who lived there when it was "discovered" by the Spaniards in 1493, had called the island *Borinquén*, the land of the brave lord, and that people from Puerto Rico were sometimes called *Borinqueños* in Spanish. The Taínos were said to be a peaceful people who were good farmers and hunters, sailors and fishermen. I even found out from the book that they played a kind of ball game using a rubber-like ball. Ball games. Fishing. I was beginning to feel a certain affection for these peoples, an identity even.

On my way to Mr. Granger's, I pulled into the Sinclair station – almost without thinking. After all, I'd promised Kate. And, Lord knows, I didn't want to give Aunt Sally any other excuse to be mad at me, regardless of what Uncle Will had said about it having just been the shock. Erik probably didn't want to see me though I wasn't really sure what I had done to make him mad. I couldn't let it bother me. After all, I was a Taíno, from the land of the brave lord.

Just in case, I decided to top off the tank. It would give me an excuse for being there and a way of knowing how Erik was feeling. He pumped the gas, cleaned the windshield, and then checked the oil. Routine service without saying so much as a word. I figured I had my answer. Keeping my promise to Kate was going to be harder than I thought. I searched for a way to bring up the subject as I handed him a ten spot for two dollars and twelve cents worth of gas. He dug into his attendant's apron.

"Can't make the change," he said, shaking his head. "Too early. I need to get it from the office. C'mon and have a cola."

Maybe he wasn't angry after all. Who could figure him? I followed him to the office, but refused the cola.

"Erik, I need to ask you something for my cousin Katie."

"Katie? You mean 'Kate'."

"Kate."

"I haven't seen her since I graduated. She must be growing up."

"She'll be a freshman this fall."

"Nice-looking, as I recall."

"Can't say," I shrugged. "She's my cousin." Cousins didn't count.

Erik looked up from where he was bent over his cash box.

"I didn't mean anything by it," he said.

"I didn't say you did."

There we were again. I just couldn't get on the right side of him, could I? He handed me my change.

"Your business, anyhow," I said.

"What'd you need to ask me?"

I stuffed the change in my pocket.

"Kate does a lot of sewing and I guess has gotten to be right good at it. She's put together a bunch of outfits and is going to be showing them on Saturday at Black River High School. Something called a 'young talents show' the Chamber of Commerce is putting on. She needs an emcee for her show. Miss Jansen suggested you."

He straightened up.

"Me? Why me?"

"She said you had a 'nice voice' and a 'proper' way about you."

He blushed. For some reason, I hadn't expected him to be so flustered.

"Miss Jansen?"

"Yeah, didn't you have her for Public Speaking?"

He looked out the window instead of answering me. "What would I have to do?"

"I don't really know. I guess Kate will write something about each of the outfits and you'll have to 'announce' them as the girls come out. You know, a fashion show."

He continued to stare out the window.

"What do you say?"

"Kinda late notice. It's already Tuesday. Saturday's only three days away."

"That's my fault," I said, without explaining further.

"Why doesn't *she* do it?"

"I guess she can't do her own show."

"What about Miss Jansen?"

"Supposed to be a guy."

"A guy? Why?"

"I don't know," I said, shrugging. "Tradition."

"You sure there's not another reason?"

"What kind of other reason could there be?"

He shook his head. "Never mind."

"Well?"

"I don't know."

"What should I tell her?"

"Don't tell her anything. Tell her I'll call her. Later tonight. I've got to think on it a bit."

* * *

I got to Mr. Granger's about eleven. I found him standing by his back door.

"Thought you were supposed to be here at ten," he said by way of a greeting.

Sheesh. I thought he didn't care about what time I was there.

"Sorry. I got hung up with something important."

"And this isn't important?"

"Yes, of course it is," I said. "But it was a family thing. I couldn't do otherwise."

"Right. Well, I've told you how I feel about families. I need you to run out and get me some grub. Got nothing left. Haven't eaten. Got no more coffee."

He listed the things he wanted me to get: instant coffee, a loaf of bread, bologna, a few tomatoes.

"Take your time," he growled. Then he disappeared into the bathroom and closed the door.

I was left standing there wondering if he were being sarcastic. But then again, maybe he was just as happy not to have me hanging around as I was not to be stuck in the dank basement with him. I no longer dared turn on the lights after what had happened after my first visit. I was about ready to go when I realized that he hadn't given me any money.

"Mr. Granger?" I called at the bathroom door.

No response. I waited a few minutes.

"Mr. Granger?" I called again. Still no response. "Sir?" I risked.

I pulled the change from my pocket. I probably had enough. I didn't know how much instant coffee was, although I thought I remembered it being pretty expensive. Well, he'd only get a small jar then. I'd get the money from him when I got back.

I wandered around the IGA picking up the things he wanted and looking out for Celia. I didn't see her. I wasted a lot of time between the meat section and aisle 14 marked "Coffee, Tea, Sugar, and Crackers." I had chosen a large package of bologna, so I picked up a small jar of coffee, in order to be sure to have enough money. Then I decided it was probably not the right decision. Mr. Granger looked like someone who needed his coffee in the morning. From what I could tell, he probably had another cup in the afternoon. Whereas with bologna, even if you like the stuff, you don't catch many folks eating it in the morning. I finally settled for a large jar of coffee and a small package of bologna. If it wasn't what he wanted, well – then, he'd just have to give me better instructions.

When I got back to his apartment, I found him lying in his cot.

"Mr. Granger?"

"Hmm?"

"Are you all right?"

"Of course I'm all right!" He rolled over and faced the wall. Despite the heat outside, he pulled his Army blanket over him.

"It's just – "

"What?"

"Well, most times when folks take to their bed in the middle of the day – "

The image of Ma lying in her bed with the covers pulled up to her chin flashed through my mind. I squeezed my eyes shut to chase the image away. When I opened them, I saw the shadowy figure of Mr. Granger fight to get the blanket off, roll clumsily out of the cot, and struggle to its feet. I raced to finish the sentence before my courage gave out.

"– it means they ain't well."

"Well, I'm fine!" he shouted. "Maybe you were expecting to find me sunbathing in the yard or in some other way taking advantage of this no-doubt 'beautiful, sunny day'? Well, I don't know if you've noticed, boy, but I'm nearly totally blind. This beautiful, sunny day for you only means for me that it's too hot for any mother's son to do a decent day's work. So, I work during the night and sleep during the day. What difference does it make to me?"

"I hadn't thought about that."

"Well, well. Now there are some things you ought to start thinking about. For one, you ought to start thinking about leaving my grub, and getting out of here so I can get some sleep."

"But Mr. Sellers is paying me for four hours and I have hardly done but an hour."

I realized when I said it that it sounded like I was doing time.

"Fine. You can stand there and watch me sleep."

He clambered back into bed. I went into the kitchenette alcove. I put the tomatoes and the bologna in the empty refrigerator and left the coffee and the bread on the countertop. I pulled the receipt from the paper bag and stuck it in my wallet. Seeing as how I wasn't even doing the work I was going to get paid for, I decided I wouldn't say anything to Mr. Granger about the money I'd spent. I'd keep track of everything on my own, time and expenses, and talk to Mr. Sellers.

When I checked to make sure the back door was closed and locked, I noticed the small pile of stones I had seen there on my last visit was no longer there. I walked back into the main room.

"The coffee and the bread are on the counter on the left side of the sink," I thought to say.

He grunted.

"The other stuff is on the top shelf of the frig."

"Fine."

"Mr. Granger?"

"What is it, boy?"

"I've been wanting to ask you something."

"Hmm?"

His voice sounded soft and far away. Maybe he was already half asleep.

"Have you ever been to Puerto Rico?"

He didn't answer me.

* * *

I hadn't really gotten an answer from Erik, either, but at least I had talked to him about Kate's show. Like I had promised. No one would be able to say I had let the family down again, that I had run away from my responsibility or was, in any other way, to blame for something going wrong. Besides, I was pretty certain Erik would agree to do it. That would make Kate happy. And by extension, Aunt Sally. And by further extension, me since maybe it would make Aunt Sally hate me a little less. I even suspected Erik had a little crush on Kate.

I drove back to the farms feeling relatively happy – at least as happy as I'd felt in a while. When I walked around to the back, I found the women in the yard. Two long sheets of black fabric were spread across the lawn. One was just lying on the short grass and the other was being held taut against the ground by Aunt Sally on one side and Ruth Anne on the other. Both were kneeling down and had their upper bodies spread-eagled across the black fabric, one corner in each hand. The position forced them to lower their heads, their noses close to the ground, so that neither one saw me walk up. Kate was kneeling by one edge toward the center of the black strip and was facing me but she was so focused on pinning lengths of black-scalloped lace to it she didn't see me walk up either. The pins she held in her tightly-closed mouth stuck out as though their sharp points were driven into her tongue. She inch-wormed her way down the length of the fabric, attaching lace as she went.

Ruth Anne finally looked up, saw me and smiled. "Hullo, Sebastian," she said, softly.

Kate didn't say anything, of course, what with her mouth full of pins. She just kept working away, concentrated on what she was doing like only she could. Aunt Sally cranked her head up.

"Thank God," she said, "I can't stay in this position a minute longer. Bass, come and hold this down for a bit."

I knelt down and grabbed one corner of the fabric in each hand. As soon as I did, Aunt Sally got up. I found that I was able to keep my chin raised, like a sprinter in starting blocks. I watched Aunt Sally walk around in a small circle, arching her back and bending her arms, her mouth stretched in pain. I remember that moment well. It was the moment I realized I had grown as tall as most adults, maybe taller. And my arms must have gotten longer. The way I usually avoided being around her, I rarely found myself standing close enough to Aunt Sally to compare our heights. I must have gotten taller over the summer, passing her up even though she was tall for a woman. Ma used to mark the growing stages of my height with a pencil on the white paint of the doorframe to my room. She'd marked Pa's height as well. To compare. He'd stopped marking our heights after she died almost as though things couldn't possibly go on living and growing after she was gone. Or maybe he was afraid to find out he was shrinking.

"Great news," Aunt Sally said after a few minutes.

Kate grunted and kept pinning.

"Someone has agreed to emcee Kate's show."

Erik must have called while I was on my way back. I thought he had said he would call in the evening.

"Erik Roth," I said, matter-of-factly. I waited for them all to thank me.

Aunt Sally rubbed the back of her neck. "Tim Kirsten," she said.

"Who?" I asked.

"He's a junior at Black River High School. Top in his class. Quarterback of the football team," Aunt Sally answered.

Ruth Anne looked up long enough to wink at me. "And apparently pret-ty dr-e-a-m-y."

Kate let out a harsh grunt. Ruth Anne laughed.

"But I thought, but I just asked Erik."

"Well, finally, it was decided that someone from Black River High School should do it. Tim was hand-picked by the BRHS principal," Aunt Sally said. She walked over to Ruth Anne. "Here, let me take over while you get the kinks out."

"Thanks, Ma. I'm all right."

I involuntarily let the fabric slip out of my right hand, the side Kate was pinning. She mumbled something between closed teeth.

"Bass, you need to hold it tight," Aunt Sally scolded. "Here, I'll take it back."

I sat back on my heels and wondered why I hadn't seen this coming, why I was so surprised. The worst thing was going to be telling Erik. I'd look like a fool. Or like I was playing games with him. He might get angry. For all I knew, we would finally have the blow up that seemed to be building for a long time for who knows what reason. I prayed he had decided not to do Kate's show. If only he would call to refuse, and beg me to explain things to Kate on his behalf. It would reverse the situation and get me off of the hook. He'd never have to know the truth.

"It was nice of you to have asked him, though," Ruth Anne said. "We all appreciate it."

I hate it when people use the word *we* when they mean *I* or, worse, when they're speaking for someone else altogether. If she meant Kate, well – I was pretty sure Kate did appreciate what I had done even if she was too busy to show it. As things were, she was so caught up in her preparations a little lapse in manners was to be expected. But Aunt Sally was a different story, I thought to myself, seething. First, she insists that I talk to Erik and when I finally do, she explains oh-so-casually that someone else will be announcing Kate's show. I was sure she had planned this last-minute change on purpose. She'd probably be pleased to see me and Erik get mad at each other.

Worse was someone else apologizing for her. Again.

"This fellow seems to be a better choice for some reason," she added.

The reason was he didn't have anything to do with me, I thought. Or with Treat's running away.

"And, you have to admit," Aunt Sally interrupted, "that Roth boy's got an odd way about him."

At that point, I would have sworn Erik didn't have brown hair and green eyes. Just to be contrary.

"Nothin' wrong with him," I said.

"Nobody said there was," Ruth Anne assured me.

"But he is a little different, isn't he?" Aunt Sally added.

"What do you mean, *different*?"

"Well, for one thing, I've never heard anything about him being on a team, playing a sport."

I shrugged. I'd barely made the cut for baseball that year.

"And for another, never hear any talk about him going steady or anything. Kate says he didn't even go to the Senior Prom."

I shrugged again. I'd had my license for over a year already and hadn't even thought about going on a date.

"And then, he seems to have had a real close relationship to Father Wilhelm."

I nodded. That was true and had surprised me a little as well.

"Especially for a boy who wasn't raised in a particularly Catholic family."

"Maybe he has become a strong Catholic on his own," I offered.

"Maybe," she agreed. "Although it looks like he is trying to out-Catholic the Pope. Head altar boy. Always hanging around

Father Wilhelm, even helping to clean the church Saturday mornings when his folks needed him at the store. He seems to have calmed down some since Father Wilhelm was transferred and he started working for the Bauer brothers. Still and all," she continued, "a gas station seems to me like a strange place for a young man with a calling."

Everything Aunt Sally said was true. But, in my mind it hadn't added up to a calling. It was true, too, that Erik had talked to me about Jesus once. We'd also talked about Superman.

"So is, come to think of it, a fashion show."

"What makes you think Erik's got a calling?" I asked.

"What else is a body supposed to think?"

I didn't know. But odd or not, it wasn't right to have had me ask Erik if it were just a matter of going out and arranging for someone else to announce the show before he even had a proper chance to answer.

"Erik is supposed to call tonight. What am I supposed to tell him?"

"The truth."

"That you asked somebody else?" I asked boldly.

Ruth Anne looked away.

"Tell him the school wanted one of their own kind to do it," Aunt Sally said.

The phone rang next door right as I was starting to eat a big bowl of ice cream – something I did pretty regularly on hot summer evenings. I could hear it ring from where I was sitting at our kitchen table. My heart jumped into my throat at the sound of it thinking it was Erik calling to talk to Kate, but then I heard my Aunt Sally call for Ruth Anne. Ruth Anne couldn't have talked for all that long, because about ten minutes later it rang again, but that time it was Ruth Anne who called for Aunt Sally. Aunt Sally stayed on the line longer than her daughter had. It was almost 9 o'clock and I was sitting over a second bowl of ice cream I didn't even really want when I heard it ring again and Aunt Sally call for Kate. I had forgotten The Boys had decided to keep the station open until 8 o'clock during the summer. They took turns staying until closing. It must have been Erik's turn and then he stayed to clean the place and take a look at the day's receipts before he locked up for the night. That was probably why he was calling so late. By the time the phone rang at our house, I had finished washing my dish and had had enough time to start feeling like a man condemned to his fate.

"I thought about what you asked me to do," he started in immediately. "And I decided I'm not the right person to do it."

I sighed so loudly that my breath whistled into the receiver.

"Don't be angry," he said.

"I'm not angry," I answered.

"I've got my reasons. I said I would call and give you an answer tonight. And so I am."

"Thanks," I said.

"I just talked to your cousin. She didn't seem too upset."

I didn't know what to say. How could I tell him that no-one really wanted him to do the show anyhow?

"Well, Kate's pretty practical about things," I said, and felt good about it because it was a true statement without being the whole truth.

"How many people know about this?"

"About the show?" I asked, stalling.

"No, about you asking me to emcee."

"Well, like I said. Miss Jansen was the one who suggested you. So I guess she knows and everyone over here." I wanted to say "my family" but found I couldn't get the words out of my mouth. "Why?"

"Because I don't want anyone saying I wimped out or that I hold a grudge or something. That's not what this is about."

"No one is going to accuse you of those things."

"Seems folks accuse me of enough things as it is," he said.

"And it was kind of late notice," I added.

"Sure was. But how are they going to find someone to do it now? Or do they have someone already?"

I didn't know what Kate told him, so I decided not to make things worse by lying. "I guess they have someone already," I said. "Someone over at Black River High School. I think they had someone picked out over there a while ago, but they didn't tell Miss Jansen or she never would have suggested we ask you." Heck, as far as I knew, I was telling the truth.

There was a moment of uncomfortable silence.

"Hey," he said, "doing anything Friday night?"

"Friday night? No," I said. When was I *ever* doing anything? "Why?"

"Want to go see a movie or something?"

I had only been to the movies once in my whole life, but not to a real theater. It was at least four or five years earlier. I'd gone to the drive-in with my folks. At the time, I thought it was pretty neat because I got to eat Cracker Jacks out of the box and stay up past my usual bedtime. My folks didn't like it much. It seemed like Ma was only at ease on the farm, not even in her own car in a drive-in theater. She fidgeted through the whole show and couldn't wait to get back home. Pa said he liked being at the picture well enough, but went out the next day anyway and made a down payment on a black and white television.

"Sure," I said, "why not?"

"Can you drive?" he asked. "I don't want to have to ask my ma for her car. She always asks me a million questions."

"Sure, I can drive. But why don't I just meet you at the station. We can walk from there."

"I wasn't talking about the Millarsburg cinema. I know another place."

"Is it far?" I asked.

"Not too far. Just the other side of Painted Creek. I can slip you some gas if you want. But you've got to come by the station in the morning, before ten."

"I'm not worried about gas," I lied. "Besides, that wouldn't be right," I said.

"It's no problem. I put gas in my ma's car all the time. Mike said it was okay long as it didn't get out of hand. And since you're driving for me, it's almost the same thing."

I agreed. But the feeling of being condemned hadn't left me.

* * *

I got to Mr. Granger's at five minutes to ten the next morning. I was back out of the door before the hour had struck. I had found him in bed. And in a particularly bad temper.

"Come back in a coupla days," he said. "I'll need some grub by then."

I left because I wasn't going to fight the old guy. If he didn't want me around, then he didn't want me around. I was just as happy not to have to stay. He was a strange old bird. Still, two things were bothering me. The first was Mr. Sellers was paying me for a job I wasn't doing. I couldn't accept that. I took a small spiral notebook out of my glove compartment and jotted down the date and time and "Asked to leave" as an explanation. I realized as I was doing it that I could just as well make something up, write down that I had done a day's work. It'd be my word against his. But, at the time, I wasn't sure if it was how I was supposed to look at things.

The other thing that was bothering me was I couldn't get my feelings for Mr. Granger to jibe with what was becoming my nearly religious fascination and respect for his *Atlas*. He was starting to ruin everything. And he hadn't even bothered to answer my question about Puerto Rico.

I drove to the library.

Miss Millar looked up as I walked in.

"Bass, glad to see you. We need to talk."

For some reason, the phrase "old biddy" raced through my mind.

I sat down at my usual table and waited for her to come over.

"Bass, I've had a call this morning from John Sellers," she said, sitting down. "He'd like to talk to you as soon as possible. Said he tried to call last night, but the line was busy."

"Is there a problem?" I asked.

She frowned. "Well, I'd rather you work this out between the two of you, but I guess I am responsible, too, since I am the one who recommended you for the job."

"What's wrong?"

"Well, it seems that Mr. Sellers drove up to check on his uncle yesterday afternoon. Nick complained that you haven't shown up to take care of him but twice since you were hired and once you got there late. And about the only thing he had left to eat was a package of baloney and a large jar of coffee. Said he was half starving. Called you 'irresponsible.'"

I shook my head. I'd been a fool to think anyone would believe me. I could throw my notebook in the trash.

"Is that what you think, too?" I asked.

She placed her leathery hand on mine.

"Bass, I've known your family for a long time. Your grandfather was a pillar of this community. I knew your pa from the time he was in diapers. Watched him grow up, trade his knickers in for overalls. And I have a great deal of respect for the memory of your mother."

I stood up, ready to give in to an impulse to run. Miss Millar held onto my arm with a surprisingly strong grip.

"I know the stock you come from. Fine Millarsburg stock."

I yanked my arm away. Even *that* was starting to make me angry. Millarsburg. Millar. That was her name, not mine. A name imposed on us like Puerto Rico was imposed on *Borinquén*. I was a *Borinqueño*, from the land of the brave lord.

"Bass Ramsey, listen to me."

She stood up. To my delight, I realized I had grown so I nearly towered over her.

"I also know Nick Granger. And I know he can be a capricious old goat," she released my arm, "who also has a genius I've never known in anyone else," she said, her voice softening.

I looked down. Why wouldn't he tell me what Puerto Rico was like?

"His nephew knows it, too. Now, why don't you go and call John. You can use my office. He left his number. It's on the blotter next to the phone."

A shiver ran down my spine as I walked into Miss Millar's office and, even today, I can't really explain why. It didn't have anything to do with my having to call Mr. Sellers. The way things had been going in my life, I was resigned to trouble. It was the office itself. There was something very still about the place, lifeless even. Miss Millar's cardigan was draped over the back of her chair. I noticed a red and white hair ribbon among the paper clips resting in a clean ashtray. A porcelain teacup sat next to a pale blue Thermos. And everywhere was the smell of lavender.

"Ah, Sebastian," Mr. Sellers said. "Good of you to call back."

He had a nice phone voice. Something told me he was probably some kind of salesman.

"Have you been having trouble with my uncle?"

"Er –," I stammered, not knowing whether to defend myself or the old guy.

"Don't bother to explain. Please accept my apologies for any inconvenience. What do I owe you?"

"Well, to be honest, I've been wanting to call you."

"Tomorrow will be a week, won't it?" he asked.

"Well, there was the holiday, and – "

I heard him clicking the keys of an adding machine. "Well, then, we'll just consider it a little holiday bonus." Click. Click. *Zing.* The paper tape must have advanced. "Any expenses. Groceries?"

"I did buy a couple of things, but – "

"Did you keep the receipt?"

"Yes, sir."

"Fine. Send it to me and I'll add it to next week's salary. Mrs. Millar has my address."

I found it funny that he referred to her as "Mrs." Everyone knew Miss Millar was a spinster.

"Gas?"

I thought of the free fill-up I was going to get. "Uh – no, sir."

"Well, you certainly aren't *walking* to Painted Creek, are you?"

"No, sir," I said. "Riding my bike, sir." I don't know why I said that. Easier, I guess, or maybe I was learning life is made up of different kinds of truth.

"Well, don't hesitate. I'll put the check in the mail right

away. Want to give me your address or should I just mail it to the library?"

I quickly gave him my address.

"Let me know if you have any problems," he said.

It sounded like he was going to hang up. "Ugh, sir?"

"What is it?"

"I don't know if I really deserve to get paid for a whole week, sir," I said.

John Sellers laughed. "You're right. You deserve more than that. You're putting up with my uncle. You deserve The Medal of Honor."

He hung up.

Miss Millar was at the check-out desk when I stepped out of her office.

"On your way, Bass?" she asked.

I had originally planned on looking at the *Atlas*, but by then I felt like getting as far away from the library as possible.

"Yes, ma'am."

She came dancing over to me, a book in her hand.

"Listen, do me an enormous favor. Surprise Nick with this," she said, handing me the book. "It just came by special delivery," she said.

The cover looked worn and dusty. I turned it over and looked at the title, *The Origin of Continents and Oceans* by Alfred Wegener.

"He's wanted it for so long and I finally got this English-language version."

She pointed to the translator's name.

"This book originally came out in Germany in 1915, I think, and was translated into English by 1922. The author revised it in 1929. We got one of the original German copies of the revision just after the war," she said, clearing her throat, "thanks to your mother."

My ma!

"I still don't know how she managed it, but she did. Nick wanted me to translate it for him. But my German has just never been up to snuff. Your dear mother tried as well, but she found the language too difficult."

Ma spoke Dutch, English, German, French, and I don't know how many other languages. She knew about music and art, was a great cook, a good farm hand, and did fine needlework. I didn't need an old biddy like Darby Millar telling me what she thought my ma could or couldn't do. Like she didn't have a lick of sense or a speck of brains. Like she was a hillbilly, a *jíbara*. Ol' Miss High-and-Mighty. Millar, of Millarsburg fame, she was fond of saying. *Geez.*

I started to say something, but Darby Millar interrupted me. "Don't get me wrong, Bass. I'm not making a comment about your mother's intelligence. This book is *very* technical, you see," she said, placing her hand on the book like a court witness places a hand on the Bible. "The revised version was translated again a few years ago and, we finally have this copy. So all these many years later. I'm so pleased," she said, beaming.

"I won't see him for a few days," I said. If at all, I added to myself. Crazy ol' codger. They would make a good couple.

"That's fine. After all this time."

"Why don't *you* take it to him?" I asked, pushing the book back at her. Seemed to me like she had gone to a lot of trouble for the old guy. And I didn't like her bringing my ma into this. Ma probably didn't want to have anything to do with the book because it was in German. Imagine even asking her! And God knows what kind of pain and suffering she probably had to go through to get the book in the first place.

"Me?" she asked, blushing.

"Sure. Why not? Don't you ever go to see him?"

She touched her fingertips to her cheek. "Oh, occasionally," she said. "I don't drive anymore, so I have to take the bus. It's not terribly convenient. I do try to go by for holidays and such. You know, Thanksgiving. Christmas. Easter. The Fourth of July."

The Fourth of July? That was just last week, I thought.

"I went more often when he first lost his sight," she added. "John used to take me."

"Mr. Sellers?"

"Hmm-hmm," she answered, dreamily.

I held the book out further.

"Oh, no. I'd rather you did it. You'll be the one reading it to him. Besides, with the way you pour over that atlas, you might just find this book interesting. A bit heavy going, though, I'll warn you," she said, smiling.

Did she think *everybody* was a moron?

"I'll figure it out," I said.

She looked a little surprised. She crossed her arms coolly across her small chest. "But all the rage again now. In the center of quite a debate," she assured me.

I pulled the book to my chest. All right, I thought. Calm down. I was beginning to spend half of my time feeling hated, half of my time feeling hateful. As I turned to go, she pointed to my habitual place at the first table by the atlases.

"See you tomorrow?" she asked.

* * *

I watched from the kitchen as Ruth Anne guided our Ford out of the driveway. I hoped she wouldn't use up too much of the gas, just in case Erik thought I'd emptied the tank on purpose. I poured myself a glass of lemonade and took it into my room, setting it on the floor next to my bed. As I stretched out on my stomach, I was at peace for the first time in a long time. The breeze coming through my window screen smelled of rain and it was a clean, summer smell. No one was around. I had nothing to do, no place to be, no one to take care of. I should have bought a comic book or borrowed something from the library. *A History of Puerto Rico*, for example. Miss Millar would have let me take it out, I was sure, even though it was a reference book.

I opened *The Origin of Continents and Oceans* and looked at the copyright page. 1966. Further down, I read that the book was a new English translation of the 1962 printing of *Die Entstehung der Kontinente und Ozeane*. I tried to pronounce the title aloud. If Ma were still alive, I would have asked her to pronounce it for me, just to hear the sound of it come from her lips.

On the next page was a short biography of Wegener. It said that he was born on November 1st, 1880 – All Saints Day, I remember noticing – to an evangelical preacher. That brought Father Wilhelm to mind. How much did he have to do with Erik's conversion? The next paragraph had some stuff about Wegener's schooling, but I skipped over it. Then, catching my interest, it spoke of how in 1906 Wegener and his brother, Kurt, carried out a joint balloon flight of 52½ hours, a record for the time. A couple of years earlier, I had read *Five Weeks in a Balloon* by Verne. I was afraid the whole time the balloon was going to collapse and fall from the sky, and the three men would get eaten up by wild animals. The book made Africa sound like a scary place, not one where the sweet smell of the savanna was carried on the wind. I also read *Voyage to the Center of the Earth*. It scared me half to death, too. I was sure the explorers were going to get trapped there. I was too caught up in the action to understand the boy was telling the story looking back on his experience which meant he had survived. Kind of like the way I'm telling this story.

I looked back at the biography. It said Wegener went on a 2-year expedition to the northeast coast of Greenland. I skipped over stuff about the jobs he held afterwards. Then, in 1912, he went to Greenland again with the idea of spending the winter there. I'd have to remember to look at the *Atlas* when I went back to the library. I needed to situate Greenland more clearly in my mind. I turned the page.

In 1914, Wegener was drafted into the army and was injured with a shot to the arm. After it healed and he returned to duty, he was injured again when a bullet lodged in his neck. The injury made him unfit for active duty, so he was employed in the field meteorological service. He'd already written the first edition of his book by 1915. I remember thinking how Mr. Granger hadn't even run away to join the army yet. The biography said that Wegener wanted to study the connection between geophysics on the one hand and geography and geology on the other. I didn't even know what "geophysics" was. There was lots of stuff about different editions of the book. I skipped over that part, too. Further down it said Wegener had planned a new expedition to Greenland with a guy who died before they could go, but I guess Wegener went anyway. By 1929, the year of the stock market crash, he had "clarified the question of the most favorable route up the inland icecap from the west coast." The main expedition began in 1930. Wegener died in November of that year, on the inland icecap. The biography was signed by Wegener's brother, Kurt.

Then there was a publisher's note to the last German edition dated 1961. I skipped over that. On the next page was the *Foreword* which I originally thought I would skip over, too, until I turned the page and noticed that it was written in 1928 by Alfred Wegener himself. So, I went back and read it.

By the second paragraph, I was already basically lost. I kept running across the phrases, "continental drift" and "drift theory," but I had no idea what either of them could mean. I skimmed quickly through the rest of the *Foreword* without hardly understanding a thing. Still, from the way he wrote, I came away with the idea that Wegener must have been a decent guy. Not stuffy or anything. Down-to-earth. On the next page was the *Table of Contents*. A quick look made me realize I would have to learn more about Wegener and his "drift theory" from some place other than his book. Chapter 2 was on, "The Nature of the Drift Theory and Its Relationship to Hitherto Prevalent Accounts of Changes in the Earth's Surface Configuration in Geological Times." *Wow.* I was going to have to dig out the encyclopedia so I could translate this stuff into normal English. I closed the book on my index finger and stretched out on my back. All this seemed like a lot of work for a rainy summer afternoon. I was really starting to regret not having picked up a comic book. Then, it was Wegener himself who saved me. On an impulse, I opened the book again and turned the page. There was a black and white photo of Wegener with his signature scrawled beneath. A wide tie was knotted sideways at his throat. He didn't look like the type who normally wore one. You couldn't see much of him from the photo, just his bust, but he didn't look particularly imposing. Smallish. Hair cut to the quick. A nice face. Even in the black and white of the photo, his tan showed through. Rugged. Like my Pa. Not one to sit around in the library, I remember thinking. Off to Greenland twice, even died there. There was something about his eyes. Clear-eyed. The photo showed that. I'd bet they were even blue. Like mine. Like Treat's.

I got up and went all the way to the living room to get the encyclopedia. A loud thunderclap startled me. Then there was the hiss of rain. And Ruth Anne is out in this, I thought to myself. I closed the window to my room and checked a few other windows to make sure the rain wasn't coming in before heading back to my reading.

I thumbed the "W" pages until I got to *Wegener*. There was only a small paragraph. Stuff I knew already from the biography I'd just read. At the bottom, it said, "See Continental Drift Theory." Doggone it! I had to get up and get another volume of the encyclopedia. In the living room, I pulled the volume marked "BR – CY" from the shelf and sat down on the floor with it. Just in case.

"The theory that continents move laterally with respect to each other was considered highly revolutionary when it was first proposed. A German meteorologist, A.L. Wegener, early in the 20th century, was the first to develop it as an integrated theory." It continued, "Wegener postulated that, beginning in the Mesozoic Era and continuing to the present, a huge primeval supercontinent that he called Pangaea (or Pangea; Greek for "all land") had rifted and the pieces had separated to form the present continents."

It then went on to talk about when and how the continents had separated. All that geological time period stuff I could never keep straight. It also talked of Wegener's celebrated theory of the "jigsaw fit" of the Atlantic continents. Jigsaw? With the word, two things raced through my mind. The first was a vision of the surface of the Earth as a giant jigsaw puzzle. I pictured the continents as painted, wooden puzzle pieces like the kind we used in elementary school to put together the map of the United States. Once the map was finished, inevitably, one of us would tilt it over until all of the puzzle pieces slid out of the thin cardboard frame, onto the table and, sometimes, onto the floor. It was one of our favorite games. In my mind, I saw the surface of the Earth breaking up in the same way, the continents sliding across the surface and becoming separated by larger and larger spaces. Several pieces crashed into each other, damaging their edges. In short, all hell breaking loose.

The other thing running through my mind was the phrase, "beginning in the Mesozoic Era and *continuing to the present.*" Was it possible the very ground I was sitting on was sliding over the smooth ball of the Earth and someday would go careening into another puzzle piece?

The article went on about how other scientists didn't agree with Wegener that the continents had split. They thought there were sorts of "transoceanic land-bridges" that had sunk, like, it said, "the fabled Atlantis." It seemed to me I remembered something from history class about Russia and Alaska having once been connected and the Eskimos having walked between the two. Or something like that.

"Other evidence supporting Wegener's hypothesis came from a comparison of the rocks on both sides of the Atlantic, which seems to indicate that the continents had been closely connected in the past, and from a study of ancient climatic zones. Thus a series of late Paleozoic sedimentary deposits known as tillites, indicating the earlier existence of ice sheets, was known to exist in South Africa, South America, India and Australia. Their distribution could best be accounted for by supposing that the continents had once been arranged to form Gondwanaland, the southern part of Pangaea, and that of the South Pole."

Gondwanaland. I repeated the name to myself several times, feeling it echo against my tonsils. What a beautiful sound.

"The distribution of Carboniferous coal deposits also indicated that Europe and the United States had been situated in an equatorial belt at the time the tillites were deposited farther south."

I stopped reading. *An equatorial belt!* Michigan! Incredible. I put the encyclopedia back on the shelf.

* * *

Ruth Anne came around to our living room, tapped once on the screened door before walking in and broke my heart in the process. I missed those times when we used to walk in and out of each other's house like that without needing to be invited.

"Thanks for the car, Sebastian," she said, handing me the keys. "I stopped by the Sinclair station and topped off the tank," she said.

"You didn't have to do that," I said. But I was a little bit relieved. I wouldn't have to do it on Friday.

"Of course I did. Besides," she added, lowering her voice, "I wanted to talk to Erik." She shrugged her shoulders. "He sure has changed."

"Erik? How so?"

"I don't know. He seems so, well – *manicured.*"

"Would you rather he looked like Mike?" I asked.

Mike, the elder Bauer brother, seemed to have been born with a mustache and grease under his nails. Kids used to say that he couldn't keep a steady girlfriend because his hands were so grimy that if he even tried to feel a girl up, his hands would slide right off. My general feeling had always been that Mike didn't care what folks said about him, and I was starting to admire him for it.

"At least with Mike," she responded, "what you see is what you get."

She looked at me a long moment before turning to go back out.

* * *

The word "manicured" was the first thing that popped into my mind when I saw Erik Friday night. It wasn't like he was in coat and tails, or anything, but, compared to the jeans and T-shirt I had on, he wasn't far from it. He was wearing a white V-neck sweater with alternating dark blue and green stripes along the neck, the kind tennis players wore, over a cream-colored short-sleeve shirt. He wore a matching pair of white cotton pants. Both the shirt and the pants were ironed to perfection. He also had on a pair of light brown tasseled loafers buffed into a mirror-like shine. He'd apparently been to the barber to have his hair razor cut. The haircut showed off his green eyes and the fine shape of his head. And he smelled so strongly of cologne that sometimes I've wonder, all these years later, if the inside of the old Fairlane, now piled in a rusted heap of wrecked cars at DiVolterra's Junk Yard and Scrap Metal in the wooded hills of Pennsylvania, still reeks of it. Erik's ma greeted me kindly enough when she answered the door, remembering to ask after Pa, Uncle Will, and Aunt Sally. His pa was still at the store. Erik told me that they, like The Bauer Boys, were keeping their store open a little later than usual, taking advantage of the long summer days to try to bring in more clients – from where, I didn't know. I think it was pretty much common knowledge that Erik and his pa had called a kind of truce. It seemed essential to their truce that they never be in each other's company for more than ten minutes. So, when one was home, the other went out. And vice versa. With a bit of luck on Erik's part, by the time we got back in the evening, his pa would already be in bed. And, I suppose, Peter Roth would be up and gone before Erik was stirring the next morning. I was just as glad not to have to see Mr. Roth. The last time I saw him was when the bunch of us showed up at the Feed & Seed in the back of Uncle Will's pick-up to interrogate Erik about Treat's disappearance. I thought Erik was lucky enough to still have both parents, but I wasn't sure, given the way things were, it was how *he* felt. Nor could I imagine old man Roth was happy to find his boy in bed each morning rather than run off because, best I could figure, Erik's pa had been wishing that very thing for the longest time.

I pulled out of the Roths' driveway.

"Take a right at the light," Erik said. "Then keep going. I'll tell you when."

I still didn't understand why we couldn't just go to the RKO in town. It was a pretty nice theater from what I recalled. I'd been there with our school a few times to see history and nature films and stuff like that. A few summers back, Father Wilhelm even had to say Mass there since the old church was all torn up. The parish had paid for a new heating system and B&C Plumbing and Heating wanted to get it installed before the weather changed or before deer season opened, whichever came first. But the seats at the theater were so soft and comfortable, everyone had a tendency to fall right asleep. And the theater was air conditioned, too. I slept through every mass that hot summer. Neither Pa nor Ma ever yelled at me, so my guess is that they must have napped a bit themselves.

"Mind if I turn on the radio?" he asked.

"Go ahead."

The radio was tuned to an all-news station out of Detroit. Ruth Anne must have been listening to it when she borrowed the car.

"Can I change the station?" he asked.

"Sure," I said. The only thing I ever listened to on the radio was Tiger baseball and to the best of my knowledge the Tigers were off that night.

The station he turned on had a lot of singing on it. Not just a lot of songs, but a lot of folks singing at one time. They were pretty peppy, too.

"What kind of music is that?" I asked. Pa wasn't much of a

music lover and Ma had only listened to classical music, which I don't like very much, so my musical influences were pretty limited.

"Gospel," he answered.

"Isn't that Negro music?" I asked.

"Yeah," he said, snapping his fingers in time to the lively beat. "I guess you could call it that."

"But isn't it like – *religious* stuff?" I asked.

The question stuck in my throat. Maybe it was an All-Time-Stupid-Question. Worse, maybe he would think I was making a backhanded reference to his calling.

"I guess so," he said. "I don't really catch all of the words." He laughed. 'But I like it anyway."

We drove for another twenty minutes or so and had just crossed the line into the city of Royalty when he suddenly called out, "Hey!" and, leaning forward, "Turn left here."

I turned onto a deserted street that was not even a half-mile long. A few cars that looked pretty broken down were parked on either side of it. If the curbs had been higher, I might have even been tempted to say that the cars were leaning against them for support. Other than a few tumble-down houses, there were only four buildings on the street, but it seemed to be the center of what there was of a town. Maybe there had been other buildings in the past and these were the only ones still standing. On one side of the street were a small grocery store and an ice cream shop with a drive-through and several wooden tables on the sidewalk. On the other side of the street was a drug store attached to a dilapidated house and a sagging wooden structure fighting a losing battle with gravity. Maybe the Earth was slipping out from beneath the place, I thought to myself. The building had a high facade right out of Hollywood's Old West. When I studied it, I realized it was a painted marquee, though the paint was peeling off.

"You can park here," Erik said, pointing to the curb in front of the building.

"Where are we?" I asked.

"Royalty," he answered, grinning. "Royalty, Michigan." He pointed to the building. "And that there is the 'Royalty Theater'."

Is this some kind of joke? I wondered. Maybe I had underestimated him. Maybe he was mad at me after all and this was his way of getting back. I threw the car back into 'Drive,' but kept my foot on the brake.

"What are you doing?" he asked. "The movie is going to start in a few minutes!"

I looked at my watch. It was about seventeen minutes after six. Seemed like an odd hour for a movie to start, but then again what did I know? It wasn't like I was a regular or anything. I looked over at the building. What seemed to be a movie poster was hung inside the entrance to the theater. But, like the charts in Mr. Granger's apartment, one top edge of the poster-board had come unfastened from the wall and was curled in on itself so that the poster showed its back to me.

"Are you going to park or what?" he asked, impatient.

"What are we going to see?" I asked back, my hand on the gear shift.

Erik grinned at me. Why hadn't I thought to ask him before? The place didn't look very respectable. Maybe it was an X-rated theater, a pornographic joint. Maybe he was going to introduce me to my first pornographic film! If that were the case, I didn't know whether to be pleased or not. Pa had said once that he would tan my backside if he ever found out I went to one. On the other hand, the thought of seeing such a film – well, excited me. The palms of my hands sweated against the hard plastic of the wheel and the gear shift. I'd seen women in bathing suits, bikinis even, but never entirely naked. And never, you know, *doing* things. Like I said, Pa had explained to me about sex when I was 12 years old, but in a vague kind of roundabout way that had left me with lots of questions. Growing up in a rural area, I had seen animals "doing it," of course, but couldn't really picture the sex act between two people. And with Treat gone, I didn't feel like I had anyone I could ask now that I was older. Plus, Pa had talked a lot about love and responsibility. To be honest, it made sex seem almost like a chore, and not the kind of wild, animal-like act I figured would be shown in a pornographic film. Was it a kind of raging? Or was it controlled by feelings of duty and commitment? I'm sure Pa and Ma thought it was the latter. They had both spoken in no uncertain terms about the sanctity of marriage and saving oneself for it. Pa had said he'd do more than tan my backside if ever I got a girl in trouble. Trouble leads to trouble, he had said. I'd have to take his word on it. I looked at the crumbling facade of the Royalty Theater. Maybe this is where Erik used to drive his mother's car when no one knew where he went. To a porn show! Although Uncle Will was right; Erik had never been known to go steady or even be particularly girl crazy. And if a fashion show or garage were strange places for a guy with a calling, what could be said about an X-rated film?

"It's a surprise. Just park the car," he pleaded.

"I don't like surprises," I said. I'd had a few too many already.

"It's good. C'mon."

"You've seen it already?"

"At least a million times. I think it was even on television. But it's better on the big screen. C'mon," he said again, opening his door.

I had to admit, I was a little relieved. If the film had been on television, it couldn't be all that pornographic. On the other hand, maybe I had just missed my introduction to sex. I threw the car into "Park" but stayed in my seat.

"You've got to tell me what we're going to see, first," I said.

"All right." He looked truly disappointed. *"Spartacus."*

"Spartacus!" I thought for a minute. "Isn't that a film about one of those Greek guys who runs around in a leather skirt and sandals and kills lots of people?" I asked.

Erik laughed. "Have you seen it already?" he asked.

"Maybe," I answered. "A long time ago."

"It couldn't have been *that* long ago. You'd only have been a little kid," he said.

"When did it come out?" I asked.

"Sixty-one, think. Maybe sixty-two."

In 1962 I was nine years old, I thought. Erik, like Treat, would have been eleven, going on twelve. Ruth Anne told me in some parts of Africa a boy of twelve gets circumcised and, from then on, is considered a man. Ruth Anne was learning a lot about Africa before she went there, reading up on it and going to conferences. I'd try to remember to look up The Congo in *Granger's World Atlas* the next time I went to the library.

"It's good. C'mon," Erik pleaded.

"What are they doing still showing it here?" I asked.

Erik shrugged. "I don't know. I asked the guy at the ice cream shop once," he said pointing across the street, "and he said he'd heard the theater had gone broke a long time ago. Said the only reason it was still open was because the folks who run it own it and live above it. He said they'd had to sell off just about everything including the popcorn machine and soda fountain to cover their debts. He also said he'd heard that somebody, out of kindness, maybe, had let them keep the copy of this film since it was the last thing they had shown, and maybe they'd be able to continue to make some money off of it. At least enough to cover lights and electricity and everything. But I think they just never got around to sending it back to wherever they were supposed to send it. They were going under anyway, so what did they care?"

I pictured the theater slipping under the mantle of the Earth and slowly melting into its hot lava core.

"You mean they've been showing this film since 1961?"

"I guess it's possible. They've been showing it for at least the last couple of years," he answered. "Let's go."

I followed him down the narrow entrance into the wide lobby of the theater. In the center of the lobby there was a surprisingly large fountain. In the middle of the fountain was the giant figure of a particularly buxom woman. She was carrying a white basket of fruit and flowers in one hand out of which water was supposed to flow down around her and into a shallow basin at her feet. Water was meant to shoot out of the stamens of one of the large flowers, but the flow had been turned off. The sprinkler ends of the system had gone rusty. Some of the gold paint was peeling from the bunch of grapes she held in her other hand, but otherwise, the fountain seemed to be in pretty good shape. And totally out of place. The wallpaper in the foyer had faded into that indefinable color that came with age. The cashier's cage was just behind the fountain. It was cylinder-shaped and enclosed in Plexiglas from the desktop to the ceiling so that a person sitting inside of it might look like he or she were stuffed into a vial. The problem was, there was no one sitting in it. Or so I thought.

"There's no one at the box office," I said to Erik. "Maybe it's closed today."

He laughed. "Nah, it's open. Trust me."

He signaled to me to move closer to the box office.

In fact, there was someone. Judging from the heavily-veined and spotted hands and fingers pinched by rings, it was a woman, probably an older woman, and one who was more than a little overweight. Her head, like her bulky arms and hands, was resting on the desk. Her off-blond curls had fallen around her face, hiding it from view. She seemed to be asleep. While we were standing there, she snored loudly enough for us to hear. Erik had to cover his mouth with his hand to keep from laughing.

"C'mon," he said.

I stared back at him, my legs unable to move.

"You mean?"

"C'mon. You wouldn't be able to wake her if you tried. Believe me." He mimicked a drinking motion.

"But we can't just go in without paying," I protested.

"I usually give a tip to her husband, the projectionist – if *he's* sober." Erik checked his watch. "At this hour, he might still be."

We entered the darkened theater. It was no surprise to find we were the only ones there. We walked down the sloping aisle into the middle of the room, then across to the middle of a row. My sneakers made a kind of sucking sound as I walked. Erik sat down and threw his feet up onto the back of the chair in front of him. I remember thinking it would have been another reason for my pa to tan my backside. I sat down. The seat of my chair tilted to the left practically spilling me into Erik's lap. I got up, stepped with difficulty over his raised legs and sat in the chair on the other side of him. This time the back of the chair felt funny, like the stuffing in it was squirting out the back.

"Here," Erik said, getting up and moving to the first chair I had vacated. "Take mine. It's the best one in the house."

I thanked him and sat down. I didn't notice much difference from either of the other two chairs, but I didn't say anything. I took it as a nice gesture on his part. He threw his feet up onto the back of the chair in front of him again.

"Might want to put your feet up," he said.

"Why?" I asked.

"Rats."

"Rats!" I threw my heels over the back of the seat in front of me. "Erik," I said, just as the movie was starting, "Why do you come *here*?"

"Where else do you have an entire theater to yourself? And it's free." He spread his arms out. "Plus, it's the only place I know still showing this film. It's one of my favorite stories in the world, although the book was better."

"You read the book, too?" I asked.

"Yeah. A couple of times." He laughed. "Shh! It's starting."

The screen suddenly went blank.

"Don't worry," he said. "Just a rough spot."

Sure enough, the film started up again, although grainy and worse for the wear.

As soon as Kirk Douglas appeared on the screen, Erik let out a whopping yell.

"Spartacus!"

"What's so great about this film?" I asked. I was more partial to Westerns. I had been hoping for a good John Wayne film. *El Dorado*, for example.

"What's so great about it? It has everything. It's about freedom and courage and love. It's about standing up to people. It's about dignity. It's about romance and poetry. Mostly, though, it's about friendship." He smiled at me.

"I thought there was a lot of blood and guts in it," I said.

"Not that much really. There's really only one big battle scene."

"Oh," I said, disappointed. "Any good love scenes?"

"Bass!"

"Well, are there?"

"Depends on what you mean by 'love scenes.'"

"You know, 'Boy meets girl. They fall in love.'"

As I was talking, slave women were being given to the gladiators for their pleasure. Spartacus was given a beautiful, doe-eyed woman. I didn't catch her name. I never did learn it throughout the entire 3-hour film. In my mind, I simply called her Celia. Turns out Spartacus had about as much experience with women as I did. I was surprised. Romans spying on him from above his cell where he was kept mocked his lack of virility. Spartacus screamed, "I'm not an animal! I'm not an animal."

"Neither am I," Erik cried out. On screen, the slave woman mouthed the words at the same time.

I looked over at Erik. "Do you know the whole film by heart?"

He shrugged sheepishly. "Pretty much. But there are some parts I like better than others."

The part I liked the best was towards the end. The slaves who revolted had been killed or captured. The Romans said they would not crucify the remaining prisoners, only return them to their fate as slaves if they identified Spartacus. Defeated, Spartacus began to stand up to turn himself in and save the others. Before he could say his name, his friend, Antoninus, a poet and gentle soul played by Tony Curtis, stood up with him and claimed that *he* was Spartacus. And before long, slaves were standing everywhere, thousands of voices crying, "I'm Spartacus! I'm Spartacus! I'm Spartacus!" Now, that was friendship, I thought.

"Did you like it?" Erik asked after it was over.

"Sure did," I said.

"We can come back again next week, if you want. I'll make some popcorn."

I walked stiffly out of the theater. I'd unhinged my hips sitting in the broken chair. I couldn't feel either foot. The old lady was still sacked out in the box office. For a minute, I wondered if she had died while we were watching the movie, but then she snorted in a bit of the stagnant air of the place which reassured me she was still alive.

"We forgot to tip the projectionist," I said.

Erik waved his hand, "We'll get him next week."

I dug into the pocket of my jeans for the car keys. Erik grabbed my wrist.

"Want a sundae?" he asked, indicating the ice cream shop with the tip of his head. "My treat."

"That's all right."

"C'mon. To thank you for driving. And," he added, "for coming with me."

"We could go to the ice cream parlor in Millarsburg," I suggested.

"They're too stingy. They're not like that here," he said.

He strode across the street without looking either way first. Royalty was that kind of town.

"Besides," I said, catching up to him. "We don't know anyone here."

"Precisely," he answered.

The guy behind the counter looked like he must have been in his thirties. In Millarsburg, there were mostly high school girls working at the ice cream parlor. Maybe the guy was the owner, I thought.

"Back again?" he asked Erik.

Erik smiled, "Yeah, and I brought a friend."

The man bent down to look through the serving window.

"How do," he said, although he didn't look terribly happy to see me.

"Evening," I said.

"The usual?" he asked Erik.

"One each," Erik answered. Then, to me, "Go and have a seat. I'll bring 'em over."

I walked over to one of two wooden picnic tables and sat down on the bench. I looked up and down the street. The town was completely deserted. The Old West style of some of the storefronts was appropriate. The place was a ghost town.

Erik was taking a long time. I heard him talking to the man, although I couldn't make out what they were saying. They seemed to be pretty good friends. When Erik finally did come over, he was carrying two of the biggest banana split sundaes I had ever seen. He handed me mine and then, sitting down on the tabletop, dug into his own.

Neither of us said anything for a time while we were eating. Good thing, too, or we might not have finished those sundaes until Kingdom come. By the time I saw the bottom of my plastic boat, eating that sundae had started to seem like work. Erik finished his up quietly, too. He'd calmed down a lot since the end of the movie. It was like he was far away.

While we were walking to the car Erik asked me, "What did you think of Antoninus? You know, the poet."

"You mean Tony Curtis?"

Erik shook his head. "Yeah, *Tony Curtis*."

"Seemed like he was pretty homesick."

"I think he just didn't feel like he belonged anywhere."

"He could have stayed with that Roman guy. Been his personal servant. It looked like he would have been treated pretty well."

"Are you kidding?" Erik screamed. "Crassius would have just used him like a slave."

"But he *was* a slave."

"Not in his mind, he wasn't. That's why he ran away."

Erik shot a look over at me. But it was too late. He'd used the forbidden phrase.

"C'mon. Let's go," I said.

I pulled the Fairlane gently away from the curb. Erik

waved to the fellow at the ice cream shop, who nodded his head.

"This is a nice car," Erik said, running his hand along the front bench.

"Thanks," I said, not knowing or caring whether it was a nice car or not. It got me to where I needed to go. I tried to keep it in good shape because it was the proper thing to do and because I was sure Pa didn't have the money to buy another car. But, given the way I had gotten my driver's license, I had never taken any real joy in driving it.

"Ed's going to help me pick out a used car," Erik said. "I'm tired of having to ask my ma to borrow her car every time I want to go somewhere."

"Besides," he continued, still guiding his hand over the vinyl seat, "I'll need it when it comes time to leave."

I took my eyes off of the road long enough to question him.

"Leave? Leave where?"

"Why, Millarsburg, of course."

"When?" I asked. "Soon?"

Memories came flooding back of the day Treat told me he was going to run away.

"Soon as I've saved up enough money," he answered.

"What about your job?"

"Mike and Ed already know when the time comes, I'm going to leave. I told them that from the beginning," he said. "But I asked them not to say anything to anyone."

From what I knew, not too many people had long, drawn out conversations with the Bauer brothers anyway. But say what you like about The Boys, they weren't known for mouthing off other folks' business.

"Besides," he continued, "I don't think God put me on this Earth to pump gas for the rest of my life. At least I hope not."

Ruth Anne had said something about "finding one's role"

after she told us she would be going to Africa. I didn't know if "finding one's role" was a particularly religious idea or not. I guessed I'd slept through a few too many masses to know. It seemed to be. God put us on this Earth for a reason, she had said, and our job was to find out what that reason is and then act on the knowledge. Erik's statement was the closest thing I had heard him come to professing the same belief. Maybe he was thinking of becoming a missionary himself. Or even a priest. I wasn't too sure, but I liked the idea a lot better than the thought that he, like Treat, was going to run away.

"Where are you thinking of going?" I asked.

He shrugged and looked down, suddenly shy.

"To a seminary?" I added.

I noticed that his hand had frozen on the car seat.

"To a – *what?*"

I was afraid to look over again. Anyway, I could hear the laughter rising up inside of him without needing to look over. When it exploded, I was a little surprised by its force. He was nearly hysterical.

"A *seminary!*" he screamed out, and, laughing, he threw his head on the back of the seat.

I stared at the road ahead of me. And realized I didn't know where I was or even how to find the way back. I've always had a sense of direction like a falling leaf, anyway. Erik laughed for a long time, almost too long, I noticed, his head resting on the back of the seat and his eyes closed. I figured he was going to have to get a hold of himself in a hurry and tell me which way to go or we'd end up in Detroit. Like a lot of country roads in the region, the one we were on was only marked with a county number, a number that didn't mean a thing to me.

"Stop here," he said finally, indicating the side of the road. "I've got to whiz."

I waited for him looking down at the dashboard. He could have gone around to the back of the car, after all.

When he got back into the Fairlane, Erik was a lot more serious. We were both quiet for a few minutes. He seemed lost in his own thoughts. I was torn between asking him directions and asking him to where, if not a seminary, he was planning on going.

"Well?" was all I could eventually manage. The memory of Treat had robbed me of my words. Would I have to keep a secret for Erik, too?

I saw him shake his head out of the corner of my eye.

"No. I'm not going off to any seminary," he said. I felt him looking at me. "Why did you ask me that? Why did you ask me if I was going to go to a seminary?"

"It's just – my aunt Sally told me that she thought maybe you had a calling."

I looked over at him. I was sure I had already missed the turn back to Millarsburg.

"Why's that?"

"Because of how close you were to Father Wilhelm."

"Everybody seems to have their own way of interpreting my friendship with Father Wilhelm. Gets under folks' skin, for some reason," he said, shaking his head. "especially my pa's."

"What about your folks?" I asked. "How do you think they're going to feel about you leaving?"

"That's just the thing. You know how things are with my pa," he answered.

"And your ma?" I looked over at him.

He examined one of the ribs in the upholstery, fingering it with his left hand.

"My ma is married to my pa," he said, looking up. "If you get my meaning."

I screwed up my courage. "Where do you think you'll go?"

"I don't know yet. Someplace far from here," he said, looking out the window. "Shit! Where are we?" he asked, sitting straight up.

"I was hoping you were going to tell me," I answered. "I think I missed the turn off."

"You sure did!" he said, turning to watch the road disappear behind us. "Like about ten miles ago."

He sat back in this chair. "Oh, well," he said. "I like to drive around. I'm not in any big hurry to get home."

"As long as we *get* home," I said. My voice must have betrayed a little more nervousness than I would have liked. I realized I had never been lost before. I'd never really gone far enough on my own to get lost.

Erik reached over and put his hand on my leg where he let it rest a few minutes before lifting it off.

"Don't worry, Bass. We'll get home."

I didn't like him touching me. It left me feeling funny. It wasn't like a handshake man-to-man. Second, it made me feel like a baby, someone needing to be comforted. It was something Treat would have done, just to get my goat. It made me almost want to reach out and crack Erik a good one. I didn't only because I sensed he hadn't done it in the same spirit Treat would have. And it made me sad because it made me realize I didn't have all that much touching in my life since my ma had died. I guess after a certain age, a guy isn't supposed to want his ma hanging around his neck. But I missed her touch. Sometimes if I went into the kitchen while she was making supper, Ma would reach out and touch my face. Her fingers often smelled of onions and herbs, and to this day the smell of onions on my own fingertips still breaks my heart. And since my pa had retreated inside himself, I don't think he had touched me at all. I still remember how protected I had felt by the bulk of his body when, as a little kid, he stood behind me while he showed me how to hold a baseball bat.

"Bass?"

"Yeah?"

"Remember the day at the station you asked me what it meant to be a man?" he asked.

"Yeah."

"Why'd you ask me that?"

I shrugged, trying to seem uninterested. "Just a question, that's all."

"But, I mean. Why'd you ask *me*? And not somebody else?"

Luckily there was a stop sign ahead. By the time I got to it, I could no longer see.

"Who am I supposed to ask?"

The tears came before I could even think of holding them back. I bawled like a baby. Erik slid over on the bench and took me in his arms, smoothing down my hair and saying, "There, there. There, now," just like a mother would. I let him hold me. I don't know where all that pain sprang up from, but once it started flowing, I had no way of stopping it. When I had finally cried everything out of me, I looked up at Erik. He was looking back at me with more understanding than I had seen in anyone's eyes in a long time. But I pulled away. I felt ashamed then, humiliated. The touching I had been in such need of suddenly felt uncomfortable. And I was exhausted. I must have looked it.

"Want me to drive?" he asked softly.

I nodded. He got out and came around to the driver's side. I barely had the strength to pull myself across the front seat. I didn't even have the power to move my own body. If only the Earth would tilt and slide me over, I thought. I don't remember anything from the ride home. I just wanted darkness, I just wanted to be alone.

* * *

Our house was dark. Erik pulled the Fairlane up to our garage door, but it was closed. I vaguely remembered Pa saying he and Uncle Will had a meeting and wouldn't be back until late.

"Should I just leave her here?" Erik asked.

I nodded glumly. I felt completely washed out, exhausted. The tastes of banana and chocolate and cherries swirled in the back of my throat. I remember thinking that probably the best thing I could do would be to go into the bathroom and try to make myself sick and that put me in mind of Treat who, after he had thrown up all of the spicy food he had eaten at Celia's camper, seemed to feel better. But I hated getting sick. It always made me panic, afraid I might suffocate to death. And without my ma there to wipe a cool washcloth on my forehead and the back of my neck and bring me a bottle of ginger ale afterwards to help get the taste out of my mouth, well – I decided I'd rather just keep on feeling sick.

Erik had just stepped around to my side of the car to help me get out, gentlemanly as ever, when Aunt Sally came out of their house. She stood a safe distance away, with her hands on her hips as though we might be dangerous or rabid or both. I prayed that the Earth would open up and swallow me whole.

"What's this?" she cried. "I should have known. You boys have been drinking!"

"No, ma'am," Erik said, trying to explain. I felt him take a step forward.

"You can stop right there, young man. You are not welcome anywhere near this house!" she said. "Ruth Anne! Come and help your cousin. He seems to have lost control of himself!"

I heard her stride off and several minutes later Ruth Anne's quick, quiet steps came toward me. Erik gently transferred my weight onto her shoulders.

"What is it?" she whispered.

"Stomach ache. Too much ice cream," I heard him say. I heard the jingle of car keys changing hands.

I didn't think about it until I was in the much wished for darkness of my room, but no one had offered to drive Erik home. There were seven miles between Millarsburg and Black River. Even Spartacus would have found that a long way.

* * *

The next morning marked a turning point in my life. I felt it as soon as I opened my cried-out eyes. I found myself lying on my back in bed or in what has always been for me a dreaded position. For several strange minutes I was lost, waiting for the realization of who and where I was to come flooding back after the amnesia of deep sleep. I felt wrung out, weak, disoriented. But oddly enough, I no longer felt vulnerable. It was like I, too, had gone to the center of the Earth, had been brought face-to-face with my own mortality and come back out the other side. I had been spewed from the mouth of the volcano, scorched by lava and scraped up by a landing on the rough outer crust of the world. But, damn it, I was alive. All this time I had been trying to make myself believe I was dead. And that meant I was even what you could call a survivor.

The farms were incredibly quiet. In those first waking minutes I remembered that it was Saturday, the day of Kate's show. I rolled over and looked at my alarm clock. It was nearly noon. I'd slept for almost fourteen hours.

I was only awake a short time and still lying in my bed when I heard a car pull into the driveway. I remember thinking that if it were Aunt Sally, she'd probably be mad as a hornet about what she thought had happened last night. And about my not being at Kate's show. Well, I thought, swinging my feet out of bed, let her buzz. I'd done nothing wrong. Besides, Erik was supposed to be the one emceeing Kate's show that day. And he hadn't deserved the reception she gave him the night before. The only thing Erik had ever done to her was tell the truth. My heart pinched a little at the thought of Kate, though. I didn't even know if her show was in the morning or the afternoon. Maybe I had already missed it.

I heard the gentle tread of feet on the kitchen linoleum. It was Ruth Anne.

"Sebastian?" she called out softly. She was the only one who would occasionally call me that rather than the nickname everyone had started using when, as a kid, I couldn't pronounce my given name. That morning, my full name sounded strong and resonant.

"In here," I called from my room. I stumbled out into the kitchen, barefoot and yawning.

"Feeling better?" she asked.

"Yeah," I grunted. "Has the show started?"

"No," she answered. "Soon. I came back to make some sandwiches and," she paused, "to see how you were feeling."

"I'm fine. Thanks." I looked around. "Is everyone at the high school?"

"Everyone but Uncle Thomas," she answered. "He had an appointment with the accountant. Said he would try to make it to the show after if he could, but that it might take a while. Ma left early this morning with Kate – I think she had the jitters and just needed to get over there."

"Kate?" I asked, surprised.

"No. Ma.' She laughed. "Kate is cool as a cucumber."

"Of course," I said grinning, proud of her.

"Of course," Ruth Anne grinned back. "Pa and I followed along later. It gave us a chance to talk." She shook her head. "I don't know whether to admire him or not. The way he carries on, you'd think everything in our family was fine. Which, of course, is far from the truth." She looked over at me. "I've been wanting to talk to Kate to see how she's faring in all of this, but there just hasn't been time. Not with her show, and everything. And Kate, God bless her, has always lived in her own world anyway. I have the feeling more and more that it's what will finally save her."

"Save her? From what?" Of all of us, Kate was maybe the one who least needed to be saved.

"From her birthright," she said, standing stock still.

I remember thinking maybe the desire for truth doesn't set us free after all. It glues us smack in our place.

"I know," Ruth Anne continued. "I'm speaking in riddles."

She walked over to me and laid a hand softly on my shoulder and I was reminded of the strange scene the night before with Erik.

"See you over there?"

The cafeteria/auditorium was nearly full. I found out from Ruth Anne that there had already been a talent show that morning. Several students had sung Broadway numbers and a pair of sisters, twins, had tap-danced. An upright piano could still be seen off to one side of the stage. Other students had read poetry and short pieces of fiction. The student leader of the marching band had given a trumpet solo. And a dozen or so paintings stood on easels around the outer edges of the room; their young artists stood next to them, blushing.

Ruth Anne told me that Kate's show was to be the final, crowning act of the day before the judges handed out prizes. It was all supposed to be over by three o'clock. I remember feeling lucky that I hadn't completely missed it.

Kate was standing not too far from the stage, dressed in a smart-fitting cream-colored pantsuit. Her golden blond hair hung like a silk curtain down her back. She was talking to a young man who was dressed surprisingly like Erik had been the night before; maybe that was the new fashion. His dark good looks and tanned skin stood out against the white of his sweater. Athletically-built, he was balanced firmly on both feet. Girls may have found him "dreamy," but he was the one who looked entranced by my little cousin who, probably to his regret, was all business. She was explaining something to him while they consulted a piece of paper on which must have been written the script to the show. Aunt Sally was racing around, giving instructions to a group of boys who were putting the runway into place and re-arranging folding chairs around it. I couldn't find Uncle Will and Ruth Anne in the audience, so I found an empty chair near the back and sat down. I decided I wasn't needed.

I looked around the room. Another pair of eyes caught mine. They belonged to Erik. He was dressed exactly as he had been the night before, exactly like Tim Kirsten. Knowing Erik, the irony of the situation hadn't escaped him. I hoped he'd had a good laugh about it. He might have been the only person I knew capable of laughing at such a thing. He stared at me a long time before nodding, like he wasn't sure that I was really seeing him. I nodded back, but was glad when he didn't show any sign of coming over to sit by me.

I must admit, I was pretty surprised by Kate's show. Right out of *Gay Paree*, or wherever it is that is the fashion capitol of the world. Real stuff, smart and elegant at the same time. I thought Tim Kirsten gave a pretty stiff performance, though. But Kate didn't seem to notice. In fact, she seemed oblivious to the whole business, concentrated on her creations. I caught her once gesturing to one of the cheerleaders who was modeling a calf-length skirt outfit. As the girl was preparing to leave the stage, Kate signaled to her that she should turn around and come back down the ramp one more time, then turn around again. The skirt swirled each time the girl turned. I guess Kate wanted to see how the fabric moved and, judging from her reaction, she was pleased. Erik was already gone when I looked over after the show. He'd done me a favor. I didn't especially want to have to face him. I did go up and congratulate Kate. She said, "I'm glad you're feeling better and could make it," which made me think that she wasn't lost in her own world as much as we tended to think. But I quickly excused myself. I didn't feel like sticking around for the awards ceremony and, as far as I could tell, my pa hadn't made it back from the accountant's yet.

I realized with a mixture of agony and pleasure when I woke on Sunday morning that I didn't have a thing planned for the day. Going to the library was out of the question, of course, since it was closed. So was the Sinclair station, the other of my usual haunts. There was probably a ball game on television, but not until that afternoon. That left the morning for me to occupy. I entertained the fleeting thought of going by to see Mr. Granger, but chased it quickly from my mind. He wouldn't be expecting me and would probably yell. Besides, I was supposed to be mad at him. I looked up at the piece of sky that showed through the rectangle of my bedroom window. The heavens were a bright white-blue. It was going to be another scorching day. The summer seemed to burn hotter that year than it had in the past for some reason even though Treat and I had spent most of our time playing outside. A car raced down the street, breaking the stifling silence, and reminding me that while I was lying on my side pondering the day ahead, the rest of the world was already up and turning. I heard my pa leave for mass. I couldn't remember when he had stopped waking me up to go with him.

I was having trouble deciding if I should get up before the heat got too unbearable or simply wait for it to drive me from my bed. I could hear the morning tones of conversation coming from the picnic table. There was the baritone of a male voice – Uncle Will's for sure – and the higher timbre of at least one female voice, maybe two. It was probably Aunt Sally. It didn't sound like Ruth Anne. And Kate wasn't one to sit around talking. Even after her fine show the day before, I couldn't imagine her lingering over the breakfast table, rehashing the show, or worse, gloating. To no one's particular surprise, she had come home with First Place and the Mayor's Medal of Merit. But knowing Kate, she was already buried under piles of cloth in the basement, stitching together another creation, looking forward to another show, yesterday's success already put into perspective and in its place: the past. I wondered where she had learned all of that.

I rolled over and looked at my night stand. My alarm clock showed 8:30. Next to the clock was *The Origin of Continents and Oceans*. Exactly where I had left it what seemed like eons before. It hadn't been pulled by any extraordinary gravitational force and gone spinning out into space. Nor had it gone crashing into the "Sports" section from Saturday's newspaper and fused with the American League standings. I guessed that meant that I would have to read it. I needed to look at it at least. I opened the book and flipped past the black and white photo of Wegener. Chapter 1 gave an historical introduction to the idea of drift theory. It mentioned that way back in 1857 a man named Green "spoke of 'segments of the earth's crust which float on the liquid core.'" I couldn't remember when *Voyage to the Center of the Earth* was written, but I thought it was after 1857. This Green fellow had advanced even the incredibly futuristic Verne. I guessed it was possible that other people had understood these things before them. Maybe primitive man even understood that the very ground under his naked feet was nothing but a hollow ball filled with liquid fire, roiling and boiling and slowly burning itself out, and not the solid piece of rock I had been mistaking it for.

I turned to Wegener's fabulously titled Chapter 2, "The Nature of the Drift Theory and Its Relationship to Hitherto Prevalent Accounts of Changes in the Earth's Surface Configuration in Geological Times." The chapter began by talking about the incomplete state of "present knowledge." Wegener had written the book in the 1920's. I wondered how much the arguments had changed since then. In the second paragraph, Wegener wrote about land-bridges, that phenomenon I vaguely remembered from school. He explained in that even-handed way of his how paleontologists felt that the numerous identical species on both sides of the oceans supported the theory of land-bridges, and then presented the pros and cons of the idea. I turned back to the black and white photo of Wegener. I wondered what kind of man he had been, this explorer and thinker. He didn't strike me as someone who would come out and slam someone else's idea even if he did find it ridiculous. *Infinitely fair* is how my mother might have judged him if she had been able to look on the photo, judged him in terms that for her were always of the highest praise. Infinitely fair, modest, thoughtful, kind. It occurred to me that she *had* seen the photograph and, like me, had probably determined Wegener to be all of those things.

I held the page close to my face as though it would help me to get his attention. His eyes continued to look somewhere off to my right. His mouth was pursed in a squeezed smile, like the photograph had been snapped just before he finally burst out laughing, no longer able to contain the little boy inside. Had he been someone who was jovial, open, talkative? He didn't seem like the type to sit brooding late into the night, his pipe burning in his hand.

"Maybe *you* could answer my question, Professor Wegener," I said aloud, trying to sound very serious. "What does it mean to be a man?" I waited a few minutes, impatient. "Huh?"

Maybe ol' Wegener didn't know either. What he did know was that the Earth's surface buckled and lurched; that oceans disappeared and were reborn elsewhere. He also knew, perhaps better than many of us, that life is cyclical and, because it is, finite. He understood that the Earth came together at some point in the long ago past, flinging moons off into space. And that at some point in perhaps the not-too-distant future, it will explode apart. I wondered if he had been a particularly religious man, having had an evangelical father and all. Maybe what pushed him towards science in the first place was the need to be the opposite of what his father was. Faith *versus* fact, belief *versus* knowledge, father *versus* son. I was beginning to believe that was the reason Erik became a Catholic. I wondered if Wegener had accepted that we "are made of dust and to dust we will return" as Father Wilhelm used to remind me on Ash Wednesday, stabbing my forehead with cinders. Wegener's body is now part of a glacier in Greenland that, for all I knew, was sliding towards me. Maybe Wegener decided that what it meant to be a man was to pursue an idea to the very limit. Even if that meant leaving family and friends and going far away. Maybe being a man didn't mean deciding how to live, but how to die. Maybe it even meant that being a man was lying down on the cold hard ground of a frozen sugar beet field hoping that life might seep out of you, too, after someone you loved more than anything else in the world had, like oceans and land-bridges before her, gone from the face of the Earth. He didn't answer me. Just sat there squelching a smile. He could laugh. He was already dead. I still had to figure things out.

"It is probably not an exaggeration to say that if we do not accept the idea of such former land connections, the whole evolution of life on earth and the affinities of present-day organisms occurring even on widely separated continents must remain an insoluble riddle."

Riddles, mysteries, questions. Was anything certain? *Evolution*. That was another thing. We hadn't even studied it in school. The word itself was forbidden. Father Wilhelm had always told us that things were the way they were because that's how God wanted them to be. It was an idea I was having trouble with, all things considered. It frightened me a lot more than the idea that things change, move, evolve and are subject to all kinds of unknown and inexact influences.

On the next page was a chart of the "yeas, nays and the difference between them" of the votes of various scientists regarding the existence of land-bridges, their location, and the geological time period when they were disrupted or broken. I noticed in a footnote that many of the names were German. Not surprising, I guess, since Wegener would probably have been most in contact with fellow Germans, but I was filled with an odd kind of pride, nonetheless.

"The land-bridge between North America and Europe was very much more irregular..."

I felt my ma and all that she was to me, slipping further away.

"These former land-bridges are postulated not only for such regions as the Bering Strait, where today a shallow continental-shelf sea or floodwater fills the gap, but also for regions now under ocean waters."

The text went on to say that some scientists of the day felt that the Earth was, in fact, shrinking, comparing it to an apple whose skin shrivels "by the loss of internal water, the earth is supposed to form mountains by surface folding as it cools and therefore shrinks internally." I noticed with a smile that one of the scientists who developed the theory was named Suess. Dr Suess, I supposed. *The Cat in the Hat. Green Eggs and Ham.* What would be a good title for the story of our shriveling, shrinking Earth? *Mother Earth loses her Girth?*

After that, I must have dozed a little, fallen back into the half-sleep of the never truly awake. My eyes moved unseeing over the text and I was pages further along before a paragraph jolted me out of my stupor.

"The basic 'obvious' supposition common to both land-bridge and permanence theory – that the relative position of the continents, disregarding their variable shallow-water cover, has never altered – must be wrong. The continents must have shifted. South America must have lain alongside Africa and formed a unified block which was split in two in the Cretaceous; the two parts must then have become increasingly separated over a period of millions of years like pieces of a cracked ice floe in water. The edges of these two blocks are even today strikingly congruent. Not only does the large rectangular bend formed by the Brazilian coast at Cape São Roque mate exactly with the bend in the African coast at the Cameroons, but also south of these two corresponding points every projection on the Brazilian side matches a congruent bay on the African, and conversely. A pair of compasses and a globe will show that the sizes are precisely commensurate."

The next page presented a "reconstruction of the map of the world according to drift theory for three epochs." On the opposite page was the same reconstruction, but seen from different angles. The first representations from the "Upper Carboniferous period" were, for me, the most frightening. The continents looked melted together, like they were made out of wax and someone had left them lying out too long in the sun. Wegener had, perhaps out of kindness for the weakness of the human heart, traced the outlines of the present locations of the continents over the mass. Africa stood out pretty clearly, and I could see the continent almost as it is drawn today. But the rest of the world, as poorly as I knew it, was a muddle. I traced the outer edges of the mass with my forefinger and got something totally unrecognizable. At the bottom of the page there were the third representations from the Lower Quaternary period. By then the continents had drifted and the map of the world was looking pretty familiar. But it was already too late. The damage had been done. I couldn't get the gobbed mass of the Upper Carboniferous period out of my mind's eye. It gave me the same feeling I'd had once when I was in grade school. I came home for lunch one day, and found Ma in the kitchen setting the table. While picking tomatoes that morning in our garden, she had gotten stung by a bee. An allergy to bee stings caused her face to swell up and become grossly deformed, like a balloon unevenly pumped up with air. One look at her made my bowels go soft. She had become grotesque, a monster in my mother's housecoat. I tried to tell myself to remain calm, that she was really my ma. I could still see the vague presence of some of her fine features. But her face had changed, a face that was as familiar to me as my own. And it filled me with horror each time I had to look at her.

While I was remembering that incident, I let my eyes trail down the text the way I did when I was trying to convince myself I was reading. It was a trick I had developed since Ma died, and was probably one of the reasons why I was getting such poor marks in school, even though I always seemed to have my nose in a book. I reached the end of the chapter and turned the page. Chapter 3 was titled, "Geodetic Arguments." I glanced over at the bookshelf by my desk where my dictionary was, half way across the room. I decided I could live without knowing what "geodetic" meant.

"We begin the demonstration of our theory with the detection of the present-day drift of the continents by repeated astronomical position-finding..."

My eyes rolled down the paragraph. I wondered if I was actually drowsy enough to go back to sleep.

"If continental displacement was operative for so long a time, it is probable that the process is still continuing, and it is just a question of whether the rate of movement is enough to be revealed by our astronomical measurements in a reasonable period of time."

I felt my lids getting heavy. I blinked myself awake. I needed to skip around, keep myself interested. Drift theory was a pretty wild idea, but dry stuff to read. Wegener should have hired a cartoonist, I thought. Made a good comic book out of it. Every fifth-grader on the planet would have been able to discuss its finer points. I thought about giving up. If I tortured myself by reading the book on my own, how would I feel when I had to read it again to Mr. Granger? I turned back to the "Table of Contents." Maybe there was an overview or conclusion where I could get a general idea without having to wade through the whole thing.

"Geophysical Arguments. Geological Arguments. Paleontological and Biological Arguments. Paleoclimatic Arguments. Fundamentals of Continental Drift and Polar Wandering..."

I must have fallen asleep because I started dreaming. I saw Wegener's representations of the continents in my dream. First, I saw the indistinguishable mass. Then, it broke up into different pieces. Then the pieces began moving over the surface of the globe, sliding slowly at first then careering at breakneck speeds. My perspective changed and I saw the pieces from ground level. One piece came sliding past me. It crashed into another one nearby. Its edges bumped up like the hood of a car after it has rammed into something. I felt myself being swept along, picking up speed. In that strange way that one watches oneself from a distance in dreams, I saw myself the size of a fairy tale giant riding the flat land mass like it was a magic carpet, gripping its edges for all I was worth. The continent I was riding was only about the size of the braided rug in my bedroom. It was white with snow. I was sitting right down on it wearing only a short-sleeved T-shirt and my favorite dungarees. I could see my shirt-sleeves blowing in the wind as I was carried forward, although I didn't feel cold. I veered northwards towards the Pole. It moved backwards and slipped out of sight, behind the curvature of the Earth. I woke with a start just as my piece of land was following it off into oblivion.

The front parking lot to the Kream-rite doughnut shop was almost empty. I looked at my watch. Almost ten o'clock. The 9:45 mass had probably just started. I had at least half an hour before the place would fill up with church-goers. I had already pulled in and around to the back and parked before I noticed the squad car. Sheriff Walker, I thought. He didn't get that belly eating Melba toasts. I hesitated for a minute before I decided to go in. I hadn't seen him since Ma's funeral. And he would forever be linked in my mind with the morning of Treat's disappearance when we all drove over to the Feed and Seed to ask Erik if had noticed anything different in Treat's behavior. Then again, I couldn't always be running from the memory of what had happened. Hadn't Friday night taught me that? Besides, I was hungry.

I walked in and slid onto the stool at the counter right next to Sheriff Walker. I don't know why. Maybe I was like one of those folks who deliberately stuck themselves with pins, burned themselves with hot irons. You know you're alive because it hurts.

"Morning, Sheriff," I said.

He turned and looked at me. His eyes widened in surprise.

"Sebastian Ramsey. How are you, son?" he asked, sticking out his thick hand.

Mary, the waitress, came up, and I ordered two jelly doughnuts and a glass of milk.

"Fine, sir. Yourself?" I asked, grasping his hand in mine.

"Fine," he said, nodding his head slowly. "Funny thing. I was just thinking about you and your family."

"Everybody's doing all right," I said quickly. I bit into a doughnut and felt the cool jelly on my tongue.

"Actually, I meant your ma," he said, looking down into his cup of coffee. He cleared his throat. "I've been thinking about her. I just passed by the cemetery this mornin'."

The bite of doughnut I'd taken got hung up on my Adam's apple. I washed it down with a swallow of milk.

"I hadn't been for a while," he said, "to pay my respects to your mother's grave. It's looking a little overgrown. No one seems to be tending it."

He didn't necessarily say this like an accusation, but it hit me like one. Pa should have been the one to tend to Ma's grave, but I knew for a fact that he wasn't. As far as I knew he hardly ever went to the cemetery and I never did. There was something about seeing Ma's name written on the headstone with those dates bracketing a life on both ends that was just too much for both of us.

Sheriff Walker took a slow sip of coffee. The afternoon of Ma's burial, he was the one who found me. Nearly three miles away. Beneath my winter parka, I was still wearing Treat's too big gray suit coat and his one white shirt, a long-sleeved Oxford, buttoned tightly at the throat and his only tie, a skinny black one that he always kept knotted and slipped over his head since neither one of us had ever learned how to properly tie it. For a couple of years, we'd passed it back and forth for important occasions. That was a system that worked fine, as long as we didn't have to go to those occasions together. I'd pretty much inherited the tie since I was the last one to have it when he disappeared. Ma's funeral was the first time I would use it. I remember it choked me at about the same place where the bit of doughnut had just lodged. After Father Wilhelm had given the final benediction, most of the others who had been by the grave site began to return to their cars. Pa took a fistful of earth and threw it onto the top of Ma's coffin. He gestured for me to do the same. The dirt was cold and dry in my hands. It made a dull sound as it hit and scattered. Uncle Will helped Pa stumble back to the hearse, but I kept walking: out of the cemetery and down the road, across fallow fields, along a stream, then finally on down the old county road.

Sheriff Walker said when he found me that he could understand my wanting to run away. That folks all had different ways of grieving. And that in some people, grief gave way to an impulse to run. He sounded like he knew what he was talking about. But, he had added, I needed to get on home. Be with my pa. Truth of the matter was, I hadn't been running away. In fact, I hadn't even realized that I was walking. It had been a reflex, not a thought, much less a real desire. Something about having thrown that handful of dirt onto the top of Ma's coffin. It was like I was burying her with my own hands.

Mary came up wielding the coffee pot. Sheriff Walker waved her off.

"Your ma one of the finest women this town has ever seen. And if I'm locking folks up in the county jail today rather than rotting in there myself, it's thanks in part to your pa."

I looked up at him. Pa had never talked too much about his childhood. Seemed like there had never been time. I'd always just taken it for granted that he and Uncle Will were best buddies like Treat and I had been, and that the extent of their universe was the boundaries of the farm. I didn't even know that he and Sheriff Walker had been friends.

"Were you and Pa close when you were young?" I asked.

"Oh," he started, tilting his head to one side, "couldn't really say *close*. Your pa is a very private person, son. Was even as a youngster. You know how farm folks can be. We were in school together, but I didn't really get to know him 'til our senior year. He was captain of this, captain of that. A fine athlete and a good-looking boy. Top student. I was pretty jealous of him. I wasn't a very good student. Didn't have luck with the girls. And things at home were far from rosy, especially by the time I was about your age. Me and my own pa didn't get on. Like a lot of boys when they start coming into their own, I reckon. Figured he hadn't done well enough for himself. He was a drill operator at the press metal shop in Flint. And I was ashamed of that. Didn't want to be like him. Can you figure that?" he asked, shaking his head. "I don't know. Maybe I thought he should have been President of the *U*-nited States or something like that. Anyway, I started hanging around with the wrong crowd just to defy him. Staying out late. Stealin' cars."

"Stealin' cars!"

"That's right, son," he responded. "Stealin' cars. One night I hot-wired an old Dodge that had been parked for ages on Vanburn Street. I think it was probably abandoned. I drove it over to Millar's Field and started doing figure-8s in the parking lot. Laying rubber and just driving like a madman. It was a warm night in the summer, maybe even around this time of year. Just after dusk. The field lights hadn't come on yet, so I didn't notice your pa out on the pitcher's mound, a bag of baseballs by his side. He was practicing his fast ball into the empty batter's box. I was driving around, making a hell of a racket when the not too surprising happened."

"You crashed?"

"Flipped her. Half-caved in the roof. She righted herself before she spun around and went slamming into the cement wall by the concession stand. Driver's side."

"Did you get hurt?"

"No. Miraculously enough. I was damn lucky. It all happened so fast. Your pa came running over to see if I was all right. Pulled me out through the broken window on the passenger's side 'cause the door was jammed. Still wearing his mitt, as I recall. No sooner had he gotten me out than the police sirens started wailing. I think someone who lived near the stadium had heard the racket and had called the police. I took off running. Left your pa standing there without saying so much as a word. I figured I was cooked. I didn't go home for two days. Got the tar beaten out of me by my pa when I finally did for scaring my ma half to death with worry not knowing where I was and for not doing my chores. But the police never came by. And no one ever said anything about the car. My fingerprints must have been all over the thing. I guess they never followed up on it 'cause they figured it wasn't worth it. No one got hurt. Nothing wrecked but the car itself – it was an old junker, anyway. As soon as I could, I went over to see your pa.

I found him out in one of your grandpa's fields, mowing down hay with a huge scythe. He was wielding the thing like a baseball bat. Cut the whole damn field by hand just to practice his swing. I didn't even have to say anything. He knew why I was there. He stopped swinging for a minute and wiped the sweat off his forehead with the back of his arm. It was the same gesture he used to wipe his brow when he was on the mound. I can see it like it was yesterday.

"'Told 'em I didn't see who it was,' he said to me. 'Told 'em I thought maybe it was someone from Black River.'"

Sheriff Walker looked over at me and we both cracked up. Black River. Our arch-rivals in baseball.

"You mean he lied for you?"

"Yeah, son. He lied for me."

I didn't think my pa ever lied.

"I didn't even really know him all that well. And I couldn't figure why he'd do something like that for me. I'd actually kind of despised him for a long time. Figured he had things I'd never have."

"Did you ask him?"

"What?"

"Why he'd lied for you?"

"Not right away. Didn't have the guts. Later, I did, though. I actually made the baseball team my senior year. Was your pa pushed me to it. Said I had a catcher's build. His old catcher had graduated. Said it'd take a goddamn bulldozer to knock me from the plate. Said we'd make a good team." Sheriff Walker rubbed at his eyes. "One day on the bus going to an away game I finally asked him."

"What he'd say?" I asked.

"Said he threw one of the hardest fast balls in the county for the same reason he figured I totaled the Dodge. Felt his guts all tied up in knots most of the time. Didn't know if it was rage, fear, frustration, or longing. Damn, maybe it was even happiness. Didn't know what it was. So he pitched himself to exhaustion. Cleared fields 'til he nearly fell over. Studied for all he was worth. And never said anything to anyone about what he was feeling. I think he understood what I hadn't yet at the time.

That all that stuff churnin' in your belly happens to every young man. Gotta wait 'til it passes."

"What if it doesn't pass, Sheriff Walker?"

"It will. Though sometimes it don't seem like it."

He dropped off his stool and threw a couple of dollars onto the counter, gesturing to Mary that it was for both of our orders.

"I'll never forget what your pa done for me. Saved my goddamn life. Of everything that has happened, I have only one real regret." He slid his cap on and checked its fit. "That as long as I live, I'll probably never figure out how to properly thank him."

* * *

I was finally going back to the cemetery. It was the one place I had avoided since the day Ma was buried. As I walked away from her grave that day, I erased it from the landscape of my mind. Since then, it had become a pain I tried to ignore, push aside. But that day I was like a person getting out of bed the morning after breaking a leg. Memories came flooding back as soon as I went through the mechanical motion of trying to stand up.

Sheriff Walker was right. Her grave was overgrown. The caretaker had mowed the grass around the headstone as best he could, but just beside it blades stuck out like hair from beneath a cap. Without thinking, I started yanking at them and worked my way around her headstone, and then went on to the headstones of my grandparents. When I had finally finished, I had a pile of springy weeds and tall grass I didn't know what to do with. I studied the headstones. My grandparents' names were cut in a different style script than the gentle curving alphabet of my ma's name. In big, block letters that could be seen clearly from a distance were the names: Bertha RAMSEY; Boris

RAMSEY. Turns out that our real family name was actually "Raumzer." Pa said that when Grandpa arrived in the United States, his name, like so many others before and after him, had been incorrectly copied onto the immigration lists. So many years later I wondered if the customs official had done it on purpose. Or had it been through carelessness or hurry? Had he misunderstood my grandpa's heavily accented English? Or had it been a way to Americanize their names to rush them into the swirling, melting flow of the young nation? I'd never know. But the effect of his act on my life was clear to me that day. Next to their graves was the grave of my mother, Christa RAMSEY, and the plot where my father, Thomas RAMSEY, would someday be buried. Who was I? A Ramsey, a Raumzer? An American, a German? How was it that in my heart of hearts I felt I belonged in Puerto Rico, that I was a *Borínqueño*?

I sat down in the grass by the graves. The crust of the Earth separated me from what was left of my ma and my grandparents. I imagined them lying in their separate coffins, unchanged, hair still combed in place and dressed the way I had last seen them. My grandpa was in his overall jeans and flannel shirt. Both the shirt and jeans were a little muddy and with tiny crystals of ice still sticking to them. And he was still wearing his International Harvester cap. I don't remember my grandma too much, so I couldn't really picture her other than the way she looked, hair done up right and a string of pearls around her neck, in the portrait that sat in an oval frame on the hutch in the dining room. Ma was wearing the navy-blue outfit she had been laid out in. Of course, all that was impossible. Just as it was impossible that their bodies hadn't changed, collapsed, started to dissolve into the varnished wood of their coffins. Not like Wegener who was lying captive forever in a glacier, the face on the page of a book still the face frozen in the ice. Thinking of him made me think how the idea of burying the dead in the ground is strange. *To dust you will return.* Or did we return to molten fire? As the continents shifted and heaved, was my ma's coffin slipping silently towards the lava-filled center of the Earth or following the pull of the poles towards the Equator?

*** * * ***

Ruth Anne was sitting at our kitchen table, flipping through a magazine.

"Hey, Sebastian," she said softly – and rather, I thought, without much emotion. "I asked Uncle Thomas if I could take a phone call here."

I took a bottle of milk out of the refrigerator. If Ruth Anne hadn't been sitting right there, I may have just chugged from the bottle like I usually did; instead, I got a glass out of the cupboard. "Want something to drink?" I asked.

"No, thanks," she said. "I hope you don't mind."

"No problem," I answered, but was surprised to find that I was actually a little annoyed. It was nearly lunchtime and I wanted to make a couple of sandwiches and get Pa to come out and eat with me, maybe talk about things.

"I shouldn't be too long. Things are a little tense over there," she said, tilting her head in the direction of the other farmhouse.

"Oh, yeah? Why?" Not that I was all that interested. It didn't occur to me that it was none of my business.

"Tim Kirsten asked Kate out," she said.

"So?"

"Ma says she's too young."

Although she was only a freshman, Kate had turned fifteen that June. Chronic bronchitis when she was six years old had kept her from school until the following year so she was a little older than most of her classmates. And it was true that she had always seemed mature for her age, like she was in a hurry to make up for lost time.

"Seems old enough to me," I said.

"Of course she is. Especially Kate." Ruth Anne shook her head. "If she could, Ma would have Kate wait until she was eighteen. That's what she tried to do with me."

"Make you wait until you were eighteen! To go out with a boy? Really?"

"Really," she laughed. "Thank God for catechism. Otherwise, I would have never met any boys!"

The telephone rang. Ruth Anne shot out of her seat.

"That's for me," she cried and jumped up to get it.

I went over to Pa's study to tell him that lunch would be ready soon, but found him curled up on the couch asleep and didn't have the heart to wake him. By the time I got back to the kitchen just a few minutes later, Ruth Anne had finished with the phone and was back at our table. She seemed subdued, and sat touching the base of her hairline.

"Everything all right?" I asked.

She looked over at me. "Oh, Bass," she said. "You're *so* sweet. Really, you are. You must drive the girls crazy. Don't you have a special girl?"

I felt my face flash hot. I didn't have any girl at all. In fact, the last time that I had come within a country mile of one, outside of school or one who wasn't related to me, was when Treat, Erik and I had gone to see Celia. She was Treat's girl. I was pretty sure of that. But that didn't keep me from dreaming about her slender, honey-colored legs, her tight buttocks under the thin fabric of her white shorts, the dark mane of her hair. To my incredible surprise and embarrassment, I felt myself getting hard. I was glad I had pulled myself up to the table where Ruth Anne wouldn't be able to notice. It'd been happening more and more often. When it first started happening, it left me feeling flushed and confused. That day, for some reason, I let myself enjoy feeling the force of my penis straining against my pants.

"No."

"You will. When you're ready," she said matter-of-factly. "Know what?" she whispered.

I could tell from the way she started that she was going to tell me something private, a secret.

"Pa and Kate know already," she began.

At least, I thought, I wouldn't have to promise to keep this secret to myself. Like I had had to promise Treat.

"What about your ma?"

"I haven't told her yet. Pa thinks it might even be better to wait until after."

"After what?"

She smiled. "After I'm married."

"You're getting married? Wow!" I yelled.

"Sh-h!" Ruth Anne waved a hand at me. "Not so loud!" She laughed. "Ma will have a fit."

"Why aren't you going to tell her?" I asked. I thought mothers were usually happy when their daughters married.

"It's a long story, Bass," she said. "And there's some stuff you don't know – I mean, 'family stuff.'" She looked over her shoulder, as though Aunt Sally might have snuck up to our kitchen window. "That's who has been calling. My fiancé, I mean. His name is Jean-Christophe. He's Belgian. I met him about a year ago when he came to our Bible study group to talk about his work in The Congo."

"Is he a missionary, too?"

"He works at the mission. But he's a lay person like me. He's an airplane mechanic, and takes care of the mission's two small airplanes. Actually, he grew up not too far from the mission. One of his brothers still lives in the capital. His parents live in Belgium, now, but I think they will come for the ceremony."

"Are you getting married in Africa?"

"Hmm-hmm," she said, nodding. "It'll be easier, believe it or not. For lots of reasons. And it will be our home, for the next few years at least so we thought it would be a good way to start out there."

"Are you ever coming back?" I felt the words catch in my throat. My penis went soft.

"Of course," she said, reaching across the table and touching my hand in that way of hers that had already become so familiar. "For visits."

"That's all?"

"My life is somewhere else now."

"And if you leave Africa?"

"Oh," she shrugged, "I guess we'd go to Belgium."

"Congratulations, then," I said, forcing a smile.

"Thanks."

That night I dreamt about Celia. It would be the first of many dreams I would have of her. We seemed to be swimming, or floating at least, submerged in clear water, water that was filled with light, a bright, diffuse and gentle light. Maybe we were swimming in the phosphorescent sea. I think now that that must be what it is like. Celia was radiant. The light seemed to catch the golden color of her skin and reflect it back. In that strange surrealistic way of dreams, we were both dressed, but our clothes and hair seemed to be dry. Her dark mane was a shiny blue-black. I was wearing my favorite dungarees and a white T-shirt just like I had when I was riding the wandering continent in an earlier dream. And just like I was dressed most days of the week. Celia was dressed exactly as she was the day we visited her family's camper, the only way I have ever known her.

I could hear myself breathing. I wasn't holding my breath like I should have been under water but breathing open-mouthed, shallow and quick. I felt myself wanting to say something to Celia. But a quiet, insistent melody, like someone humming, drummed in through the water and forced me to remain silent. I tried to move towards her, to close the distance that separated us. But I was never able to. Without appearing to move, she retreated from me every time I willed myself forward. She smiled a bright, gap-toothed smile that made me want to crush her in my arms. Instead, I saw them floating near me independent and detached and unresponsive.

A piercing sound invaded the calm water. The humming stopped. Celia looked panicked, then retreated, disappearing into the brightness of the sea. When I woke up, I realized that the sun was shining through my bedroom window almost directly into my eyes. Aunt Sally was in the driveway, honking the horn of her car impatiently calling for someone, Kate or Ruth Anne, to hurry up.

CHAPTER FOUR

"I didn't know there was, like – *hair* on 'em," I said.
Erik looked up from his book.
"On what?"
"Tits."
He made a face.
"And your nuts, dodo brain?" he said, turning back to his book.
I hadn't thought about that. I turned the page.
"Wow!"
The next photo was of two women. Both were naked except for wide, studded black leather belts and matching black leather cowboy boots. They were holding each other at the waist, and had their upper bodies turned toward the camera. Their faces were close, almost cheek-to-cheek. They weren't exactly kissing, but touching the tips of their tongues. Both had the outer foot resting on a short, three-legged stool. Their legs were spread open; their pelvises thrust toward the camera. I held the page up to Erik who tore himself painfully away from his book. He cracked his gum in quick succession, three times.

"I don't know why guys drool over that stuff," he said, lazily. "Pretty awful if you ask me."

I looked at the picture again. Both women were heavily made up. Black highlighted in royal blue showed around their eyes. Their long, white-blond hair was teased up high behind their heads so that it looked as though it were standing up on its own. Their lips were smeared with red that stood out against the almost sickly paleness of their skin. It was true that they weren't exactly what I would have called "beautiful." And neither seemed to have the natural charm and grace of someone like Celia. But both had full, voluptuous bodies and heavy breasts that nearly spilled from the picture. Then, there was that pose.

"Maybe it's better in real life," I said.

"What?"

"*That*," I said, pointing to the place between one girl's legs.

"Possible."

I knew then that Erik didn't have much more experience with women than I did, despite our age difference and the relative freedom he enjoyed by having parents who were more often at their store than at home. I was kind of surprised. And it sure didn't explain those long drives he took. Compared to the physical way Treat had been drawn to Celia like a magnet to metal, Erik seemed strangely indifferent to women. Maybe he was just shy when it came to that kind of thing.

"I didn't mean to *embarrass* you," I said. I was pleased to have found just the right mocking tone. I hadn't been like that before. A few hard-ons had transformed me.

"You didn't *embarrass* me," he answered sharply. He made a point of going back to his book and looking particularly concentrated on his reading.

I hadn't come all the way there that morning to be ignored.

Worse, Erik wasn't even paying attention to the dirty magazine I had found in the office. Treat would have been all over it.

"What are you reading?" I asked glumly. It seemed like Erik was always reading. Probably wasn't much else to do sitting around waiting for folks to drive in. And I noticed lately that he seemed to have graduated from *Superman* comic books to real paperbacks.

"It's a play," he said, showing me the cover.

"Who's Afraid of Virginia Woolf?" I read aloud. "Who's afraid of the big, bad wolf, the big bad wolf? Who's afraid of the big, bad wolf, the big bad wolf? Not me!" I sang, sticking a thumb to my chest.

Erik smirked. "Bravo," he said.

"What *are* you afraid of, anyway?" I asked, brandishing the magazine.

"I'm not afraid of anything."

"Are, too."

"*Am* not."

We stopped and looked at each other, realizing, I think, how childish we sounded.

"So why is it bothering you that I'm looking at this if you're not afraid?"

He rolled his eyes. "It's *not* bothering me. Go ahead and look. If that kind of thing turns you on."

"It doesn't turn you on?"

"Not really."

"Why do you buy these things then, if you're not interested?" I asked.

Erik stuck his nose further into his book.

"It's not mine," he grumbled. "It's Mike's. Some kind of biker magazine."

"Oh," I nodded, turning the page.

The same two women were in the next photograph in a

similar pose, but this time a man stood between them, with one arm around each woman's waist. All three were looking at the camera, mouths half-opened in what I guessed was meant to be a seductive pose. The two women had changed their leather belts for ones made out of a fabric that looked like leopard skin, although I bet myself it wasn't really. The man standing between them was shirtless, and showing off an incredibly muscular chest. He was wearing a piece of cloth over his private parts made out of the same fabric as the women's belts. There was a fake banana tree in the background.

"Lucky guy!" I said.

"Who?"

"The guy in this shot."

Erik slid his feet off of the desk.

"Give me that thing," he said, reaching out his hand.

I handed him the magazine. He studied the photo for a long time without turning the page and then handed it back to me.

"Well?"

"Well, what?"

"Pretty sexy, huh?"

"I told you what I thought about those women."

"Then what about the guy?" I asked. I had meant it as a joke.

Erik was up and at me before I had time to react. But he struck at me in wide, lateral arcs, his fists half-opened like he didn't really want to hit me. I defended myself easily.

"You hit like a sissy," I teased.

Erik slumped suddenly to the ground and covered his face with his hands. For a moment, I thought maybe he had hurt a hand or an arm slapping at me. But when I saw his shoulders jerking up and down, heard him draw in a long, deep breath, I realized he was sobbing.

"Erik?"

Seeing him like that reminded me that only a few days before, I had been the one crying and he had been the one to comfort me. Like a true friend. But I found it impossible to put my arm around him, to hold him the way he had held me. Plus, I felt pretty bad. I figured I must have really hurt his feelings. I hadn't meant to go that far. I bent down next to him and pressed the fingertips of one hand to his back.

"I was just joking," I said.

He nodded his head up and down.

"I was just joking," I repeated. "Really."

He turned and pressed his face into my chest, throwing both arms around my waist and holding me tightly. I drew up and took my hand from his back. My arms hung stupidly at my sides. My first thought was to secretly pray that neither Mike nor Ed would show up and find us like that. How could I explain when I wasn't even sure myself what was happening? In the meantime, I found myself trapped in Erik's embrace. Maybe someone would drive in for gas and save me. I waited what seemed like a long time for the bells to ring in the office as imaginary tires rolled over the rubber hose by the pumps. But there was only the sound of Erik gasping for breath between sobs. He had told me a million times: Mondays were quiet.

He released me a bit and I hoped that meant that he had pulled himself together. I waited for him to get up and return to his chair. Instead, he turned his face towards mine. His lips were almost touching my cheek when I finally reacted. Through the sheer force of my panic, I broke free from him and was up and out of the office in a fraction of a second. I threw the Ford into gear and left a patch of rubber that ol' Sheriff Walker would have been proud of. But I didn't think about that until much later. My hands were shaking on the wheel. My knees felt all jiggly. I hadn't gone far when I had to pull over to the side of the road and collect myself. I got out of the car and did a few deep-knee bends. My mind raced. Had he really been trying to kiss me? Did that mean that he was a – ugh, what was the word? A *queer*? Was it because I had gone to the movies with him? Because I had cried and let him hold me in his arms? Then what did that make me?

I remember Ma telling me once that when she was a young teenager, she and her best friend Maria used to practice kissing in her parents' barn. They both wanted to be ready, she had explained, when the real time came with a boy. And I knew that my ma hadn't been a *girl* queer. Now that I knew he was as inexperienced as I was, I figured Erik had just wanted to practice his kissing. Those pictures had probably excited him after all. Got him thinking. I myself had never kissed anyone, play kissing or not. But beginning not long after our visit with Celia and her family, I had begun practicing on my pillow at night, alone in my twin bed. Clutching the downy cushion, I experimented with just the right way to take my imaginary woman in my arms and pull her toward me. I pressed my face into hers and kissed her open-mouthed, feeling the cottony fabric on my tongue. My pillow-woman was deeply in love with me. I knew that because she told me so all of the time. Without ever really imagining a face, I knew my pillow-woman was beautiful. Starting that summer, my pillow-woman's face became identifiable. It became Celia's.

I finally convinced myself that Erik had been trying to tell me something. His mouth had been as close to my ear as to my lips, hadn't it? In that case, he wouldn't have been trying to kiss me after all. But tell me what? A secret, maybe. I was filled with the strange and sudden hope that he had been trying to tell me where Treat was. I was more and more sure he knew. He and Treat had gone back to the place where Celia and her family had camped together the day after the three of us had been there. Knowing Treat, he had probably already decided by then to run away. It only made sense he would tell Erik. They had been next-to-best friends. In that case, Erik had not only kept the truth from Sheriff Walker, he had kept it from me, which was a yellow-bellied thing to have done. That would explain why he had broken down when I called him a "sissy." All of this time his lack of courage had been weighing on him. That might even explain why he and I had become friends. That would explain a lot of things.

I hopped back into the Ford with the idea of turning around and forcing Erik into a confession, making him admit to me that Treat was in Puerto Rico. But I had to decide against it. It would have to wait until the next day. It was going on ten o'clock and after the conversation I had had with Darby Millar on Wednesday, there was no way I was going to be late going to Mr. Granger's. Especially seeing as to how I was of half a mind to tell him off.

The front door was open, like I had found it on other visits, but the back door was closed and the pile of stones had mysteriously reappeared next to it. I found Mr. Granger sitting in the desk chair, his back to his work table and facing the door. He was holding a thick book in his hands.

"Mornin'," I said, ducking in.

He held the book out towards me.

"I want you to read from this."

It amazed me how Mr. Granger didn't trouble himself with niceties like saying "hello." I picked up the stool and carried it towards where he sat. I remembered the last incident with the stool.

"I've got the stool," I said, setting it down noisily in front of him.

"Of course, boy," he growled. "D'you think I expect you to sit on the confounded floor? Here, take this, before it breaks my arm off."

I took the book from him. *Shorter's Encyclopedic Dictionary*.

"What is it you want me to look up?" I asked.

"Whatever you want."

"I beg your pardon?"

"Whatever you want, confound it. I don't give a flip. Start in the A's if you don't have any other ideas."

"You mean – you want me to read to you from the *dictionary*?"

Mr. Granger stuck his chin out at me. "You're supposed to be my reader, aren't you?"

"Yes, sir."

"Then read."

"From the *dictionary*?" I repeated.

"That's what I said."

"But I have this here book that Miss Millar – "

"I know," he said. "She told me. Give it over."

He stuck one hand out and I placed *The Origin of Continents and Oceans* in it. He turned and let the book drop onto his work table before turning back to me. "All right. Go ahead."

"Actually," I said, clearing my throat, "that book is pretty interesting. I looked at it some." I felt sorry for old Wegener.

"I'm sure it is. Go ahead," he said, gesturing toward me.

I looked down at the cover of the dictionary.

"But isn't reading the dictionary kind of – boring?"

"I didn't ask your opinion, boy. Read."

"Yes, sir."

I opened the dictionary on my lap and loosely flipped through it looking for a place where I might want to stop and read something. I didn't find one. I could hardly see a thing in the shadowy basement. And I couldn't get over it. Reading from the dictionary. What a crazy idea.

"Can I turn on the light?"

"No!"

I turned pages noisily.

"But, I can't see to read," I complained. "I'll turn it off when I leave. Honest. I promise."

"Don't ever promise, boy," he said. "Anything. You'll almost always regret it."

I was reminded of the promise I had made to Treat. "I can't see," I repeated.

"Confound it! Stop whining. I hate whiners," he added under his breath. "Go ahead and turn it on. But if you don't turn it off when you leave, I'll hang you by your heels!"

I ran to the light switch near the door, flipped it on and raced back to the stool.

"Where's the fire, boy?" he asked, tilting his head to one side.

"Sorry."

I continued to thumb the pages of the dictionary. "Are you sure you don't want me to read from that other book?"

"Yes, I'm sure. The dictionary is good reading."

"But that other book is probably better," I insisted.

"Listen, boy. When I was your age – "

Oh, *brother*. A "when I was your age" story. Aunt Sally was good at those.

" – a dictionary was about the only book we owned. And it wasn't even a fancy encyclopedic one like this one. My parents were simple folk. Not much for book learning. Not much for leisure, either. Listened to the radio some. We didn't have a television back then."

I was only half listening. What did I care about life before television? I didn't want to have to read from the dumb ol' dictionary. I was sorry that I hadn't been more serious about reading Wegener's book. There it was, lying unopened on the table the way Wegener's body was frozen silent in the ice. I might never learn all that he had to say. Mr. Granger didn't have a thought for Wegener.

"Wasn't much to do nights after chores."

"Didn't you have homework back then?"

"Homework?" he grunted. "Heck, boy, I quit going to school before I was wearing proper britches. Couldn't have been twelve years old."

"Cool."

"Oh, I don't know about that. That's how things were at the time. You didn't ask questions. If I had to do it all over again, I might have stayed in school. Wasn't too bad a student, all things considered. Didn't exactly have what folks nowadays might call a "good learning environment." My folks weren't educated. My pa couldn't read the back of a dollar bill, if he'd had one to spare. Didn't think learning amounted to anything."

"You read from the dictionary so you could learn?"

"Basically taught myself how to read. Learned a lot of things from that dictionary. I used to spend hours looking at it. Kind of like the way you stare at maps."

I felt myself blushing. Miss Millar must have told him.

"Yes, sir."

"Don't 'yessir' me."

I continued flipping through the dictionary, self-conscious and glad again that Mr. Granger couldn't see me.

"Why do you waste your time lookin' at that atlas?"

Waste my time! It was hard to understand. The very man who had drawn those maps now calling looking at them a waste of time.

"But they're *your* maps, Mr. Granger."

"Exactly. So who better to tell you to stop looking at them?"

"But why?"

"Bunch of lies, I tell you."

"Lies?"

"Maps show you what to see, boy. And how you're supposed to see it. Don't ever forget that."

"But they also show you how to get places. Like how to get from here to Millarsburg."

"Yes, they do," he acknowledged.

"And then they show you different, faraway places. Exciting places. Places you've never been to, but someday you might want to go."

Mr. Granger tilted his head to one side. I was beginning to get his ticks down. When he stuck his chin out at me, he was looking at me. Tilting his head to one side meant he was thinking. Or maybe listening for silences.

"And you've got an idea about someplace you might want to go?"

I felt my heart thump in my chest. For the first time since I had learned of the existence of *Borínquen*, the land of the brave lord, someone was finally asking me the one question that I had been wanting to hear. Was I brave enough to say it, and mean it? Could I actually tell him I wanted to run away to Puerto Rico?

"How about someplace like 'The Boondocks'?" he asked.

I laughed a bit too loud. I hadn't realized the old guy had a sense of humor.

"You think that's funny, boy?"

"That's not a real place," I said.

"I can show you a map with 'The Boondocks' on it."

"But it was probably just a joke. Or a mistake."

"You wouldn't figure it was too funny if you drove around looking for the place. Would you?"

Seemed like a good enough joke to me. And I could imagine Treat cracking up over it. Anyone driving around for hours looking for a place called "The Boondocks" probably deserved it. Right?

"No, sir." I was getting pretty good at lies myself.

"Most maps are meant to lead you around by the nose, boy. Not guide you. Almost a blessing not to be able to see them anymore."

I had somehow forgotten. Mr. Granger couldn't even look at his own maps. They couldn't make him want to travel to someplace exciting, someplace like Puerto Rico. Hadn't he said that he never left the house anymore, except to go into his own backyard?

"Did someone really put 'The Boondocks' on a map, Mr. Granger?"

"I'm telling you they did."

I laughed, and shook my head. Imagine.

"Just like somebody put 'Easy Street' on a map."

"Easy Street!" I howled, "but that's just – "

Nick Granger struggled to his feet. He felt the far right edge of the wall map of *The City of Painted Creek*, followed it to the bottom right corner, and then slid his finger across the yellowing paper. "Look here," he said.

I got up, carrying the heavy dictionary with me to the wall map. Mr. Granger's dirty fingernail was pointing to a short road.

"Easy Street," I said.

Satisfied, Mr. Granger shuffled back to his chair and fell into it.

"Notice anything about it, boy?"

I looked more closely. "It's a dead end," I said.

"Hah-hah," he screamed, slapping his thigh.

"But Easy Street doesn't really exist," I said.

"It's on the map," he answered.

"But you're the one who put it on there," I said at the same time the realization came to me. "Why did you do that, when you know it doesn't exist?" I heard my voice catch like cloth on barbed wire. I was sure he did it just to make fun of people.

"Maps are just a bunch o' lies, I'm telling you."

Lies? Then what if the *Baia Fosforescente* wasn't real after all? Maybe it had only been put in the *Atlas* to make fun of me. Who could believe such a wild place really existed? But, then again, it was Mr. Granger who had put it in the *Atlas*. I looked hard at him hoping he would feel me glaring.

"Why did you do that, Mr. Granger? Put a place on the map that doesn't exist, I mean?"

"Read, boy, and stop this confounded discussion."

"You have to answer me first," I said.

He stuck his chin out at me. I don't know who was more surprised, him or me, by my stubbornness.

"Just to make fun of people?" I asked.

He fidgeted in his chair. "No, of course not. Part of the trade. It's a way of protecting your work. At least it was back then. Might still be for all I know. If somebody copied your work without your permission, say. They're probably not going to notice that you've stuck the name of some little, non-existent dead-end street on there somewhere. Then you got them."

"What about those folks who drive around looking for that street?"

"Look at the map again, boy."

I was still standing right next to it. "Okay," I said, turning.

Millarsburg was east of Painted Creek. The far-right corner of the map coincided with the edge of town. "Easy Street" was located somewhere in between. I looked for a landmark. Just to the north of "Easy Street" was a main thoroughfare. East Baker Road. Then Spruce Street that led off to the old dump. Then – it couldn't be. "Easy Street" was the dead-end road that led to the place where Celia and her family had camped.

"There's nothing out there. It's in the middle of nowhere. Does that look like a place you might want to go?"

My heart shrunk in my chest. *Jurutungo*. Somewhere that was nowhere. How could I tell him that I had been there and that it had changed my life?

I slunk back to the stool and hung myself over it. I looked hopelessly through the dictionary for a few minutes.

"Arrh! Stop flipping those pages and go to one letter. 'A,' for example. That ring a bell, boy? It's at the very beginning. 'A' as in Australia! Antarctica! Alaska! Albania, if you must."

The names came firing out like gunshot.

"I'd bet those are all pretty exciting places," I said. "I mean, I like looking them up in your *Atlas*." I was lying again or exaggerating at least. I hardly ever strayed from the page on Puerto Rico.

"Tell you what, boy. All those places feel the same to me in that book," he said, without the slightest hint of sadness. "What good is the *Atlas* to me now? As far as I'm concerned, it might as well be filled with blank pages."

I turned back to the section on words beginning with "A," chose a page at random and slid my finger down the page to a stop.

"*Aneurysm.*"

"Gad, no."

I flipped back toward the front of the book and repeated the same gesture.

"*Absinthe.*"

"Charming. Find something else."

"I thought you said anything."

"Within reason, boy. At my age I don't need to hear about health trouble. And 'absinthe,' as pleasant as the word is in the mouth, is toxic on the tongue. If I didn't know better, I'd think you were trying to kill me off."

The thought has crossed my mind, I said to myself.

"What, then? You need to give me an idea, sir."

"How about something having to do with language, speech – writing."

"Writing? In the 'A's?"

"Of course, boy. Use your gourd."

I thought for a minute.

"I got it. 'Alphabet,' I said proudly.

"That's it, boy."

"Why that, sir? I mean – beggin' your pardon – you can't see writing, either. Any more than you can a map."

"But I can hear, boy. I can hear you read to me. Maps need to be seen, and that's why they're dangerous. The eyes play tricks on a body."

"But I could describe a map to you."

"How?"

"By describing – by using – "

"Words?"

"Words lie, too, Mr. Granger."

"That's true, boy. That's why words need to be spoken. Because sometimes, *sometimes* – you can hear those lies. Fight 'em if you want. Ask questions. A map is done, complete. And most of the time when you're looking at one, it's because you don't know a place all that well or at all. How can you question the map, then? That's why we get away with putting places like 'Easy Street' on the map. Who really knows other than the handful of people who actually live near that spot? And they probably get a good chuckle out of that kind of thing. I know I would."

I had to admit, what he said was true.

"And then there are all those things a map don't show. Those 'silences' I was telling you about."

"But sometimes things go left unsaid," I suggested. "Things that shouldn't."

Things like: "Don't go. Don't die. Don't run away. Don't leave me."

"That's why you need to start learning how to read silences, boy. Then they can't surprise you anymore. Now, go on."

I turned to the word "alphabet." "It says that writing was probably created in Western Asia some 5,000 to 6,000 years ago."

"Read, boy, don't interpret."

"Okay, okay," I said. Geez.

"The first known writing was pictorial in origin and only much later did writing systems acquire the capacity to reflect or run parallel to the words and sounds of speech."

I stopped and looked up at Mr. Granger. Maybe that was enough. We could get on to something else.

"Go on, boy," he said.

"Initially Greek was written from right to left like Phoenician, but later changed from left to right. The reason for this development is unknown. There was, however, for a time a technique in which letters were inscribed on stone with one line running from left to right with the letters facing one way and the next line from right to left with the letters facing the opposite way. This technique was known as 'ox-turning' because it worked on the same principle as an ox ploughing a field and was efficient since it avoided the need to track back across a wide surface."

"Hey!" I said, involuntarily.

"What is it, boy?"

He started struggling to get to his feet.

"No, sir," I said, to keep him in his place. "I mean, it's just that's pretty interesting."

"Hmm," Mr. Granger nodded. He let his body's ballast

shift back into his chair. "That's right. You're a farm boy. That ought to be something you can understand."

I pictured Pa driving the tractor out in the fields, turning up the earth and piling it into mounds to prepare for planting. Back and forth, back and forth. Slowly. Methodically. I understood then how much love there was in that act. It hurt me to remember how Treat and I used to race the old John Deere on the back lot, slanting across the hardened ridges, cutting across space, going against the sense of the land.

I read on until the end of the article on "alphabet."

"What do you want me to read next, Mr. Granger?"

He let out a bit of a snort. Actually, it was more like a snore that had gotten cut off. I'd caught him dozing.

"Whatever you want, boy," he said gravel-voiced.

"Can I go out of the 'A' part?"

"Why? What do you want to know about?"

I didn't think there would be much about Puerto Rico in the dictionary. Besides, Miss Millar let me look at *A History of Puerto Rico* at the library. What did I want to know about?

"Maps."

That woke him up.

"Stop insisting, I'm telling you!"

I ignored him. "What's it called again, making maps? I always forget the real word."

"Cartography. And the person who makes the maps is called a 'cartographer.'"

"That's it. Cartography. I want to read about that."

"No!"

"You asked me what I wanted to know about. That's it. That's why I'm here."

"You're here because you're getting paid to be here."

"But I only come here because you're a cart-o-gra-pher," I

said with difficulty. "I only accepted because it was to work with you."

"Don't flatter me, boy."

"It's true, Mr. Granger. I want to know about places – about *a* place. A place you drew in your maps."

I quietly opened to the "C" section and slowly turned pages to get to the word "cartography." I'm sure now that Mr. Granger must have heard me turning those pages. But he didn't say anything.

"You want to learn about maps, boy? I'll tell you something you probably didn't know." He stuck his chin out at me. "You're sitting on one."

I looked down at the stool beneath me.

"This stool – is a map?"

I closed the book on my index finger marking the page with the definition of cartography."

"Not right now it isn't. It's serving its intended function as a place to park your backside. But when you return it to its rightful place on those hatch marks over there," he said, waving his hands, "it gets magically transformed into something else. Technically speaking it's not a map, but a landmark. But I use it as a guide, the way one is supposed to use a map."

I turned and looked back at that part of the room. Of course! Why hadn't I thought of it before? The stool was normally placed at the intersection of the front door, the kitchen, and the work table. It was how Mr. Granger found his way around in this studio apartment. It was a map of his everyday world.

"Maps don't always have to be that thing you're staring at in the library. Maps can be lots of things. Things that you can touch, rather than just see. Even things from everyday life. In fact, I'm one of those people who thinks they should be. You know why that ox-plowing business you just read to me is so interesting? Because it shows us how, when people were learning to write, they imitated the one other thing they really knew how to do, the thing that was important to them: farm. They took an example from their everyday lives.

"It's known, for example, that Eskimos whittled pieces of wood into the shape of the Alaskan coastline that they then carried around in their pockets. Long before Christopher Columbus had ever reached them, American Indians knew the exact configuration of the islands of Hispaniola, Cuba, the Bahamas and others because they plotted them out using beans. Pacific Islanders attached shells to the midribs of palm leaves to create navigation charts. In the Philippines, folks measured distance by how many chews of a betel nut it would take to get from one place to another."

"A what, sir?"

"A 'betel' nut. B-E-T-E-L."

"What's that?"

"Look it up, confound it," he screamed. "As best I can see, you got the dictionary on your lap. And stop calling me 'sir,' will you?"

I stared at him. "Only if you stop calling me 'boy.'"

My heart pounded in my chest. Mr. Granger stuck his chin out at me. I looked back at him. He pulled his chin into his chest.

"So, what is it?" he asked, lowering his voice.

"I'm looking," I lied. The unsaid "sir" hung in the air.

I kept my index finger on the page with "cartography" and flipped quickly to the "B" section and found the word.

"The leaf of – "

"Stop!"

"What?"

"I said, 'Stop.'"

"But I thought you wanted me to read you the definition of 'betel nut'!"

"I know what a betel nut is. I'm pretty sure you don't. And you definitely aren't going to learn much about betel nuts or anything else if that's how you read the dictionary."

"But – "

"Read everything if you want to learn something, confound it. Start from the very beginning."

"I did."

"Don't contradict me. The *very* beginning. The stuff that's usually in parentheses or brackets."

I looked down at the dictionary again and, for the first time, really noticed all of the notations that came before the actual definition.

Mr. Granger interrupted my thoughts. "I'm legally blind, remember? Tell me what you see?"

"But there's all kinds of stuff, Mr. Granger. Italics and abbreviations and numbers and whatnot."

"Don't whine. I just told you I don't like whiners."

I shook my head. Not only was I going to have to read from the dictionary, I was going to have to read every stupid semi-colon and period in the thing.

"I don't think my dictionary at home is like this." I said.

Then again, what did I know? I'd never really paid any attention before and often didn't bother to look things up if I didn't know the meaning. I remembered all of the unfamiliar words I'd seen in the Wegener book just the day before and the ocean that separated me from where I was resting on my bed and the bookshelf where I kept my dictionary.

"That's possible," Mr. Granger said. "And it's a shame."

I was wary of his being so agreeable. It wasn't like him.

"Most of the dictionaries used in schools probably just note whether a word is a noun, verb or adjective."

I snuck a peek at the definition for the word "betel" and saw the abbreviation *"n"* just after a bunch of weird-looking letters between slash marks that I now know are meant to help with pronunciation. That was followed by "M16". I had no idea what that meant and I sure wasn't going to ask Mr. Granger because he would just probably make me look it up. That and the rest of the stuff between brackets like Port. f. Malayalam *verilla*...

"If you flip to the front, there's usually a guide on how to use a dictionary like the one you have in your hands."

Just to keep the old guy happy, I turned to the front, flipping the pages as noisily as I could. There it was, a guide to using the dictionary – twelve-pages long! After that, there were four whole pages explaining the abbreviations and symbols. Sheesh That dictionary was like the mucky bottom of the Harlow River. The more you tried to get out of it the more you got sucked in.

"All that leave you cold?"

"How's that, Mr. Granger?"

"Confound it!" He reached behind him and picked up the aluminum cane. I'd forgotten about that cane. He gave it a good whack on the ground. "If you look at maps the way you read the dictionary, then you might as well be as blind as I am!"

I didn't say anything. Tears stung at my eyes. I think he must have understood my silence because when he began speaking again, he had lowered his voice.

"Look," he began. "You want to know about cartography? Then you need to learn to pay attention to details, symbols, notations. Just like when you look up a word in the dictionary."

I shrugged. What did I care what a betel nut is? Something somebody somewhere chews to measure distance. Then it struck me.

"But wait a minute!" I said. "How could a chew of betel nut

be used as a measure? I mean not everybody is going to chew it the same way. Some might chew it faster so they would chew more betel for the same distance. Or a fat person might walk slower than a skinny person and maybe chew more betel nut. It's all relative," I added.

I thought I sounded very grown-up.

"Of course it is, b– . Exactly. That's *exactly* what we're talking about."

I noticed it was as hard for him to stop calling me "boy" as it was for me to stop calling him "sir." I guessed the important thing was that we both were trying.

"What *are* we talking about, Mr. Granger?"

"About how maps are relative. They are about *relationships*. One thing in relation to another. That stool is a map for me because it defines the relationship between the sections of this apartment, divides space that I can't see but that you can distinguish because you can see."

"The stool would help me find my way around at night. With the lights out."

Mr. Granger shrugged. "That's true. But not with the lights on. In fact, it's probably even something that would get in your way in the daylight. Right? That's another thing you want to remember. A map is most important to the person who needs it. But it might not necessarily be to other people."

I pulled my index finger from the book. I realized that Mr. Granger was giving me his definition of cartography.

"Don't you see? A map can be anything. A piece of wood. An old bar stool. When primitive peoples had to find their way around, you think they picked up a confounded quill and a piece of parchment and drew a bloody bunch of abstract lines on it? Those lines probably wouldn't have meant squat to most of the population. Don't get me wrong, now. I'm not saying representational maps didn't exist way back when," he said, waving his hand. "Explorers and colonialists had indigenous peoples draw them in order to learn how the hell to get around!" He pointed over to the corner of the room where scrolls of paper lay on the floor. "Someday, I'll have to show you my collection. All I'm saying is a bunch of squirrelly lines on a piece of paper or hide aren't the only kind of maps that have ever existed.

The kind of maps you're always looking at haven't been around all that long. Took folks going up in planes during the second world war, taking pictures before it really started developing."

At that point in my life, I'd never been up in an airplane. The first time I did, many years later, I half expected to see hatch marks outlining the States the way they did on maps even though I was an adult and should have known better. And not even one month after my conversation with Mr. Granger, I drove across the State line for the first time and was surprised, looking out the window of the Fairlane, not to see the famous dotted lines painted on the ground.

"But people probably climbed to the tops of mountains or went up in hot-air balloons," I argued. I thought of Wegener and his brother.

Mr. Granger shook his head. "Not high enough, not enough distance to make a map of a large area. But that distance also creates distortion, just like the photo that's used to make it."

"Can a pile of stones be a map, Mr. Granger?" I asked.

Mr. Granger yawned and stretched his arms. "Why don't you get along now," he said. "I need to get some shut-eye."

"Can it? Like the one near the back door?"

"Mind your own business," he grunted.

That was it. That pile of stones near the back door was

some kind of map as well. Like the stool. A blind man's map. But a map of what?

Mr. Granger stood up and walked stiffly over to his cot. He was under his blanket before I knew it.

As far as I could tell, he still slept during the daytime.

"What should I do with the dictionary?"

"On the table," he mumbled.

I banged one of its aluminum legs when I grabbed the stool.

"You can leave the stool there," he said, "for when you come tomorrow."

"But," I said, "I thought it was your map of this apartment."

"Don't need it. I know this apartment inch-for-inch," he said, turning on his side. "That's another thing you got to remember about maps. Comes a time when you don't need them anymore."

"Why do you put the stool on the hatch marks then?"

"To get in other people's way."

I had to laugh. Crazy old bugger.

I walked to the door and flipped the light switch. The room grew thick with darkness.

"Is it hard being blind, Mr. Granger?"

I heard him clear his throat. "If you're talking about not being able to discover 'exciting places,' as you call them, anymore, I'll have you know that John Hanning Speke was virtually blind when he stumbled onto the mythic source of the Nile at the northern end of what he named Lake Victoria. And 'stumbled' is apparently the word. By all accounts, the man couldn't find his backside with both hands – almost a professional at losing his bearings. And I'm pretty damned sure he wasn't following a map. Now get out of here!"

CHAPTER FIVE

I dreamt about Celia again that night, as I would almost every night from then until – well, until just after the accident. In fact, that time it wasn't really much of a dream, more like a flash; a mental picture that was so disturbing it woke me up straight-away from that sticky sweet morning sleep I just didn't feel like leaving. In the dream, I was at the Sinclair station like I had been the morning before. I was looking at the dirty magazine, at the picture of the two girls with the man standing in between them. And I was talking to someone nearby, someone I couldn't see in the dream. I guess it must have been Erik, although it wasn't entirely clear what I was saying to him. After I spoke, things didn't happen the way they had the day before. Erik and I didn't fight over the comment I had made to him about the man. Maybe I didn't even make it. Instead, we both laughed at something I said, and, still standing with the magazine in my hands, I turned the page.

On the next page was a photo of a woman in much the same pose as in the other pictures we had already seen, but she was alone and without the fake decor and safari get-up.

Instead of having dyed blond hair and a jaundiced complexion, this woman was raven-haired and honey-toned and surrounded by a soft light that reflected off her skin as though it were polished brass. And most importantly, she was wearing neither boots nor belt. She was simply and elegantly naked. It was Celia. I looked at her face and felt a weight crush my chest. She was smiling in that gap-toothed way of hers that made her all the more beautiful. I couldn't help myself, couldn't stop my eyes from roaming all over her. I followed the long lines of her body down to that place between her legs where a tuft of curly black hair rose just above her exposed femininity. I had the crazy thought then that I was glad *I* wasn't blind. John Hanning Speke be damned. Here was the mythic source of the Nile, that place where all life begins. And more than anything else, I wanted to get there. I felt myself getting excited, hardening. I heard the sound of flowing water, a river running, and could feel the sound carrying me off. As my pleasure rose, I felt my penis straining, felt the liquid excitement flowing to its tip. For one brief second, I experienced the thrill of an erection begin to wash over me until it reached the head of my member together with all the life-giving juices in my soul. It startled me awake. I jumped from my bed to run to the bathroom. I realized as I looked down into the toilet bowl and fought to keep my tears from dropping down and mixing with my urine, that one second longer and I would have wet my bed like a child.

I might have stayed in the bathroom like that for a long time, might have actually let myself stand there and cry and piss and maybe even masturbate until I had wrung myself completely dry. But the desperate sadness of my mood was interrupted by loud voices coming from the kitchen next door. Shouting – an argument – carried over on the cool morning breeze.

"As far as I know, I'm still the mother around here," Aunt Sally screamed.

"Ma," Ruth Anne pleaded, "it's just an afternoon picnic."

"I told her that she is too young to date."

"There's a whole group of them. It's a good way for her to get to know the kids in her new school."

"It's a good way to get to know Tim Kirsten!"

"You were the one who was so impressed by him. Good student and all."

"This is different!"

"Ma, you can't protect her forever. Kate is very grown up, very mature for her age."

"That's exactly what worries me."

"I meant very 'responsible.'"

"If she's so responsible, then why are you the one doing the talking for her?"

There was a moment of silence, and then I heard Ruth Anne say, "Because I know things she doesn't."

"And you will be so kind as to keep that information to yourself!" Aunt Sally shouted.

"Ma," Ruth Anne pleaded.

"Just because you gave up your studies to run off and play Florence Nightingale. And now you're going off God-knows-where to get married to God-knows-whom. That's your own business. But Kate has talent, *real* talent. And I'm not going to let her ruin her life because a handsome boy swaggers onto the scene, takes her by the hand and invites her to a picnic in Baxter Park!"

That was it. Ruth Anne must have told her that she was getting married, far away, to a stranger. I had a feeling the argument was more about Ruth Anne's upcoming marriage than about Kate spending an innocent afternoon with the young Kirsten.

"You're going to have to let her go sooner or later."

"I'll let her go once she's old enough and on the right path!"

"You can't live your life again through Kate – or through any of us. You have to let go."

"Stop telling me what I can and cannot do. Who says I'm trying to live my life again through her?"

"I am. And I should know. Because you tried to do it with me. And the result was that it – " Ruth Anne's voice caught in her throat. "It just made me want to get away."

Aunt Sally's voice was raw with rage. "And now I'm responsible for your foolish behavior."

"We can't live with your frustrated dream. Why do you think Treat – "

Ruth Anne didn't have time to finish her sentence. Aunt Sally cried out – a cry like the one I heard from the bathroom the day Treat disappeared. I heard a door slam and a car engine turn over. I looked out of the small bathroom window just in time to see Aunt Sally pull out of the driveway.

I got myself cleaned up and ready to go to Mr. Granger's. Pa was sitting at our kitchen table with his hands over his ears and his nose in a cold cup of coffee looking for all the world like he was trying to shut the world out. I downed a glass of orange juice and slipped out the door as quietly as I could. The truth of the matter was I was almost looking forward to going back to see Mr. Granger, especially after the morning's events at the farms. I wanted to look at maps. I wanted to dream about Puerto Rico. I wanted to think about Celia. I wanted to get as far away as my mind could take me. Plus, I thought that the previous visit with the old guy had been a success. I'd learned something about cartography and had what almost felt like a real conversation with Mr. Granger. I had stood my ground on certain things, and he seemed to have respected that. And reading from the dictionary wasn't so bad after all. I still wanted to read from Wegener, though. All of that "shifting continents and wandering pole" stuff had me puzzled and I was sure that Mr. Granger could sort it out for me.

As I drove along, I thought about the scene I had heard in the kitchen that morning. Ruth Anne's mention of Treat had had a strange effect on her ma. Ruth Anne seemed to know why Treat had run away – and seemed to put the blame square on her ma's shoulders. Until then, I thought I was beginning to understand something about why Treat ran away, too, but I had been figuring that it had something to do with Celia and Puerto Rico and not being a *jíbaro* and with being free. Something about being a man. What did Aunt Sally have to do with all that?

To my surprise, I found the door to Mr. Granger's place closed when I arrived. Not only closed, but locked. My first reaction was to worry that something had happened to him. Maybe he had fallen and broken a bone or had taken sick and been carted off to the hospital. Or worse. *I told that nephew of mine that I needed someone to come about once a week, buy me some grub, make sure I'm not laid out flat with little green worms crawling out of my eyes.* My heart raced. But wait, I thought, he wouldn't have taken the trouble to lock the door before falling to the floor and dying, would he? I hesitated before knocking once, and then pulled his key from the pocket of my jeans. What I saw when I opened the door was even more unexpected than anything else I could have imagined. The back door of the apartment was also closed. Mr. Granger's work table had been cleared off, pulled to the center of the room, and covered with a bright tablecloth. A flickering light came from a single white candle at its center. There were serving dishes of cold chicken, green beans and tomatoes, a big bottle of RC Cola and a basket of purple grapes. There was also a fancy, decorated cake.

Mr. Granger sat on one side of the table in his work chair. For the first time since I had been going to see him, he had changed his shirt from the rough black wool button-down he usually wore to a cotton polo-shirt that was a faded gray but looked clean. He'd combed his thin white hair to one side and his face was red as a berry liked he'd scrubbed it a long time. Facing him and perched delicately on the stool on the other side of the table was Darby Millar.

It was in retrospect that I remembered the scent of lavender in the apartment. There was no doubt about it. Miss Millar was all dolled up. Her hair was done differently than usual and she was even wearing make-up, something I noticed she never did at the library. Her manner of dressing for the library was very somber, austere even, whereas that day she was in a flowery, flowing robe that was very festive. Her back was slightly turned to me. She seemed to be holding something in her hands that I couldn't see. Mr. Granger cocked his head to one side as I walked in. Miss Millar turned and looked coyly at me.

"Why, hello, Sebastian," she said softly.

Mr. Granger grunted. "Ah, it's the urchin."

"Nick, really, don't be naughty," she said, waving a finger at him.

He shrugged and bit into a chicken leg.

"Come in, come in," Miss Millar said. "Would you like some chicken?"

I groped for my stomach. It wasn't even ten o'clock in the morning. I was starving, but chicken didn't sound good. And there was no way I was going to sit down and eat with the two of them.

"No, thank you," I said. I started backing up towards the door. "I beg your pardon," I said. "I didn't know anybody was here."

"I'm here," Mr. Granger said. His mouth was full of chicken.

"I meant that I didn't realize you had company, sir. I'll just be on my way."

Miss Millar slid off the stool and turned towards me. "I would have told you, Sebastian, but I didn't see you at the library yesterday."

As she stood, I saw that she was holding a paperback in her hands. Its cover was a reddish-orange that looked familiar. I looked more closely. It was Wegener's *The Origin of Continents and Oceans*. She was reading it to him. She was reading Wegener's book to him. After all the fuss she had made about giving me the book, about wanting *me* to read it – and to read it to Mr. Granger. After she made me believe it was something I could share with him, something only two like minds could understand. What a liar she was! What a traitor. And so was Mr. Granger. Pretending not to remember her name and then stuffing himself with her home cooking. I felt sick. I had to get out of there. I reached for the door handle.

"See you tomorrow at the library, Bass?"

I looked back at her. The library. Come to think of it, why wasn't *she* at the library? She was always acting as though it were the center of the universe. She must have read my mind.

"It's closed today, exceptionally. For a special occasion," she said, smiling. "It's Nick's birthday." He waved a greasy chicken leg at her. "And we celebrate it every year together, don't we?"

Mr. Granger grunted again.

I pulled the door to the apartment closed so hard the handle nearly came off in my hand. I heard Mr. Granger call out, "Urchin!" as I walked up the steps to the sidewalk. Imagine Miss Millar closing her beloved library to celebrate the ol' bugger's birthday in that dank basement. I couldn't believe it. I wondered if the honest taxpayers of Millarsburg knew that. It was an outrage. I wouldn't be able to go look at the *Atlas* or *A History of Puerto Rico*. And all that because of the ol' bugger's birthday. Plus, there was the whole scene at the library about taking the Wegener book to Mr. Granger when Miss Millar knew she would be there herself the following week. And Mr. Granger wanting me to leave the stool the day before. Of course! It was because he knew Darby Millar would be coming for his birthday. What a silly fool I was to believe a thing either of them ever said to me.

Once outside in the bright summer sunshine, however, I had the urge to laugh. What a scene. Could it really be that Miss Millar was in love with the old guy? Maybe she had been for a long time. The ol' bugger and the spinster. It was something right out of a movie.

I drove to the Sinclair station. It was too bad Erik didn't know Nick Granger. I was dying to tell somebody, and knowing the way Erik felt about movies – at least *Spartacus* – he probably would have gotten a kick out of the whole thing. I pulled into the station, and had another surprise. The Bauer brothers were there, but Erik was nowhere to be seen. Mike was filling up the tank of Buster Millar's Chevy pick-up. Buster was Darby's nephew and took care of what was left of the family farm on the outskirts of town. I always thought Buster wore his inheritance like a truck tire around his neck. I could see Ed Bauer through the plate glass window to the office. He was on the telephone. I parked the car near the air pump just off to the right side of the station.

"Hey, Mike," I said, going over to him.

He stuck out a black-stained hand – which I shook – and then went back to pumping gas. I waited until he had finished, replaced the gas nozzle, collected the money, and Buster Millar had pulled out before saying, "I was looking for Erik."

"Not in today," Mike said.

Well, I'll be hanged, I thought. What was *he* celebrating?

"Day off?" I asked. It wasn't worth speaking in complete sentences to Mike. He pulled a paper towel from the dispenser and wiped his hands.

"Sick."

"Sick? What's he got?"

Mike shrugged his shoulders. "Didn't say. Sounded funny, though."

I backed the Fairlane out of the station so that I wouldn't make the bells ring in the office by driving past the pumps. A few minutes later, I pulled into the Roths' driveway. The place looked closed up like nobody was home. Neither of their cars was in the driveway. Erik's parents were probably at the store. I went up to the front door and knocked. No answer. I knocked again. Still no answer. Maybe Erik had just wanted the day off, but hadn't wanted to ask for it. That was strange. I'm sure they let him have a day off now and again when he wanted one. Maybe he had something he wanted to do, but didn't want to have to tell The Boys what it was. I decided to ring the doorbell. If he were really sick, then he probably just wouldn't answer it. Anyway, I was pretty sure he wasn't home. I waited a few more minutes. I was just about to walk back to my car when I heard the front door creak open. I couldn't see very well past the screen and into the darkened house. The brightness of the sun was blinding me. I squinted. There was someone standing there in the shadows.

"Erik?" I asked.

The screen door opened out from the inside. I recognized the straw-colored hair on the arm pushing it open. It was Erik. I stepped inside the house. It took a minute for my eyes to adjust to the light. I looked back at him.

"What happened to you?" I asked.

He stood there looking at me without saying anything. His

face was a disaster. His left eye was blackened and he had a cut above it that ran up through his eyebrow and all the way into his hairline. His nose was swollen and yellowish-purple and looked like it was broken in about three places. His bottom lip was cut open and puffy. There was some dried blood sticking to the wound. I could see his tongue through his open mouth. It looked like he had trouble closing his jaws. His cheeks were discolored and scraped up. He held a cramped hand out to me. I took it gently. He was wearing the same outfit he'd had on the night we went to the movies and the afternoon of Kate's show. Seemed like it had become some kind of uniform for him. He wore it like a badge. The front of the V-neck sweater was stained with blood. Both the white shirt and the cream-colored pants were smeared with grit and wrinkled. One pant leg was torn at the knee. He was still wearing his penny-loafers but they were covered with dried blood and dirt. He turned and limped into the living room. He mumbled something to me, but I didn't understand.

"What did you say?" I asked.

He looked back at me. He spoke with difficulty. I noticed he was missing a few teeth.

"Geez, Erik!"

He shook his head and didn't say anything. He motioned for me to follow him. He walked stiffly through the living room and into their kitchen in the back. In the kitchen, he filled a glass of water from the tap and drank some of it slowly. Even that looked like it hurt. He rinsed his mouth out with the rest and spit it out in the sink. It poured out of his mouth the color of honey-vinegar.

"Where are your folks?" I asked. Someone should have been there taking care of him.

"At...the...store," he said. It seemed to take all of his energy to speak.

"At the store!" I said. I figured I'd seen a lot of things over the past couple of years, but that took the cake. "They just left you like this?"

"They – don't...know."

"What do you mean they don't know?"

Erik made a face as he swallowed. It seemed like the words came out of his mouth long after his lips stopped moving, like an old film whose soundtrack had gone haywire. "I didn't get in until nearly daybreak. I left the keys to Ma's car on the table and went into my room," he said.

"Why didn't you get them to help you?"

He shook his head.

"Why not? What happened, Erik? Did you have an accident?"

He shook his head again. It was like playing Twenty Questions with a mute.

"What, then?" He looked away from me. "Did you get beat up?"

He waited a minute before nodding.

"Dang, Erik. You should tell the police. I'm going to call Sheriff Walker."

"No!" he said. He laid his hand on my arm. His knuckles were scraped nearly down to the bone.

I didn't know what to do.

"Then let me take you to the hospital," I said.

He shook his head. No.

Hang him. I couldn't figure him. "You can't just stay like this."

Erik's face crumpled. I think he was crying, but I couldn't really tell. His eyes were almost swollen shut and his mouth was all dried out. His tongue was sticking half out like he couldn't get it back inside. I might have actually taken him in my arms then, I felt so sorry for him. But I was afraid to touch him. He was bruised all over.

"I can call Father Wilhelm," I said. He nodded. That was a good idea. "You got the number?" I waited while he limped into his bedroom and came back, holding an address book in his hand. I took it from him.

"W?" I asked. My question reminded me of having read the dictionary with Mr. Granger the day before. Erik nodded. I opened to "W," found and dialed Father Wilhelm's number. A stroke of luck. He was in.

"Father Wilhelm? This is Bass Ramsey."

He couldn't keep the surprise out of his voice. "Bass Ramsey! How are you?"

I explained to him that I was at Erik's house and described the state I had found Erik in. I also told him I didn't really know what had happened. Erik didn't want to tell me. He seemed to have been beaten up, but didn't want to go to the hospital nor to the police. Father Wilhelm didn't seem very surprised. He told me I needed to get him cleaned up and into bed, maybe get him to drink a little broth or bouillon.

"Can you do that?" he asked. "Just run a warm bath. Maybe try to clean his wounds as best you can. Be as gentle as possible. I'll be up from Ypsi as soon as I can."

I covered the receiver with my hand and told Erik what Father Wilhelm had said. Erik looked at me like I was his last hope on Earth.

"Can you do that?" Father Wilhelm's voice sounded into the earpiece.

"Yes, Father. I can do that," I said. I hung up and looked at Erik. "Let's get you cleaned up," I said.

While Erik walked slowly to the bathroom, I ran ahead and plugged the tub and started running the water. I touched it to make sure it wasn't too hot. I looked around the bathroom. Erik would need a place to sit. I couldn't have him standing in the state he was in while we waited for the tub to fill. I raced into the kitchen and grabbed a chair and carried it back to the bathroom. Erik walked in and sat immediately down on the chair like all the forces of gravity in the world were pushing down on his head. His hands were a mess. Every movement seemed to cause him excruciating pain. I didn't want to do it – but I was going to have to help him get undressed. I probably even needed to help him urinate before getting him into the tub. I let him rest a minute on the chair and tested the water again. The temperature was fine.

"Be right back," I said. I ran back into the kitchen and opened a few cupboards. I found a Tupperware container that looked about right and carried it back to the bathroom.

Erik looked up at me. There was so much sorrow on his battered face I could hardly bear to look at him. He reached up and touched the point of the V of his sweater and gave it a slight tug.

"I'll help you get undressed," I said to him. "And get you into the tub and take care of you. Don't worry. It's no big deal," I lied. In fact, my knees were shaking. I lifted up the Tupperware container. "Do you need to pee?"

Erik mumbled something I didn't understand but took, for some reason, for a "yes." Then he closed his eyes. I noticed goose-bumps on his forearm.

"Cold?" I asked.

He nodded.

It was almost a blessing I didn't realize until later that Erik must have been in shock.

The temperature was heating up outside and even in the house it was already stuffy, but Erik started shivering. I walked over and closed the window above the toilet and then shut the door. He was so doubled over with pain it didn't seem possible that I'd be able to get his trousers undone, much less actually get his penis out and help him to urinate.

"I'm gonna – ugh, open your fly," I said stupidly.

I opened his trousers, reached into his briefs and pulled out his penis. I have to admit noticing, not without some satisfaction, that his penis wasn't very big. In fact, it seemed even smaller than mine, though, I guess, part of the reason it seemed all shriveled up had to do with his suffering. I rested it against the side of the Tupperware container and said, "Go ahead." He peed a few drops, then a few more, but it was far from the torrent I had been expecting.

I waited a little while then asked, "That all?"

"I peed myself," he said. "After." The humiliation. It was true that he smelled a little of piss.

"Don't worry about it," I said. I set the Tupperware container in the sink.

"Let's get you undressed," I said more to myself than him. "Erik," I began, taking a deep breath. "I know you're hurt, but you need to try to relax otherwise all of this is just going to hurt more. And I need you to lean back otherwise I'm not going to be able to get your pants off."

He took a deep breath and seemed to gather together all of his forces. Every half inch of movement backward seemed to send shots of pain through his body that made him jerk forward. He tried several times, caught between wanting to lean against the chair and the pain doing so caused him. I wanted to guide him, but I didn't dare touch him any more than was necessary.

"Take your time." I said. "There's no rush. We got all the time in the world."

That seemed to calm him. I checked the temperature of the water and actually went out into the backyard to have a pee myself. I was feeling pretty nervous. When I got back into the bathroom, Erik was resting against the back of the chair. His shoulders drooped as though leaning back had completely drained him of energy. I cut the water off in the tub.

Erik's head was resting against the top wooden slat of the chair. His eyes were closed. If I could just get him to slide down a little further, I'd be able to slip his pants off while he braced himself on the chair. The shirt and sweater after that would be a piece of cake. I told him what I wanted to do and asked him if he thought he could slide down. He nodded and began his slow, glacier-like movement down the chair. I thought of the way Treat used to tease me whenever we foot-raced down East Baker Road and, like always, he beat me.

"Geologically-speaking, you're pretty fast," he used to say.

I thought of Wegener's shifting continents. The Upper Carboniferous. The Lower Quaternary – or was it Tertiary, I couldn't remember. I touched the water again. I was almost sorry I hadn't run it hotter. It was cooling off already. By the time I actually got Erik into the tub, the water might be too cold. I plunged my hand into the tub and lifted the drain to let some of the water out. I had a heck of time getting the darn thing back in. Then I ran a stream of boiling hot water until the overall water temperature was pretty warm. When I turned around, I realized Erik was half off of the chair and was having trouble holding on. I slipped his pants and underpants down to his knees in one quick motion and told him to sit up again. I'd take everything completely off once he was resting on the chair. He groaned as he strained to get his backside onto the seat. He wasn't going to make it. I was going to have to help him. I put my hands under his arms and lifted him up. He was pretty light. He cried out.

"Sorry," I said.

"It's okay," he said weakly.

I took off his shoes, socks, pants and underpants. When I

went to throw his pants off to one side, I noticed what I hadn't noticed before. The seam in the seat of his trousers had been ripped open. His underpants were bloodstained. I took off his sweater, shirt, and undershirt and threw them into the same pile. His chest and thighs were covered with bruises.

"Geez, Erik," I said. "How many of them were there?"

"Three," he whispered.

I shook my head. Dang.

I got Erik to stand up and lean against me so that I could help him lift one leg into the tub.

"Too hot?" I asked when his foot touched. It sprang back.

"No," he said, but I wasn't sure. I was going to have to take his word on it.

I helped him lower himself gently into the water and then released him. He slid down up to his chin. He didn't even have the strength to keep himself upright. But I couldn't stand there and hold him the whole time.

"Look under the sink," he said.

I propped him up on his elbows, maybe the only parts of him that weren't bruised and swollen, and opened the cabinet under the sink. There was a short plastic bench in there, the kind mothers used for babies, I guess, to help them sit upright in the tub. I couldn't help smiling at the two, small round indentations for the baby's bottom. When I lifted it out, I noticed that there was a suction cup at each corner. I got Erik back into a standing position, and left him wobbling on his own while I pushed the baby's seat down into the water and secured it at about the middle of the tub. I helped Erik sit down again, lifted his legs over the seat and braced his buttocks against it. His head remained just above the water. Perfect. Now I could see to getting some broth warmed up and maybe letting him rest a little bit in the bath.

"Okay like that?" I asked. I was kind of afraid to leave him alone. There was a small transistor on the glass shelf above the sink. I clicked it on. It worked. I turned the volume up as loud as it would go and then turned it off. I set the transistor on the chair next to the tub and pulled the chair close so that the radio was easily within Erik's reach.

"I'm going to see about making you some soup. If you need me, just turn on the radio. Okay?"

He nodded, but seemed half asleep.

I went into the kitchen and opened cupboards until I found the place where Mrs. Roth kept her dry goods. I dug around in it until I found a package of bouillon cubes. Then I found a mug and spoon, filled the kettle and put it on to boil. I ran back into the bathroom and found Erik in the same position, so I went back out and into his room. His bed was still made. There was some blood on the bedspread. That was going to have to be a problem for someone else, I thought. I turned down his bed and fluffed up the pillows against the headboard. I found his bathrobe hanging on the inside of his closet door and carried it back to the bathroom. He opened his eyes when I walked in.

"We need to clean out some of your cuts," I said. "Father Wilhelm said so." I grabbed the soap from the sink and found a washcloth hanging on the towel rack nearby. "I'm going to try not to press too hard, but if it hurts, just tell me."

I wasn't going to have to worry too much about that. Erik stifled a scream at the slightest contact. Before getting it all soapy, I wet the washcloth and dabbed it around Erik's lips and then squeezed it out into his mouth which was dry as a bone. For some reason, I was reminded of images of Christ on the cross and the guard squeezing a sponge of vinegary wine into the mouth of Jesus. I remember how Erik had talked to me about Jesus. About Jesus and Superman. The water gurgled in Erik's mouth.

"Just spit it out."

He struggled to bring the water up. He couldn't purse his lips.

"Or, heck, just swallow it. It's just water."

The kettle whistled on the stove.

"Be right back."

I mixed up a mug of bouillon and carried it into Erik's room where I set it on the night stand next to his bed. It could cool while I got him out of the bath. Back in the bathroom, I sponged off his face and forehead but decided not to try to wash his head. He had a lump the size of an egg in the back. Then I soaped up the washcloth and gently wiped down his arms, legs and chest. I even swiped it quickly over his groin since a little blood had trickled all the way down his chest and into his pubic hair. And then, well – there was all of that piss. The water became tinged with color. The mug of bouillon had cooled down to a good temperature by the time I got him out of the tub, dried off, and into his robe. I helped him stumble into his room and climb into bed. I had to hand-feed him his bouillon by the teaspoon. I thought we'd never finish that mug. When we finally did, Erik let his head drop back against his pillow. For the first time since I had found him that morning, he seemed almost at peace.

"Bass?"

"Yeah?"

"Thanks."

I felt kind of embarrassed. Heck, it was only normal.

Father Wilhelm still hadn't arrived. "Can you sleep?"

He shook his head. "Don't think so."

"Do you want me to leave you alone?"

He looked over at me, his eyes wide.

"I mean, in your room." I think he thought I wanted to leave the house.

He shook his head. "I don't want to be alone."

"Well," I started. Where did that leave us? We couldn't very well talk. He was tired and had trouble speaking. And he didn't seem to want to discuss what had happened. We could listen to the radio, but there wasn't a ball game on until that afternoon. "I could try to find that music station you like," I suggested.

"No, thanks." He lifted a hand to his head. "Headache."

"You want some aspirin?"

"Please."

I found aspirin in the medicine chest. I filled a juice glass with water in the kitchen and carried it back to him. I might as well have asked him to swallow a brick. "Hang on," I said, "I'll try to mash it up."

Back in the kitchen I started going through drawers. I was getting to know Mrs. Roth's kitchen as well as my own. Ma used to have a thing that looked like a hammer that she used for pounding meat. Aunt Sally didn't have one. Mrs. Roth might. I rummaged through a drawer with utensils. Eureka. I set the pill on the Formica counter and gave it a good whack. Part of it went flying off someplace, part of it stuck to the knobby end of the hammer, and the little that was left on the counter had actually turned to powder. At that rate, I'd have to pound up the whole bottle. I went back into the bathroom and got a couple of more tablets. This time, though, I wrapped them in a kitchen cloth before smashing them with the hammer. Success. I spoon-fed Erik the powder and then lifted the glass of water up to his mouth. He swallowed quickly, but made a face.

"Tastes pretty bad, huh?"

He nodded. There was a little bouillon left in the mug. I spoon-fed that to him as well to wash away the bitterness. Now back to the problem of what to do until Father Wilhelm arrived.

"I could read to you," I said shyly. "If you want."

Erik looked like he was trying to smile.

"I've been reading to this guy. I haven't had the chance to tell you. This blind guy over in Painted Creek. So, it's no problem, if you want. Would you like that?"

"Very much," he said.

I looked around his room. "Anything?"

There were some paperbacks on a bookshelf next to his desk, stuff that looked serious like that book he was reading the other day at the station. I didn't really feel like reading any of that. There was a big dictionary, but I wasn't going to read that, either. There was the *Guinness Book of World Records*, but that would only be interesting for a little while. If I had known, I would have bought the *Millarsburg Eagle* for him. He was always reading it at the station. I squatted down to look on the bottom shelf. There were two tall stacks of *Superman* comic books.

"I could read you one of your *Superman* books," I said. "But, you've probably read them all already."

"That's okay," he mumbled.

I started going through the stacks. Might as well read one I hadn't read. I checked the titles. *Superman meets Al Capone*. Nah. Given the state he was in, better not read anything too violent to Erik. *Superman Goes to War!* Not that, either. I was tempted by *The Bizarro Invasion of Earth*, but I'd read it already and it was also about death and destruction. I needed something a little more upbeat. I laid my hands on a *Giant Superman Annual* featuring *the Superman Family on Krypton*. That might be interesting. I didn't know too much about Superman's early life on Krypton, other than, like everybody else, that his father had sent him off in a space rocket to save his life before the planet blew up. I checked out the "Table of Contents." No title grabbed me any more than any other. I decided that I'd just start at the beginning. *Krypton Lives On*. It was the story of what Superman's life would have been like if Krypton hadn't exploded and he hadn't been sent to Earth in a space rocket. I noticed, for some reason, at the bottom of the first page that it had been published in 1962 and that the company that had published it was located in Sparta, Illinois. When I mentioned this to Erik, he smiled and nodded. I didn't know whether to curse Mr. Granger or thank him. I'd never look at a book the same way again after the way he had made me read the dictionary to him. Here I was reading copyright information in a *Superman* comic book!

Erik was lying back with his eyes closed, so reading the comic book to him was almost like reading something to Mr. Granger. In a way, it was even harder than reading to Mr. Granger because I had to try to make Erik see the pictures, too. But Erik seemed to like the idea, so from the very first page I took the trouble of describing the scene to him before reading the dialogue. It was tiring. I realized after about the third page or so that I was completely out of breath. So, I was pretty happy when I looked up and noticed that Erik had fallen asleep. I crept out of his room and closed the door quietly behind me. I decided that I would finish the rest of the comic book on the Roths' back patio. I even helped myself to a glass of iced tea from a pitcher in the refrigerator before going out. I figured the Roths wouldn't mind.

Once I started reading, though, I almost regretted not having taken the *Bizarro Invasion of Earth*. Thanks to a gift from Batman and Robin, Superman is able to visualize on his "Super Univac" what his life would have been like if he had been able to stay on his own planet, Krypton, with his parents, Jor-El and Lara. I couldn't help but be reminded of my own life, and how different it would have been if my ma was still alive. Amongst other things, Superman learns that, if Krypton had not exploded, his mother would have had another boy, a baby brother. I knew that I would never have had a baby brother since Ma couldn't have any more kids. But I had been like a baby brother to Treat and still would have been, if Treat hadn't run away. Kal-El, which is Superman's name on the planet Krypton, has to choose another world where he will do a good deed using a space telescope and *long-range power rays*. He chooses, of course, to do his good deed on the planet "Earth" which he selects from a map of the galaxy that also includes planets called "Zornia" and "Dyon III" and "The Blue Planet." I remembered that in the film, Spartacus, too, refers to a map of *his* universe, a map of Italy. Seemed like no matter what I did those days, I found myself faced with a map. In the Superman story, Kal-El wants to become a spaceman and explore those other worlds surrounding Krypton, but the "skill machine" selects him to become a dispatcher for the other spacemen who get to leave Krypton. Some days, I felt a lot like Kal-El. I watched while other people explored new places or simply left me alone in the universe.

I heard a car drive into the driveway. I walked around to the front of the house and recognized Father Wilhelm's black Ford sedan. He popped out of the driver's side. A thin, blond-haired man with gold-rimmed glasses appeared from the passenger's side. He was carrying a black physician's bag. I shook Father Wilhelm's hand.

"Bass, this is Dr. Novak. He's come to see about Erik. How is he?"

"Sleeping," I said, shaking the doctor's hand. "I did everything you said."

"Bass," Father Wilhelm said, "you've been more than helpful. I'm sure Erik will never forget you for this."

"Yes, Father," I said. I could have crawled under the car. I felt so embarrassed.

TERRA FIRMA

"I need to ask you to do one more thing. Something very difficult."

"What's that, Father?"

"I don't want the Roths coming home this evening and finding Erik in this state, not knowing that something has happened. And I can't stay very long. I called the store before coming here and – well, Mr. Roth hung up on me before I could say anything. I need to ask you to go to the store and see if you can talk to Mrs. Roth, preferably out of ear shot of her husband. Gently tell her what happened and let her know that Dr. Novak and I are here."

"But I don't really know what happened, Father."

"Tell her just what you know then. Tell her the truth."

"Which is?" Like the hollow ground underfoot, I was coming to understand that the truth wasn't always what it seemed either.

"What you told me. How you found Erik. All that you've done."

"Okay, Father." I handed him the *Superman* comic book. "Could you put this back in Erik's room?"

He took it in both hands like an offering. "And Bass, it might be better if you don't come back with her."

Mrs. Roth was behind the counter at the Feed and Seed. I had always liked their store. It had rough-planked floors that seemed like something out of the Far West. And a kind of pungent, earthy smell that hit my nostrils as soon as I walked in the door. The coast was clear. Mr. Roth was in the side lot showing a used tractor to somebody. The Roths kept a few pieces of farm machinery that they sold on commission. Mrs. Roth looked startled to see me.

"Hello, Bass," she said. "What a nice surprise."

I got a cold feeling in my stomach and head like I had eaten too much ice cream too fast. She wouldn't think it was such a nice surprise once I told her what I had to tell her. I stood there a minute looking at her. She had mousy brown hair that she always had fixed in the same puffy style and lacquered into place with hair spray. She wore green horn-rimmed glasses that Erik once told me were made out of bone and which were considered very *avant-garde* in our little town. When she was young, she used to paint. The Roths had several of her watercolors hanging in their house. I thought they were pretty good. But as time went on and the store expanded, Mr. Roth needed her more and more to help with sales and inventory. She had put up her brushes. I had never noticed before how much Erik looked like her.

"I got some bad news, Mrs. Roth," I said.

She listened to me carefully as I told her about her son. Only once did she betray any emotion by looking off to the side through the plate glass window to where we could see Mr. Roth gesturing as he talked to the client about the tractor.

She touched my arm gently. "Thank you, Bass," she said.

As I was pulling out of the parking lot of the Feed & Seed, I noticed her walking slowly towards the side yard, wringing her hands.

* * *

The early afternoon heat was sweltering. My T-shirt was sticking to me. I went to my room and pulled it off, then stretched out on my bed. I was beat. Before I knew it, I fell asleep.

It seemed like I could hardly close my eyes anymore without dreaming of Celia. Sure enough, during that afternoon nap, I dreamt of her again. Like in other dreams I'd had of her, I kept trying to get to her, to reach out and touch her, but was never able to. In this dream, we were standing in some kind of grove. The sun was very hot. Celia was dressed in the same shorts and top. I was dressed the same way I had been that afternoon at Erik's. A door frame stood between Celia and me. It was golden – gilded, I think, is the word for it – and had neither screen nor glass, just a beautiful wooden frame that stood upright between us, suspended in the air I don't know how. I kept trying to walk through the empty frame, but couldn't. Each time I took a step forward, it slid backwards. I even tried going around it once, but the frame moved along with me, and I always found it between me and Celia. No matter what I did. I began to get very frustrated. Celia stood there smiling demurely, looking at me. The golden door wouldn't let me pass. I became so angry that I grabbed the frame and tried to yank it away. It didn't budge. Finally, in desperation, I smacked the wood hard with my fist. One, two, three times.

I woke up. Someone was knocking.

"Sebastian?"

It was Ruth Anne.

"Come in," I called.

She walked in and sat on the foot of the bed.

"Sorry to wake you," she said.

I ran a hand across my face. "What's up?"

"Listen. I've decided to leave early."

"When?"

"Tomorrow morning. First thing. I'll go to Mission headquarters in Des Moines. I've got a ton of paperwork to do, anyway. And the person in charge of travel for the mission said he could probably get me on an earlier flight out than the one I was supposed to go on. I think I've done enough damage here."

I began to protest. She put a hand up to stop me.

"Besides, I'm anxious to see Jean-Christophe. And even though things are starting to settle down in the region, I'm always worried that trouble will break out again soon."

"What kind of trouble?"

She felt for the nape of her neck. "It's a young nation. And there's been a lot of agitation, a lot of anger and emotion, even violence. But I think that happens whenever anyone or anything is struggling to define itself or set itself free from something else. Whether it's a nation or a person." She smiled meekly. "Look at me and ma."

I laughed.

"Or look at what's been going on in places around the world. Puerto Rico, for example."

I sat straight up. "What's going on there?"

She considered me for a minute. "You know what? I think I'm going to get you a subscription to *Time* or *Newsweek* or *The Christian Science Monitor*. A kind of belated birthday present. Would you like that?"

"What's going on in Puerto Rico?" I insisted.

"Well, in a nutshell, there's been a struggle between the people who want the island to remain a commonwealth. There are those who want it to become a State. And there are the *Independentistas* who want it to become a nation in its own right with its own government, and its own flag. There are a lot of people tired of being governed by what they consider a foreign power with a different culture and language. What's interesting for me, when I compare things to where I will live, is that Puerto Rico is an island with its own natural borders – even if the population is made up of descendants of Indians, Africans, and Europeans mostly of Spanish descent. The problem in Africa is that the boundaries are always shifting, that they're so arbitrary. People from the same tribe sometimes live in two different countries whereas people with very different cultures and even different languages are supposed to be co-citizens."

I pictured the map of the world. Instead of shifting land masses, the national borders started moving. I imagined Mexico pushing northwards until it had taken over the southern United States or the Michigan border dropping down to take over a part of Ohio. Would that mean that an Indians fan would have to start cheering for the Tigers? Or that a Texan would have to change his passport without even moving out of his house?

"This decade has seen so many changes. I can hardly even keep up with all of the name changes."

Borínquen. The land of the brave lord.

"Why do names change like that, Ruth Anne?"

"It's a way to assert oneself, I suppose. In the same way that naming something is a way to dominate it or possess it. Look at Katie wanting to be called 'Kate' now. It means that she's growing up, and doesn't want to accept a pet name that Ma gave her when she was a little kid."

I nodded. The name "Bass" was just fine with me.

"Speaking of Ma," Ruth Anne continued. "She won't be back until later. I think she needs some time to herself. I need to ask you another favor."

"Go ahead," I said.

"I wanted to know if I could borrow your car again," she said, looking at her watch. "I need to buy a few gifts before I go. And I don't really have time to get around on Kate's bike." I dug into my pocket and handed her the keys.

"Thanks, Sebastian," she said.

* * *

"Bass?"

"Yeah, Uncle Will?"

"Come here for a minute, would you?"

Uncle Will was sitting at the picnic table, nursing a glass of lemonade. I think he and Pa had worked in the vegetable patch in the morning, because there was a colander of green beans in our refrigerator that had been washed and rinsed, but still needed to be snapped, and a couple of almost-ripe tomatoes on the window sill that hadn't been there when I left to go to Mr. Granger's house that morning. I didn't know where Pa was, but that wasn't unusual. For as much contact I actually had with him, I could have been living alone.

"I guess you probably heard what happened this morning."

I shrugged. "More or less." I didn't want him to know that Ruth Anne and Aunt Sally could have been arguing in *our* kitchen for as much as I'd missed of their fight.

"There's something I should tell you, man-to-man. And then maybe you'll understand a little better what's going on. Maybe you'll even understand what I think the real reason is that your cousin ran away. And you'll finally understand that it wasn't your fault. Okay?"

He swallowed and took a deep breath. "Your aunt and I dated for a while before we got married. I wanted us to get married when we both turned eighteen because I already knew by the time I was sixteen that I loved her and wanted her to be my wife, but my pa wouldn't allow it. He said I was too young and he needed me on the farm. Your pa had gone off to fight. Your grandpa would go through a lot of trouble to get an exemption from service for me on the grounds that the farm would go under and since we were contributing a good part of our sugar beet production to the cause, it was accepted. He said he'd already given up one son. Grandpa wanted me to wait until I was twenty-one to marry Sally. By that time, he figured I'd be more mature, your pa would be back and the war would probably be over. We could all work the farm together. I felt cheated because I wouldn't get a chance to fight like your pa did. I figured that made me less than a man."

He stopped and took a deep breath. "I didn't want to wait because I knew what my pa didn't and that was that your Aunt Sally wasn't all that keen on getting married. She was working after school as a seamstress and had done all kinds of volunteer work for the war. She said that when she turned eighteen, she wanted to strike out on her own, open a notions shop and do tailoring. She was very independent and very self-assured for a small-town girl, especially for someone that young. Kate takes right after her. And Sally was very caught up in the war movement. All those young men in uniform seemed to impress her. I even worried," he said, shaking his head, "that she'd kind of fallen for your pa in his absence. She begged me to read the letters he sent home and even asked for a picture he'd sent of himself – saying it was for a scrapbook she and some girlfriends were putting together. The thought of your pa coming home worried me. We didn't know yet that he had met your ma. All of those soldiers coming back in their handsome uniforms. And there I was, just a farm boy. I figured if Pa made me wait to marry your aunt that I would lose her. So, I did the only thing I knew how to do at the time to prove my manhood."

I sat there looking at him and waited.

"One summer evening we were in Baxter Park. Just the two of us. It was getting late and I knew I had to get your aunt back home. We were necking and petting and – well, I just let myself get carried away. I was like a madman. I think Sally was too frightened to stop me. Or – I don't know – your aunt was always very modern in her thinking. Or maybe she just didn't really consider the consequences. I had, though. I had. The result was that we found out only a few weeks later that she was pregnant. We had to get married, then. At the time, it was the thing to do. I don't even know if your aunt loves me," he said, the words catching deep in his throat. "I know that she has always resented the fact that she had to give up her dream of becoming a seamstress or maybe even a fashion designer. She has always hated farm life and has never missed one opportunity to remind me and the kids of that. We told Ruth Anne she was a 'honeymoon baby,' but I think she understood pretty early on that her life started under – well, less than ideal circumstances. Sally has always been particularly hard on her. I guess Ruth Anne is a living reminder of what she felt she had to give up. That's why I can't – won't – object to Sally's going back to school.

"And she was always on Treat not to do what I had done. Always talking to him about what it was like for her to be stuck on the farm. I think he finally ran away because he had a vision of the farm being like a prison. He sucked up that idea with his baby's milk from your aunt's nipple. But I can't say I can blame him. I've got only myself to blame, and my selfishness." He was quiet for a moment. "So now you know," he added.

I didn't quite know what to say to all of that, but I understood then why Pa had always insisted about what he'd do to me if I ever got a girl into "trouble." I'd always figured until then that Pa feeling that way mostly had to do with him being raised in a strict Catholic family and having his beliefs and all. It never even crossed my mind that it was because Uncle Will and Aunt Sally had to get married and that Pa saw and understood the consequences of their forced union long before I would ever learn what "to get a girl in trouble" meant.

* * *

Ruth Anne was up and gone before I was awake. I have the fuzzy memory of feeling a warm kiss on my forehead which I incorporated, of course, into the dream I was having of Celia at the time. She actually kissed me, I thrilled, if only in a dream and if only on the forehead. In that dream, Celia and I were sitting on a park bench much like the ones in Baxter Park. But instead of looking out over the dark, curving alley of water that was Black River, I dreamt we were looking past palm trees and a sandy expanse of beach to the sea just like I'd seen a couple doing once in a travel poster for Florida. When I woke up, I found a note from Ruth Anne on my night stand that said she hadn't wanted to wake me to say, "good-bye." We would see each other again soon, she promised. Maybe someday, she had added, I could even visit her in Africa. There was an address where I could write to her, if I wanted.

I felt especially lonely that day. It's strange how quickly you get used to somebody. And then they're gone. I think we all felt Ruth Anne's absence that morning, felt it in a way none of us ever had for Treat. Plus, there was still the hope that Treat would come home again whereas Ruth Anne's departure that morning felt very final.

Her leaving also coincided with the beginning of a period of change for me. From then on I would spend more and more time at the library and with Mr. Granger. Erik, the only real "friend" I'd had that summer – and, in fact, the only real friend I had had since Treat ran away – would remain house-bound until late in the summer. He quit his job at the Sinclair station and it was like he had gone into hiding. I received a note from his mother saying that she and Mr. Roth had greatly appreciated all that I had done. Erik even sent along a note of personal thanks, but asked that I not visit. Not just yet. Emotionally, I think he was still very shaken up. And his physical condition was worse than I could have ever imagined. He had sustained a couple of broken ribs and a mild concussion and had suffered some internal bleeding. I was told that he might never fully recuperate the use of his right hand. Dr. Novak continued to treat him on occasional visits north, accompanied, of course, by Father Wilhelm who visited me once as well. Mr. Roth apparently accepted these visits silently. And Sheriff Walker had, I'd heard, agreed to keep his nose out of things. Erik had been attacked in Black River which was in a different jurisdiction. So, at the family's request, Sheriff Walker turned a blind legal eye to what had happened, though word spread fast enough so that most folks knew.

As the month of August approached, I was reminded, as I had been the year before, of that fateful visit with Treat and Erik to Celia and her family's campsite. I knew I wouldn't be able to help myself. I knew that I would go back to the campsite time and time again to search the ground for clues, hoping and fearing each time I turned at the blue spruce that I would find the ramshackle Holiday camper back in its place, propped up on an empty beer keg like it was that day. And each time I would be disappointed. One afternoon, though, I thought I saw Celia. After I had finished reading to Mr. Granger, I stopped in for a burger at a diner in Painted Creek. I'd been there once before. That afternoon there was a girl behind the bar when I walked in. She was wearing a white cook's apron around her thin waist. She stood with her back to me talking to the owner, Hank, with whom I'd had a friendly conversation about baseball the first time I'd gone there. I only saw the girl's profile and that for only a fraction of a minute before she slipped into the kitchen. She had the same build as Celia, was the same height and had the same blue-black sheen to her long hair. I sat for the longest time, toying with my food, hoping she would reappear, but she never did. I didn't have the guts to ask Hank after her. Most folks don't usually take kindly to snooping and some folks less kindly to flirting. Maybe she was even Hank's daughter – or worse, his girl. Or maybe she was a townie with Chippewa blood in her and I'd just humiliate us both by asking to meet her. I tried to put her out of my mind.

On the positive side of things, Mr. Granger and I were getting along better and better. I'm not saying there weren't times when he didn't yell or act strange or send me away before I had a chance to get a foot in the door. And there were the times when I would arrive and find him in his bed. On those occasions, he would send me out to buy bologna and tomatoes, or kippers and saltines. Sometimes, he'd ask me to go buy a bag of hot cashews. I continued to read to him mostly from the dictionary. I wouldn't finally read Wegener until after Granger's death when the book came back into my possession. But Mr. Granger was more and more willing to talk to me about cartography and graphics, drift theory and the idea of the Pangaea or the "all land" theory that Wegener had represented by the gobbed land mass I had seen in his book. I especially wanted to know the reason the continents had broken up. Granger told me many scientists believed that heat had built up beneath the great block of land, exploding it apart.

"And could the continents explode again?" I asked.

"Hah-hah!" he cried, smacking his cane on the ground. I think the idea pleased him. "Afraid of finding yourself stranded on some little piece of turf in the middle of the sea?"

"Could they?"

"Alas, probably not," he said, frowning. "If it's true that it was heat that broke up the land mass in the first place, the pressure was released. Kind of like taking the valve off of a pressure cooker."

I remembered the magical disc on Ma's pressure cooker. It spun off vapor in a long, whistling *shoosh*, before bursting into periodic *rat-a-tat-tats* that Treat and I used to pretend were machine gun fire and that sent one of us diving behind the davenport, the other behind the easy chair.

After nearly each of my discussions with Mr. Granger, I raced to the library to look at the *Atlas*. I began to look at the map of the world more carefully. Mr. Granger even let me stay on in the basement apartment one morning while he slept and look at one of the maps in his personal collection. It was a reconstruction of an early map of the world, a flat Earth surrounded by ocean waters, found in the first book on geography written in the 6th century BC. Mr. Granger later told me that by the 3rd century BC, the view of the world had greatly changed. The ancient Greeks had already understood after studying eclipses that the Earth was neither flat nor completely round. They gave its shape a special word. Mr. Granger made me look it up in the dictionary. *Geoïde*. A shape that resembles no other, a word with only one meaning. *"The earth's figure,"* the definition read, *a hypothetical solid figure the surface of which corresponds to mean sea level (and its imagined extension under land) and is perpendicular to the direction of gravity at all points."*

"Point zero!" Mr. Granger said gleefully. "Zero altitude."

"You mean, 'ground level'?" I asked.

Mr. Granger's legs danced an arthritic little jig. "*Sea* level, urchin," he said, tapping a hanging foot on the ground beneath his chair. "Which is sometimes even *under* the ground. And sometimes," he continued just as happily, reaching out his short arms, "above our heads!"

"Above our heads!"

"Of course, neophyte. At times, the planet has been almost entirely covered with water. And someday probably will be again."

"Someday soon?" I asked.

"Not in my lifetime," he laughed.

"But in mine?" I imagined the drifting of continents and

the rebirth of oceans like the changing of seasons. It would happen quickly and catch us unaware.

Mr. Granger considered me for a moment. "Maybe. If you live to be a hundred."

"I hope I don't then," I said, which wasn't necessarily the case. I had always secretly hoped I would live forever.

"Don't worry, urchin. In a hundred years it wouldn't be up over your head. Probably just up around your ankles like a leaky basement. The folks who'll be hurting the most are all of those society folks with fancy, water-front property. Ploop. Their beaches will be under water."

I saw the palm-lined beach of my dream. Puerto Rico. "Could islands disappear?" I asked.

"Of course,'"he answered.

"Forever?"

He shrugged. "Forever for us."

That was long enough for me.

During another visit, he told me the Earth's shape was precisely what makes it so hard to map.

"How can you represent something spherical by something flat?" he asked me, wrapping a piece of newspaper around his fist. Maps were full of errors, distortions, miscalculations, he told me. Especially, he added, because maps are drawn by cartographers of all nationalities. If a cartographer places his own country at the center of his world map, he will end up distorting the size and diminishing the importance of other places. Just look at the world map in your geography book, he suggested. He said he'd bet on the fact that the United States is much bigger proportionally than it is in reality. Our seemingly gigantic country could fit inside the African continent, he continued, not rival it as many maps seem to suggest. The Belgian Congo alone, he explained, was a third the size of the U.S. The Belgian

Congo was where Ruth Anne lived. I looked up her town one day in the *Atlas*. It was called, *Mbuji Mayi*, which she told me means "black water" because of the water in a nearby river. A black river, like the one I drove across nearly every day.

Once Mr. Granger showed me one of his maps. I would learn later that it was the one that had gotten him into so much trouble with, as he had called them, "the powers that be." It was the world as a giant, twisting sea shell. The spirals themselves marked longitude, twirling and disappearing around the earth. The cone-shaped ends represented the poles. Most of the surface of the shell was painted blue to designate ocean waters. Pieces of brown hinting at land masses could be seen before disappearing into the curve of the shell, pieces too small to identify any one place.

"Whad'ya think, urchin?"

I could never tell when Mr. Granger was joking. I hunched up my shoulders. "Well, you can't see anything – I mean, besides water."

"What else do you want to see?"

"Land. Continents."

"Which ones?"

"All of them, I guess."

"Impossible, urchin. Told you that. You gotta choose."

"But, I can't. I mean, if I chose some, the others would be left out – or, we'd only see a part of them."

Mr. Granger shrugged.

"But it's not fair," I answered.

"Whoever said cartography was fair? When a cartographer makes a world map or a map of any kind, for that matter, he makes choices. He chooses what goes in and what stays out. Every time he makes a choice, practically no matter what he does, he messes with someone's idea of the world because a map can only represent one view at a time. When he tries to put the whole thing on there, some places get squished or squashed and other places get stretched out of proportion. From the very beginning, making a map of the world has been pretty much impossible. Look what happened with Columbus."

"You mean because he thought he had found the way to India?"

"Who could blame the fool?" Mr. Granger asked. "He was following a cockeyed map. And not the right one at that. That one would come later. Renaissance scholars found Ptolemy's mapping textbook, *Geographica*, some 1,000 years after it had been written. It was one of the things that guided Christopher Columbus. Problem was that other than for the Mediterranean area, Ptolemy only really had an armchair notion of the world, like most people of his day. At that time, common thought was if you went south of the equator, you'd melt. The old gent's cartographic miscalculations had added an additional 50° to the east-west measurements of the world. Instead of India, Columbus ran smack into *Guanahani* or El Salvador."

I found El Salvador on another map, and trailed my finger across the Caribbean Sea to the island of my dreams.

"Didn't Columbus discover Puerto Rico, too?"

"On a different trip, as I recall," Mr. Granger said, sticking his chin out at me.

I ignored him. "He must have thought it was a pretty wonderful place and all. I mean, he even changed its name to show that he thought it was a rich port."

I was glad to have remembered Treat's translation of its Spanish name. I was learning stuff. I wasn't just another teenager happy enough to live in his own little world. Mr. Granger had to see that.

"That so?" Mr. Granger tilted his head. "What was it called before?"

I straightened up. "*Borinquen.* The land of the brave lord." I waited for him to congratulate me.

"And after that?"

"After what?"

"Borinquen."

"Puerto Rico, I guess," I answered.

"Guess again, urchin."

"Columbus didn't call it Puerto Rico?"

Mr. Granger clucked his tongue. "He called it *San Juan Bautista* after Saint John the Baptist. Or just plain ol' San Juan, if you like."

"But that's the name of the capital!"

"Indeed. Which also happens to be a port city. A *puerto.*"

"Mr. Granger?"

"It was the island that was originally called San Juan. The port was named Puerto Rico by Ponce de Léon because he was so impressed by the bay he found on the north coast."

"Then how did it get to be that the city became San Juan and the island be called Puerto Rico?"

"Damned cartographers!" Mr. Granger banged his cane to the ground. "You and your confounded cartographers!"

"They switched the names around?"

"Didn't do it on purpose, I'm sure," he snarled. "Not like putting 'Easy Street' on a map. Worse than that. Got the confounded things mixed up. Way back in the sixteenth century. A classic example of how a mistake by a couple of distracted mapmakers can have a lasting impact on our lives!"

* * *

That afternoon at the library I re-read the introduction to *A History of Puerto Rico* and discovered, to my surprise, other things that I hadn't bothered to read very well before. First, I learned that my beloved Taíno Indians weren't exactly native to the island, either. They were immigrants like the rest of us. Although, it was true that they were the ones who had welcomed Columbus to the island, they had come from what is now Venezuela. And if *Borínquen* was the land of the brave lord, the Taínos apparently feared a couple of things. One was the god *Juracán* whom they thought was responsible for the violent storms and tropical cyclones of the West Indies. They were also afraid of the Carib Indians who often invaded the island and, apparently, made a meal of their prisoners. *Carib*, it said, meant "cannibal" to Christopher Columbus and his men. The Caribbean I had traced my finger across that very morning was transformed in my mind into a sea of man-eating waters. The Taínos had a diet more to my liking: corn on the cob. I found out that the Island's original Indians were called the Araínos or "the ancients" and they had been fishermen. They were conquered by the Igneri who were farmers and pottery-makers. Later came the Spaniards, then the British, the Dutch, the Spanish, again, and the Americans. I looked back to the *Atlas* and studied what had become the familiar shape of Puerto Rico, floating like a piece of torn flesh in the sea. The Spaniards forced the Indians into laboring the sugar cane fields. Slaves were brought from Africa for that same reason and the slavishness of the labor was passed from generation to generation. Those were the same sugar cane fields Celia's father had worked as a boy. The same ones he had escaped from to a San Juan *barrio* just to end up in a tannery, the same island he had abandoned for *Nueva York*. A history of dominance and abandon. Treat was right to go there, I thought. To go there and stay. Stay there out of love for that place.

One day, I finally got up the courage to ask Mr. Granger again if he thought Puerto Rico was as beautiful as I imagined it and learned another painful lesson in how the world is drawn.

"Puerto Rico?" he asked as though it were the hot, molten center of the Earth. "Never been there."

"Then how could you draw a map of it?" I wanted to know.

Mr. Granger stuck his chin out at me.

"By God, urchin. You don't expect me to have visited every place on Earth I've ever drawn a map of. I belly-crawled across much of France and that'll do me for the rest of my life. Nothing like a little foreign war experience to cure one of the travel bug!"

His response actually put me off cartography for a while. I'm sure, now, that is exactly what he meant to do. On the next visit, while he was sleeping, I actually spent time looking up words in the dictionary. Words like "urchin." Mr. Granger seemed to have traded it in for the term "boy" when talking to me. I didn't say anything to him because I could tell he didn't mean any harm by it. It was almost like punctuation for him. And, I had to admit, his sentences sounded naked without it. Plus, it didn't make me angry the same way the word "boy" had. Maybe because I didn't really know what an urchin was. I found out from reading the dictionary that it was a word that came down from the French word for "hedgehog." When I looked up what a hedgehog was, there was a drawing of a cute little thing that almost looked like a porcupine. The first definition of the word was: *"young boy or girl, especially one poorly or raggedly dressed."* That couldn't be what he meant. Mr. Granger had never seen me. He couldn't possibly have any idea what I might look like or how I might be dressed. Unless Miss Millar had told him. And you could hardly say that Mr. Granger seemed interested in clothes, anyway. He had to call me that for another reason. *"A mischievous child or youth."* That couldn't be the case, either. What had I ever done to hurt the old guy? The definition also mentioned "sea urchin." I imagined the blue-green waters off the coast of Puerto Rico. I thought of the "ancients" who probably risked their lives to fish in those waters. *"A small animal with a prickly, heart-shaped shell."* That was better. My heart in the sea. But if it were prickly, like a porcupine, it meant no-one could come near it. Spines were good protection. But they also kept others at bay. Maybe that was why I felt so lonely.

CHAPTER SIX

I don't know why it was to Father Wilhelm that I finally decided to talk about love. The love I thought I felt for an island I had never seen and for a girl whose face was quickly becoming a wispy memory. Maybe it was because he started talking to me about love first.

"Do you know what love is, Bass?" he asked. He had stopped over to see me shortly after Erik was attacked while Doctor Novak was at the Roth's house.

I tried to explain as best I could, but thinking about Celia made me nervous. I didn't want to get hard sitting there talking face-to-face with a priest. I talked instead about my parents' marriage. That had been true love, I was sure.

"Do you think love can only happen between a man and a woman?"

"People can love animals, too," I said. "Like, I used to love our dog, Reilly, before he died."

Father Wilhelm smiled and I felt stupid.

"That's right, Bass. All the things of this world are worthy of love." He cleared his throat. "What I meant exactly was, do you think two men or two women can love each other?"

I thought for a minute. Father Wilhelm wasn't one to set traps like Mr. Granger. There had to be a good answer to his question.

"I love my pa," I said, choking on my words. "And I love my uncle Will."

Father Wilhelm nodded. "What about another boy?"

"I miss Treat," I said, not quite able to admit how much I had loved him.

"Someone who's not a relative."

"You mean like Erik?"

"Yes, like Erik."

"I guess you could say I love him," I muttered, shifting in my chair. I was glad no one else could hear me. "He's my friend."

Father Wilhelm patted me on the shoulder. "And I know Erik loves you, too. Erik loves other boys, too. But in a different way than he loves you."

"What kind of different way?"

"Like you love Celia."

I was right. Erik *was* a queer.

"Do you think that's wrong?" Father Wilhelm asked.

I shrugged. How was I supposed to know? People talked like it was wrong. Seemed kind of strange to me.

"I'm supposed to think it's wrong," Father Wilhelm continued, touching his priest's collar. "But somehow I can't really. For me it's more important that people be capable of love – any kind of love – than for them to not be capable of love. No matter what. The diocese here doesn't agree." He winked. "That's how I got that super-fast transfer to another parish." He waved his hand. "But that's another story. Erik has been in counseling with me for a long time to try and understand his feelings. To try and understand if this is a phase, or a real life choice. It's not been easy for him – for either of us, really. It's hard from the church's point of view not to feel like I should condemn him. But I don't really see that as my role. And it's hard for him not to want to condemn himself. Do you understand what I'm saying, Bass?

It's true, of course, that he has gotten little support at home. Mr. Roth prefers to deny that his son might be a homosexual. And like all young men, regardless of their – uh – tendencies, Erik has started to experiment with sexual relationships. He asked me to tell you what he hasn't been able to tell you himself. He was attacked that night coming out of a – well, a place where men go to meet other men. He was beaten up by a gang of youths who called him a 'freak' and a 'pervert.' They molested him with a piece of pipe. His physical condition has been, as you know, very serious. And psychologically, I'm worried for his recovery. He was just getting to the point of beginning to accept himself. And others will only accept you once you've accepted yourself. Erik's going to need your friendship more than ever. I hope you don't abandon him."

Father Wilhelm's words echoed in my ears a long time after he had left. I didn't think myself capable of abandoning a friend. But then again, Erik had already tried to kiss me once and I didn't like that. At least that's what I was pretty sure he was trying to do. What if he tried something again? That wasn't being a very good friend to me, since I didn't want him to. Even if I had never been kissed and wanted to know what it felt like. And what if – the idea was like a punch in the gut – he was in love with me?

As the month of August slipped out from beneath my feet, I became more and more fascinated by the idea of love. Father Wilhelm had asked me if I knew what love was. Was love about losing someone like I had my ma and Treat? Or was it loving someone other people didn't think you should and getting hurt because of it, like had happened to Erik? – or even Kate who had soured her relationship with her mother by going to that picnic with Tim Kirsten after all. Was it even loving someone so much you were able to do almost anything so that they would be with you like Uncle Will had done to keep Aunt Sally? Or leaving everything you had to be with that person in some faraway place, like Ruth Anne had for Jean-Christophe? Or even, I was sure, like Treat had for Celia.

What was it about Celia, Father Wilhelm had asked me on that visit, that made me so sure I was in love with her? *What was it about anyone?* I wondered. But, in fact, I think I knew what it was – or at least part of it. Celia, like Puerto Rico itself, was that imaginary place I could go to in my mind where I was strong and handsome, courageous and admired. It was an alchemist's pot that turned lead into gold, a young boy into a man, a shy and hesitant observer into a confident participant. That was the magic of the dream. In the back of my mind, I guess I must have always known that it was only a dream.

What if that meant I was never going to be loved back?

* * *

I sat at my customary table one day at the library and watched Darby Millar. Maybe she had been in love with Mr. Granger all of these years. And he had never loved her back. That would be hard. It would be like me looking for Celia all of my life and never finding her. And never finding anyone else like her. I wondered if Mr. Granger had ever kissed Darby Millar. *Blech*. She had a face like a sack of flour. Pasty white. And what did Miss Millar possibly see in the old guy, anyway, that would keep her hanging on like that for so long?

"Indeed, Nick is quite a character," Miss Millar acknowledged. I had been trying to extract the secret of what it was that attracted her to him. I thought maybe it was because he was so different. I told her one afternoon very matter-of-factly that Mr. Granger was one of the most unusual people I had ever met. Which was the complete and total truth.

"Nick has always liked being different. I think that tendency has become even stronger since he lost his sight. It's become like a personal crusade for him to try and teach the seeing world that 'sight' does not necessarily equal 'power.' It's a way, I guess, for him to affirm himself. I almost feel partially responsible!" she laughed.

"Responsible? In what way?"

"I was visiting Nick regularly during the period when he was just starting to adjust to his blindness. It was a very difficult time. Imagine, a man whose life's work had been drawing and designing maps, to suddenly no longer be able to see. And Nick who has always been so independent – never wanting any family or anything, always living alone – a confirmed bachelor. There he was, suddenly dependent on someone to take care of him."

"His nephew?"

"No, dear," she said, smoothing down her skirt. "Me. As I'm sure you've guessed, I've always had a great deal of feeling for Nicolas Granger. I certainly wasn't going to abandon him in his time of need. And it hurt me terribly to see him so defeated. That's when I remembered the H.G. Wells story."

"The War of the Worlds?" I asked.

"No, no," she laughed. "About the one-eyed man. You don't know it?" she asked. "You know, the proverb, 'In the valley of the blind, the one-eyed man is king'?"

"Yes, ma'am."

"Wells wrote a story called, 'The Country of the Blind' that gives a twist on that saying. Don't you know it?"

I shook my head.

"Oh, dear, you really should read it. Wells was such a master."

She scrambled up from her chair and disappeared into the stacks. She came back with a book in her hand, a collection of short stories by H.G. Wells.

"I thought *The War of the Worlds* was pretty neat," I said.

"What a panic it caused when Orson Welles adapted it to radio," she commented. "It was in '38, I believe. Just before Halloween. People actually thought we were being invaded by Martians. My, what a terrible moment. But a lovely one for literature." She smiled brightly.

I read the story, "In the Country of the Blind," sitting right there at that table. It was true that there were things in it that reminded me of Mr. Granger. Like his sleeping during the day when it was hot and working at night. And the way his apartment was such an obstacle course so that a seeing person was always stumbling over stuff. And how, too, well – there wasn't much to look at and how I was always having to ask Mr. Granger to put on the light because, when you walked into his place, it was dark. Funny, though, how you don't feel much sympathy for the lost mountaineer in the story who arrives in the village and wants to take it over. He thinks he is better than the villagers because he can see. But, when he describes the mountains surrounding the village to them, they think he's a fool and a madman prone to hallucinations. And no matter what he does to tell them of the world outside their valley, they do not believe him. Their world ended at the village's encircling stone walls. They were certain, too, that a smooth rock dome covered their heads.

I didn't think about it until recently when, one summer afternoon, I re-read the Wells story. I noticed how the villagers of the Country of the Blind were not unlike the tenth century cartographer who developed a map of the world known as *Terrarum Orbis*, a map that is in the form of an "O." A symbolic as well as geographic representation, the *Terrarum Orbis* is a circle with a "T" in the center that represents Christ's crucifix. Within the "O" is the finite and walled-in world as described in the Scriptures. At the top of the circle is Asia; Europe is to the left and Africa to the right. Adam and Eve stand in the part representing Asia, or earthly paradise, conspicuously covering their genitals with their hands while the serpent looks on.

One thing bothered me about the story, though. Or rather, bothered me to know that Miss Millar had read the story to Mr. Granger. At the end, the mountaineer has finally submitted to the idea that, in the Country of the Blind, he had no chance of being king. For the love of a village girl, he is almost ready to accept an operation that would remove his eyes that the village medicine man said would "cure" him of his visions. Instead, he makes a desperate and almost unintended "escape" from the village. Once outside its walls, he rediscovers the painful beauty of the natural world and even thrills at the "minutely beautiful orange lichen close to his face" as he lies on the ground. Later, he sleeps under the limitless sky looking up at the stars. Clearly, the story is meant to make us appreciate the world around us – the seen world, that is. What cruelty to have read it to Mr. Granger. I remember thinking that it was like Miss Millar wanted to punish him for something.

After I had finished reading, I went to return the book to Miss Millar. She was in her office, reading, her glasses perched on her nose. I probably should have waited before going in, but I didn't. The door was open, so I knocked on the door frame leading to her office and walked right in before she had a chance to say anything. I guess I must have startled her. She certainly looked surprised. I handed her the collection of H.G. Wells stories. As I did, I noticed that she was reading one of those dime-store type romance novels. The kind with the pastel-colored painting on the cover. I knew what those books were like because Aunt Sally had raised a holy ruckus one day when she found one in the kitchen. Kate said a friend had lent it to her, but that she hadn't read it. It didn't interest her all that much, she had said. Aunt Sally forbade her to ever read it or another one like it and ordered her to return it to that friend lickety-split. Those novels, she hollered, did nothing but put silly ideas in a young girl's head.

Miss Millar snatched the Wells book out of my outstretched hand and laid it on her desk over her book.

"Well, what did you think?"

"Pretty neat," I said. "Makes you see things differently. Like the world turned upside down."

"Hmm," she said, nodding. "Nick, of course, was very inspired by it. I think that was when he started his secret project."

"Secret project, Miss Millar?"

"Oh, you know. That dreadful black thing he is always hunched over. Won't tell a soul what on earth it might be. I suspect it's some kind of map, a map meant to be touched –you know, for a sightless person. But a map of what? Lord knows!"

"Where did he get it?"

"Why, he made it, dear. Sculpted it himself out of modeling clay and then had me and his nephew take it over to the Art Department at the college where they molded a fiberglass version of it. Nick taught sculpture there for a while after – well, after he stopped making maps. Nick is actually quite an artist. I'm sure if it hadn't been for the war, he would have been a very famous sculptor. I was hoping when he made it that it meant he would start sculpting again, but he didn't. It was quite a disappointment, as I'm sure you can imagine."

"What is he fixin' to do with it?" I asked. "Whatever it is."

"His nephew tells me that Nick actually intends to take it to Washington. I bet he wants to show it to someone at the Smithsonian Institution or the National Geographic Society or some such place. Personally, I think he wants to redeem himself in the eyes of his peers. Map-making for the visually-handicapped is becoming an increasingly important area. And who is better placed for such a thing than a blind person with cartographic training? His nephew, of course, has refused to take him and thinks the idea is just outlandish. I actually entertained the idea of accompanying him by bus myself, but with the library and all, I just couldn't be absent for any extended time period. I am needed here," she said firmly.

* * *

"Been talking to the old gal again, haven't you? What's -er name."

"I think you know her name, Mr. Granger," I answered.

Nick Granger swung around from where he was hunched over the black, molded plastic. His hands hung in the air. "That's right, urchin. I do. In fact, I know it almost better than my own. And I should. Her old man made me write it a million times, in a million ways, on about a million maps of this county. I've written it forwards and backwards, upside down and inside out – in big, bigger or gigantic letters depending on the political ambitions of the old man at the time. *Millars*burg. *Millars*burg. Ad infinitum. Ad *nauseum*. Know it? You bet I know it!"

"I was sure," I said.

"I wouldn't be half surprised if you told me it was etched right here on my forehead," he continued, dragging a forefinger across his skin. "Millarsburg. Population of one – yahoo. Everything with the name 'Millar' on it belonged to the old man.

Everything except me, that is, but it wasn't for his lack of trying."

"I guess you didn't like him very much."

Nick Granger jutted his chin out. "Like him? I *despised* the man. Know what the ol' biddy wanted me to do coupla years back? *Sculpt* him. Sculpt a bust of the man so she could put it in the library. I told her I couldn't remember what he looked like. Rot! He was dead and I was going blind. She said, 'Do it from memory.' Who wants to remember that confounded megalomaniac, anyway? He tricked me into coming here when I was down on my luck with empty promises of being able to do something innovative. Together, we would 'reinvent cartography' he told me. He would give me all of the tools I needed, he said. Humph. The only innovation he was interested in would have made Copernicus turn over in his grave. Old man Millar wanted nothing less than to reinvent the configuration of the universe by putting Millarsburg at the center and making everything else turn around it. He didn't like it when I finally did a mock up to scale and he found out what an insignificant little divot his namesake actually is! I still don't know who snitched about the print type," he added, almost to himself.

"What does it matter about that?"

"I used Old English, urchin. Old English is for archeological sites. You know, for places buried in the sand, stuck in time. Places where they keep mummies," he screamed. "Mummies like his daughter!"

We both laughed, but then Nick Granger turned serious. "People don't like it when you mess with their cosmography."

I didn't ask him what "cosmography" meant. I was afraid he would make me look it up. Along with meg-a-lo-whatever.

"That's how I finished off my career anyway."

"Because of Mr. Millar?" I asked, confused.

"No, urchin. By messin' with people's ideas of the planet.

Folks have gotten too used to Mercator's projection. Look here," he said and showed me where I could find a copy of the famous projection among the scrolls of maps in the corner.

"Know what I think it is about that projection that continues to appeal to folks?"

I stared at what I realized was a familiar rendering of the map of the world stretched across an even grid. "No," I said.

"First of all, it's orderly. Folks don't like to think that the world is a jumble. Mercator laid it all out, nice and neat and smooth. A perfect, self-contained little universe."

I thought about the villagers in *The Country of the Blind* and how they believed their world included a smooth dome overhead.

"Like an egg," I suggested.

"Exactly, urchin. The "mundane egg" as the world was known in the Middle Ages. Smooth, perfect, unwrinkled. And all of those philosophers and priests trying to explain away the existence of mountains!"

"What's wrong with mountains?"

"Genesis doesn't mention them, urchin. Weren't you an altar boy?" he asked me, tilting his head to one side. When I didn't answer him, he continued, "They somehow had to be created *after* Adam and Eve were chased from paradise. So, they must have been the result of an earthly evil. Folks were sure that demons lived in their hidden crags."

"But mountains are beautiful," I said. "I mean, I guess they are." I'd only seen pictures of them.

"Think so? Why do you think globes are smooth and round?"

"Maybe because when folks started making them, they didn't know how to make globes with mountains on them. But you could change that," I said, brightening. "I mean, you're a sculptor, too. Right? You could make a globe of the whole world, with bumps and everything."

"I'm not interested in the whole world, anymore," Mr. Granger answered, turning around and letting his hands fall back onto the black plastic. "Besides, people wouldn't like it. Someone already thought of that idea way back in the 17th century, anyway. A guy named Burton. Wanted to show folks what a 'rude lump' the Earth is. Probably got ridden out of town on a rail, like I did."

"For making maps with mountains on them?"

"For just making folks *think* about mountains. For most folks, mountains were like blemishes on the earth's surface. Signs of our earthly imperfection. It'd be like sculpting a face with warts on it or a bust that showed the person actually carried one shoulder higher than the other. Or was just plain old ugly – like old man Millar himself. A curse on his name!"

I thought of Wegener. "But mountains are caused by the continents drifting, aren't they? It's not our fault."

"If the continents are drifting – and I think they are – it means that the world is not what we thought it to be, urchin. Use your noodle. Think of the word you just used. Fault. A lot of geological activity, like earthquakes, is attributed to faults. A *fault* is a failing. Something bad or wrong. A fault is a crack in the earth, a defect. I figure that's why folks always took so hard to Mercator's projection. It was not only neat, it looked stable. Nothing sliding across the grid, nothing giving any idea of the push away from the poles or the tug of the equator. Nothin' shiftin' around, getting stretched out. Problem was, Mercator's map is being used in lots of ways that were never intended. That projection was never meant to be an exact representation of the land masses. You can see that Greenland is way out of proportion," gesturing in the thin air. "But that didn't matter back then. It was the waters between those land masses that mattered to folks those days. Mercator meant his projection to be used as a navigational chart. The important thing was getting folks to *terra firma*. He probably didn't care a flip about what happened once they got there or how far that land stretched away towards the poles. He probably couldn't have cared less if it were all one big glob."

"The Pangaea," I said, reverently, thinking of Wegener's body frozen in the Greenlandic ice.

"What say?"

"I was thinking about drift theory," I answered. "About Alfred Wegener. You know, the book Miss Millar had me give to you and that – " I hesitated, "she was reading to you on your birthday." I couldn't help it. I sounded hurt.

"If it makes the ol' bird happy. Better than to listen to her chirp."

"But I thought you just said you agreed with him that the continents are drifting."

"I do, urchin. But what difference does it make to me now? My career is over. That book might have had a bigger impact on me if I had been able to read it when it first came out. 'Twas your mother got it for me, as I recall."

"You knew my ma?" I asked.

"Who didn't know your ma?" he asked, his voice softening. "She was sublimity incarnate."

For once I didn't need a dictionary to understand a big word. He was talking about my ma, after all.

"Miss Millar said she asked my ma to translate the book for you," I said, my voice failing. "But I guess she couldn't do it."

Mr. Granger tilted his head. His eyes tick-tocked skyward. "The old biddy's gone daft. She gave it to one of her desiccated friends at the University who sat on it like a hen does an egg – only a lot longer. Didn't agree with her vision of the world, I guess. By the time she lifted her arse off of it, I couldn't show my face in a barn without the horses turning their backsides to me. My days as a cartographer were over."

"But why did Wegener interest you – I mean, as a cartographer?"

"I told you, urchin. I never wanted to be a cartographer. I wanted to be the antithesis of cartography, the Antichrist of cartography. That's the reason your man Wegener appealed to me. No nations, no states – no Millarsburgs. Just one big lump!"

"Is that why you started sculpting?"

"I started sculpting so I wouldn't wring someone's neck. 'Therapy' is, I think, the term folks use for it nowadays. Doesn't matter. Cartography's days are numbered, anyway because of aerial photography and those confounded computers. I may be blind now, but I can see it coming. We were the scribes of our time, urchin. Nobody needed scribes anymore, either, once folks learned to write."

"But you could sculpt maps – you know, like for the blind."

"I'd sculpt a ruder lump than Burton could have ever imagined. I'd sculpt all the countries together so that folks wouldn't know where they were!" He reached for his aluminum cane and banged it on the ground.

"A gobbed mass," I said, more to myself than to him.

"A gobbed mess!" he answered. "Hee-hee! Wouldn't that be fine!" He sighed and settled back into his chair. "But, like I said, I'm not interested in the whole world anymore. I think we should take a lesson from Voltaire. Cultivate one's own garden. All this flying up in the air, going out in space is only going to cause trouble one day. No, urchin, *terra firma* is what matters most to me now. I'll soon be six feet under."

Like most Americans in 1969, I was caught up in the NASA space program. That year, Neil Armstrong was the first man to walk on the moon. Space exploration was for me a natural extension of the spirit of men like Wegener, Wells, and Verne. I couldn't let Nick Granger's sour grapes destroy my newfound heroes.

"But maps helped the first explorers. And they help us to explore."

"Help us to exploit, you mean."

I didn't know if I meant that at all. I was in over my head. "Explorers are courageous," I countered.

"Maybe. But Christopher Columbus never would have left home if it weren't for the fact that Ptolemy's map made him think the ocean was a heck of a lot smaller than it actually is. He might have been a lot less courageous if he had realized how far he would be from land, if it weren't for another confounded map that gave him the wrong idea that the ocean was just a little puddle of water and he could come ashore any time he wanted. Early explorers and mariners *were* courageous, urchin. That's true. But you know that when the Phoenicians started sailing the Mediterranean, they never let land out of sight. The Italians made charts called 'portolanos' whose sole purpose was to get folks from port to port."

"San Juan is a port," I said. "San Juan, Puerto Rico." A *portolano* would take me there, I thought.

"I never heard a body jaw on about a place before as much as you about Puerto Rico. What's the point, anyway?"

"I want to go there."

"Then go. And quit yapping on about it."

"But Mr. Granger!"

"You heard me, urchin. What are you waiting for, someone to come down from the heavens and carry you off? When a man decides he wants something, he needs to act on it. Otherwise, he's not a man."

"But I'm still young," I protested.

"You need to do these things when you're young. Don't

wait around 'til you're old and blind like me and have to depend on someone else to take you where you want to go."

"Miss Millar says you want to go to Washington."

Nick Granger swung around. "The ol' biddy talks too much for her own good. What business is it of yours, anyway, urchin? Unless you're planning on taking me," he said, tilting his head. "Got a car, don't you?"

"Yes, sir," I said. The "sir" had slipped out. He waited. "But school is going to start."

"Right. Wouldn't want to miss all of that book learnin'," he said, mocking. "Might have to learn something from the dictionary like I did!"

I was surprised to find myself looking for excuses. I had been dreaming of going away ever since Treat left. "But I don't know how to get there."

"What?" he screamed. He reached out and grabbed Mercator's projection from my hands. "I told you, boy, you might as well be as blind as me."

The word, "boy," cut like a knife.

"I just meant – "

"Got your nose in a map and your feet in cement. What's the point, I ask ya? If you think maps are so great, then put them to their intended purpose. Maps are meant to be used, urchin. You said it yourself, they're meant to get people to go places, see things, conquer worlds. Buy, sell, trade! You think they're just meant for decoration like that Mondrian painting of your mother's."

I remembered the abstract painting in my parents' bedroom. "You mean that yellow and blue and red and white one – with all of the squares and rectangles on it? That one?"

"That's right, urchin. That one. *Broadway Boogie Woogie.* Great title." He tapped a foot on the floor.

"How do you know that my ma had that painting?"

"Because, urchin. I was the one who gave it to her. It's just a reproduction, of course, but I wanted to thank her for the book. And it was – " he laughed heartily, "– a wedding present."

"My pa doesn't like it."

"No offense, urchin. But a man like your pa can't understand it. He was too much in love with your mother and too much in love with his land."

"And could my ma understand it?"

"Oddly enough, she might have been able to understand the artist better than his art. That's the kind of irony Mondrian would have appreciated. Mondrian fled from a world gone crazy, like she had. I've always been a fan of Mondrian," he said, turning to the black plastic and stroking it. "Know why? Because his abstract paintings were an end in and of themselves. The thing I liked about them was that they never represented anything."

He turned back to me. "And the thing I liked about your ma was that Millarsburg wasn't *a* place for her, it was *no* place. Which was exactly where she wanted to be and exactly what I've always thought of Millarsburg."

"Do you think my ma would want me to go to Puerto Rico?"

"I probably didn't know your ma well enough to answer that, urchin. But I did know her well enough to know that she probably wouldn't approve of you wanting to do something and not doing it."

As I was leaving that afternoon, I asked Mr. Granger if Washington, DC was on the way to Puerto Rico. He said it all depended on what kind of map you were following.

* * *

The last thing I expected was to find Erik there when I turned at the blue spruce to the spot where Celia and her family had camped. He had his ma's wagon and was sitting cross-legged on the hood looking around him as though maybe he was expecting the thing to lift off into the air like a flying saucer. I was sure that he'd already seen me by the time I saw him, so I figured there was no good reason to back around and pull out like I'd made a wrong turn or something. That campsite was a place you went to on purpose.

I got out of the Fairlane. "Hey, Erik," I said, walking over to him.

"How you doing, Bass?" he answered. He started to lift up his right hand, thought better of it, and extended his left hand. I took it in my own right hand. We stayed that way for a moment, almost like we were holding each other onto the ground. When we finally let go, we both stood there quietly. Neither of us seemed to want to break the silence. The camp was deserted but reminded me of church after mass – you could almost hear the echo of voices over the burned grass.

"I've decided it's time," he said.

"Time for what?"

"Time for me to leave."

"How do you know? I mean, how do you know it's time?"

"Oh, I've been feeling this way for a while. But I've been afraid to really do anything about it. Afraid to show who I really am. But other people like me are starting to and all of that has kind of inspired me."

"What has?"

"Well, for example, in June some folks – men *and* women – resisted police outside a homosexual bar in New York City. Stood up for their rights, you know? Stood up for their right to love who they wanted. I need to stand up for my rights, too."

"You did and you got beat up for it," I said.

"Did Father Wilhelm tell you that?"

I looked out across the vacant lot. "Shouldn't he have?"

"Yeah, he should have. I asked him to. So you would know about me. Who knows? You might even know other people like me without realizing it."

"Girls, too?" I thought of the way Celia's lean muscles worked under her translucent skin.

"Why not?"

"I didn't know girls could be like that," I said.

Erik laughed. "I hope you don't think all women are like those biker girls!"

"No, 'course not," I said, but decided that I needed to change the subject quick. "Where will you go?"

"San Francisco, I think. I've heard that there's a community out there for me. And Dr. Novak says he knows some people who could put me up for a while until I get on my feet."

"Will you go soon?"

"Yeah, I think so. I just got this," he reached into his pocket and pulled out a folded letter. He handed it to me. I looked at the return address. The draft board.

"What's this?"

"A strangely lucky break. It's an exemption." He lifted up his right hand. "Possibly permanent damage. Can't fire a gun. There's a war going on, you know."

"Yeah, yeah," I said, too quickly.

"I didn't mean it that way."

"I know," I said. I was feeling a bit sore. I picked up a rusted beer bottle cap and turned it over in my hand.

"Just a pretext, if you ask me," Erik continued. "The Army doc was just like Superman. What I mean is that he had x-ray vision. Saw right through me. I don't think they want to have to deal with sissies in the war." His smile hiked up one side of his face.

"Good thing for you, if you ask me. Seems pretty awful. I've been seeing it on the news," I said.

I had, but Walter Cronkite could have been speaking a foreign language for all I understood of what was going on in Vietnam. I did notice that there was usually a map projected onto the screen next to him during Cronkite's daily report on the war; it showed troop movement. It was Mr. Granger who told me that, earlier that year, President Johnson had said that he would no longer bomb north of the 20th parallel, which I had come to learn was three degrees to the south of the Tropic of Cancer. But otherwise, the map of Vietnam didn't mean anything to me because Vietnam was another place that existed on a part of the globe that was turned away from me, like the dark side of the moon. It was on a page in the *Atlas* I had never once thought to examine. I also remembered what Mr. Granger had said about how going up in planes during the Second World War had revolutionized cartography.

"Are you flying out there?" I'd never been up in an airplane. For me, it was one of the most exciting things that could happen to a person.

"Nah, driving. Know what? Ol' Granny Stein is going to give me her car!" he laughed. "I guess she's moving out to Arizona into some kind of old folks' home not far from where her son lives, and says she won't be needing it anymore. Says her grandson doesn't want it, so she's just as happy to give it to me since I used to help take care of it. Said I was almost like a grandson to her." He looked away, his eyes glistening. "She probably wouldn't say that if she knew."

"I bet she would," I said. I watched a tear run down the side of his face.

"Thanks," he said.

"Think that old clunker'll make it all the way to San Francisco?" I asked.

"Ed and Mike think it will. The engine might fuse into a block by the time I get there, but it doesn't matter. I can junk it once I'm there." He looked up at me. "I'm not planning on coming back."

"Ever?"

"Ever's a long time. As close as I can get to 'ever,' I guess, 'though I'll probably want to come back some day to see my ma. She's takin' this all kinda hard. My leavin' and all, I mean. I think," he stopped and cleared his throat, "I even think my pa's kind of takin' it hard."

"So why don't you stay?"

"Like I said, it's time. What am I going to do if I stay in Millarsburg, anyway? I don't feel like pumping gas for the rest of my life."

"Seems like a pretty good job to me," I said.

"It was," he said. "And I sure needed it. But it's funny, you know. I used to get this crazy idea. There I was filling up tanks so that folks could drive around in circles for about a week and then come back so I could fill up their tanks again so they could go driving around in circles again. I always felt like I was putting them on a merry-go-round. Around and around they went, but they always ended up back where they started."

"Is something wrong with that, do you think, Erik?"

He shrugged. "I don't know. Guess it depends on what you want. I mean, look at Mike and Ed. They've got their garage and their customers and they work on their engines. They seem pretty happy in Millarsburg. But I don't really belong, you know. I don't belong here."

"Do you think you'll belong in San Francisco?"

"Won't know until I get there," he answered. He looked at me. "Hey, you should come out and visit. You're not planning on staying in Millarsburg for the rest of your life, are you?"

"No way!" I said, more loudly than I had meant to. "In fact, I'll probably be leaving soon myself."

I said it like it was a long-standing project. In fact, I had only seriously considered it that morning.

"Leaving? For good?"

"Maybe."

"How's that?"

"You remember I told you how I was reading for this blind guy over in Painted Creek? Well, he's a famous cartographer and he's got some super secret project that he's supposed to take to National Geographic and I'm going to drive him to Washington, D.C."

"You're going to Washington?" Erik asked, crinkling up his nose.

"Well," I said, casually, "I've been thinking that once I leave Mr. Granger in Washington, I'll just keep going on my own."

"To where?"

"Puerto Rico," I said.

"Puerto Rico!" he repeated. Erik looked around him before looking back at me. "From Washington?"

"Well, you know. It's just a place to start."

"Then what."

"Then I'll – I'll run away like Treat."

"It'll kill your pa."

I couldn't let myself think of that. "My pa died when my ma died, Erik. He'll feel better about it when he knows I've gone there to be with Treat."

"Gone where?"

"To Puerto Rico," I repeated. Was he thick, or what?

"What makes you think he's in Puerto Rico?"

"Isn't he?"

"You think he's gone to Puerto Rico because of the people we met here?"

"Because of Celia," I said. "She was from Puerto Rico, wasn't she?"

Erik wrinkled up his nose. "I think she was from Detroit."

"But Treat told us she was Puerto Rican," I protested.

"She is, I guess," he said. "Kinda like we're German." He studied me. "Are you going to Puerto Rico to look for Treat?"

I shifted to the other foot. "I might run into him," I said.

Erik smiled. "Bass, Puerto Rico's a small island, but it's still a pretty big place. And you're not even sure he's there."

"Where else would he be?"

Erik turned away. After a few minutes he said, "Besides you can't leave that old guy alone in Washington. Didn't you say he was blind? How's he going to get back?"

"I didn't think about that," I acknowledged. "But he's famous – at least, I think he is. And he's got like this important project, so he'll probably just stay. Besides, he asked me to take him. He didn't say anything about wanting me to bring him back. Besides, I'm not coming back." I hadn't thought about having to bring Mr. Granger back again. The truth of the matter was that there was a lot that I hadn't considered.

"Bass, can I give you some advice?"

Erik's face was squinched up like I'd never seen it before. Like he was in pain. He hadn't even looked that way after he had gotten beaten up.

"Sure," I answered.

"Don't go to Puerto Rico to look for Treat."

"You don't think I should go to Puerto Rico?"

"I didn't say that. I said, 'Don't go to look for Treat.' Go for yourself, if you want to. That's what Treat would want, I'm sure."

"But then he and I could be together again. Like we used to be."

"Know what I think?"

I shook my head.

"I think that wherever he is, Treat probably wants to be alone for a while. To get things straight in his mind."

"But we were best buddies," I said. I felt my throat closing around the words.

"And I'm sure he still thinks of you as his buddy. But if Treat ran away, I'll bet it was because he wanted to be on his own."

I thought about that for a minute. The sun seemed especially bright to me that day. My vision became a blur. The migrant workers' camp melted into confusion. "Do you think he'll ever come back?"

"Like I said, 'ever' is a long time. Maybe, once he gets things straightened around."

"What kinds of things?"

Erik shrugged. "Things."

"Erik?" I hesitated. "Treat's not like – " I couldn't quite say it.

"Like me?"

I nodded, ashamed.

"I don't think so. Didn't you see the way he was drooling over that girl?"

"You mean, 'Celia'?"

"Whatever."

"Yeah. Yeah, I saw him. Maybe they're married now."

Erik wrinkled up his nose. "Married?" He shrugged. "Yeah, maybe."

But he didn't sound too sure about it. Erik promised to come over to say good-bye before he left for San Francisco. As I walked to my car, he called out to me.

"Hey, Bass?"

"Yeah?"

"Would it bother you if he were?"

"If who was what?"

"If Treat were like me?"

I shook my head. "Just wanted to know."

***

I sat on the patio and drank a big glass of lemonade. Erik was leaving. Treat was gone. Puerto Rico might be a big place, but my world was getting smaller with each passing day. Even ol' Granny Stein, the longest living resident of Millarsburg, was pulling up stakes. I thought about Mr. Granger's wanting to go to Washington. I could take him. I could drive him there in the Fairlane. That would make him happy. And it would get me out of Millarsburg until I could decide exactly what I wanted to do. It sounded like a good plan. What could go wrong?

Quick! I needed to think. What would I need? I'd never really traveled anywhere before. There was one problem. I didn't have much money. I had saved what I'd earned working for Mr. Granger, but maybe that wouldn't be enough to get me all the way to Puerto Rico. In fact, I didn't even really know how much money I would need. Maybe lots. Pa told me after Ma died that I had something called a trust fund, but I didn't know how much was in it. It didn't matter, anyway, since I couldn't touch it until I was eighteen. I couldn't wait that long. And I was sure that Mr. Granger wouldn't want to wait that long. I felt numb and had, I realized, been feeling that way for a long time. I was sure if I stayed in Millarsburg that numbness would only get worse. I was also pretty sure that I was not past saving myself only because the memory of a hot afternoon with a Puerto Rican family was the one thing that still moved me.

Next thing I knew, school was fixing to start. It was late August, but the sun still hadn't lost its bite. I found myself one evening sitting at the picnic table after supper with the fragrant grass smelling strong and sweet, and the croaking of frogs filling up the empty night air, suddenly faced with the prospect of a new school year – and one without Treat, without my ma, even without Erik. The thought left me feeling like there was nothing but open water ahead of me. I was scared. I wanted to run. I might have done just that, gotten up then and there from where I was sitting and taken off like a madman down the road if Pa hadn't come up behind me. I didn't even hear him come up. But then again, Pa had become as transparent as the evening breeze; half of the time you only knew he was there because *other* things moved when he was around.

"Hot today, wasn't it?" he asked, almost shyly. I agreed that it had been. It was on just this kind of day that Treat, Erik and I had ridden our bikes to the family's campsite. Summer was blowing one of its last blasts. It always got wild hot just before the season blew itself out. Fall would be on us before we knew it. That was probably why school was on my mind that morning. It was on my pa's as well.

"School will be startin' soon," he said, sitting down.

Like a lot of schools in the area, Millarsburg High School started before Labor Day in order to make up in advance for the inevitable number of snow days we had each winter.

"Yes, sir," I said. My voice was so hollow you could have stuck your finger through it. I'd pretty much decided right then and there that I was going to take Mr. Granger to Washington and then, somehow, go on to Puerto Rico. But there was one thing that was bothering me more than I ever could have imagined, and that was leaving school. For one thing, I had never pictured myself as a drop-out. Even though I had never been a great student, the idea of dropping out of school was twisting up my insides. And I knew how my pa would have felt about it if he knew. To him, being a drop-out was even worse than being a *jíbaro* because he figured you were more or less born into poverty, whereas being a drop-out was, in my case, at least, a kind of choice. Maybe the first real important choice I would have to make – after having chosen to keep quiet about Treat's running away, that is. The sorry thought crossed my mind that Treat, my friend and idol, was a drop-out, too.

"I was wondering if you were needing anything," he said.

I pretended to think for a minute. How would I be needing anything? I wasn't planning on staying around long enough for that.

"I don't think so," I said.

"Sure? New dungarees or shoes or something? Got enough T-shirts?"

It was true that if I was going to be starting my life over in Puerto Rico, I was going to be needing a few things. I'd outgrown just about everything. Like Treat's old dungarees and T-shirt I had worn to rags. But there was no way I was going to let my pa buy me new clothes just so I could wear them while I was running away.

"Sure," I said.

Pa looked at me hard. "Are you thinking about college?" he asked.

The word stabbed at my heart. A drop-out can't go to college, I thought. And as far as I could figure, most runaways didn't run in that direction.

"I don't know yet," I lied.

"The community college over in Black River is a pretty good one, you know."

I looked over at him, but Pa was staring at his hands. It took me a second to understand just what he was trying to say. Folks went to the community college for any number of reasons, but the reason that most of the people I knew, including Ruth Anne, went to the community college rather than to the state university or even the liberal arts college over in Painted Creek was purely financial. Those other schools were just too expensive even if you paid "in-state" tuition. The farm must be doing worse than I thought. If that were the case, then maybe I'd even be doing my pa a big favor by going to Puerto Rico. He could sell his half of the farm to Uncle Will and move into a smaller place, maybe closer to town. He could take a job at that nursery or one selling tractors or, heck, maybe even get hired at Roth's Feed and Seed. He wouldn't have to worry about paying for my school and buying me clothes and things. He could sell the pick-up truck and buy something smaller, more economical.

"Been a long time since we've been over to Black River, hey?" Pa said.

I knew he meant going over there to fish. When Treat and I were just little kids, he and Uncle Will used to take us over to Black River to catch blue-gills and sunfish in the shallow waters near the small dam at one end of the river. I'd never been on the other side of that dam and as I sat there watching my pa I realized that I had never bothered to find out where the Black River went. Did it flow into some larger river? Work its way out into the Great Lakes? Snake through the Saint Lawrence Seaway and spill out into the Atlantic Ocean? Merge under the thin shelf of land with all of the other waters of the earth until there was only that and nothing more, only the never-ending sea to drift upon?

"I know the past couple of years have been hard on you," he continued. "They've been hard on all of us. But we've survived, haven't we?"

"Yes, sir," I said.

He smiled weakly.

"Pa? Would it be alright if I took a little trip?" I asked, and then wished I hadn't.

"What? What do you mean a trip? When? You know school starts next Thursday."

I tucked my chin into my chest. "I don't know yet when. It's for my job," I said.

"What job?"

"You know. I've been reading to that blind guy over in Painted Creek. He's got an important meeting in Washington, but can't go alone because of his being blind and all."

"Can't someone else take him? A relative? What blind guy?"

I ignored the last question. "I guess not. He's only got a nephew and his nephew's real busy. And it'd be a shame for him to miss the meeting because he'll probably become really famous."

"Famous? For what?"

"He makes these maps for blind people," I said. "And now he's supposed to go to Washington to show them to somebody."

"To someone in Congress?" he asked.

"I think so," I said. As long as I was telling whoppers, I decided I might as well make them good.

He considered that for a minute. "Well, it would no doubt be a good experience for you. But I don't like the idea of you missing school. How long will you be gone? About a week?"

"I reckon. Maybe more."

"Shouldn't be much more," he said. He calculated, counting on his fingers. "A couple of days to drive there, a day or so for his meetings, and then a couple of days to drive back."

Funny how folks always figured I was coming back.

"Do you think you can drive that far by yourself? That's a long way, and you don't have that much experience driving. You'll need to be careful. Make a lot of stops."

"I will," I assured him.

"What about money? Is this fellow paying for expenses?" he asked. "You know, gas, hotel, food. Washington is an expensive city from what I understand."

"Yes, sir," I said, way too quickly.

He knitted his eyebrows together. "I'd like to meet this fellow, before you go."

"You would?"

"Of course. You don't think I'm going to let my son go off just like that without knowing who's going to be responsible for him. Do you?"

"'Course not."

That was the thing I couldn't possibly let happen. One look at Mr. Granger and Pa wouldn't let me out of his sight, much less out of the city. Mr. Granger reminded me of a character in a movie I saw once: the guy who lived in the church tower and rang the bells.

"I'll have to see, though, because I know that he's real busy."

"He can't be so busy as to not be able to present himself to your family!" Pa shook his head. We could invite him to supper. Invite your aunt and uncle and cousin over. You know, get together as a family. Like we used to."

Nothing was like it used to be, I thought.

But the idea of getting together "like we used to" must have stuck in Pa's brain because he went out and bought a big watermelon and invited Uncle Will and Aunt Sally out to the picnic table later that evening to eat it; Kate had gone to an early movie with Tim Kirsten.

"Sebastian has some news," Pa said.

"What kind of news?" Uncle Will asked. He spat out a couple of seeds.

I went through my spiel again, but this time with as much seriousness as I could muster. I needed to make this trip seem like an important opportunity for me. Something I couldn't possibly risk letting pass by. Uncle Will watched me closely as I spoke. I got the feeling he wasn't swallowing my story any more than the watermelon seeds.

He asked some of the same questions Pa had asked about who was going to pay for what and where we were going to stay, and then went quiet. But he never stopped looking at me like he'd caught me at something.

"What do you think, Will?" Pa asked.

"I say Bass is old enough to know what he wants," Uncle Will said.

"But he's just a boy!" Aunt Sally said.

"The past couple of years have forced us all to grow up a lot, haven't they, Sarah?"

I had never heard Uncle Will use Aunt Sally's first name before. She seemed stricken by it.

"You and I," he continued, "should know better than anyone else that keeping someone from doing what their heart tells them to do just causes a lot of pain and resentment. Shouldn't we?"

Aunt Sally turned and looked at me like she was seeing me for the first time. And, strangely enough, it was like I was seeing her for the first time, too. The wild look in her eyes that I had often mistaken for hatred or anger was something else. Fear? Panic? The desire to run? Or another desire that she had always somehow managed to keep in check: the overwhelming impulse to cry.

She rose, and walked to the barbecue where she stuffed the watermelon rinds and soggy paper plates under the grill. Before disappearing into the house, she looked at me a long time, and then said, "Be careful. We want you back in one piece."

* * *

That night I went in to say good night to my pa. It was something I hadn't done in a long time. Maybe I was half expecting him to ask me to tell him the truth. Maybe that was even partly what I wanted. But he didn't, even though I was pretty sure he understood that I was planning on going away. For good. Events would be such that, in the end, it wouldn't matter. Instead, he talked about what he knew of Washington, even though he'd never been there. He gave me driving tips and the name of someone to see over at AAA before I left so that I could go and get a good road map. Then he told me that he was actually kind of jealous of me, taking off like that, going somewhere.

"Funny how things turn out," he had added. "I never thought I'd ever be jealous of *that*."

He also told me that finally he didn't see any reason for me to have to bring Mr. Granger around. Mr. Granger used to even be something of a local personality.

"You know him, then?"

"*Knew of* him," Pa answered. "When a stranger comes and settles in a small town like Millarsburg, everybody knows it. And plenty of folks resented the fact that an outsider was being brought in to work on the town planning commission. It didn't take long for most folks to figure out, though, that old man Millar had brought him in mostly to try and marry off his daughter. It wasn't long before Granger became the laughing-stock of the community. Once Granger figured out himself what was going on, he and the old man were at each other all of the time, like cats and dogs.

Granger gave a lecture at the library once, as I recall, before things blew up. The girls went – your ma and Sally, I mean. It was a lecture about the influence of the war on different movements in art or painting or sculpture or something. Flew right over the top of most people's heads, from what I gather. Sally came back relatively early, alone. She got tired of waiting for your ma, I guess. Said she left her standing there talking to Granger. Miss Millar apparently shooed them out of the library so she could close up, so your ma invited him to supper. They seemed to have some kind of understanding."

"About art?" I asked. I thought of the abstract painting Mr. Granger had given to Ma.

"About a lot of things. About art. About music. About the war. About what it means to be a stranger."

"Aunt Sally's not from here, either."

"Sally is not so much a stranger in Millarsburg as she wants to be. Sally's always figured that there's some other place on this earth where she should have lived, some place where she would have been happier. But events conspired to keep her from getting there." He shook his head. "And in the meantime, there was no way she was ever going to be happy where she was." He took a deep breath. "So go on your trip if you have to go, son. I don't expect that anything I could ever say or do could ever keep you from it – and things around here would only be worse if I tried. But you need to know that this is your home and will be for as long as you want it."

I drove over to Mr. Granger's the next morning so lost in thought that I drove right past his house before I realized it. So, I would take him to Washington, after all. He would be pleased. Then I would go on to Puerto Rico. Somehow. I would do it. I was determined. His door was closed and the basement apartment dark. As I opened the door and walked in, I felt something lightly knock against my head and heard it roll like thunder. Instinctively, I reached for the light and switched it on. A piece of poster board hung down from the top of the door. I was just about to examine it when I heard an animal-like growl come from deep inside the apartment. I swung around and saw that Mr. Granger was curled on his side on his cot, a shapeless heap under the weathered army-issue blanket. The sound I had heard was coming from him. He was snoring – or at least pretending to. It didn't matter. His message was clear. He was having none of me that day.

But he hadn't left me entirely alone. That was the next thing I noticed, couldn't help but notice. From floor to ceiling were maps. They were tacked all around the apartment, except in the kitchen alcove – food for the mind, not the belly – and covered nearly every available inch of wall space. Most of them were *mappaemundi*, world maps: reproductions, copies, originals, mock-ups; even pages torn from dictionaries, encyclopedias and textbooks – modern, ancient, and, in one case, anticipated since it bore the date, 100 million A.D. It looked like a draft drawn, I guessed, by Mr. Granger himself and reminded me surprisingly of Wegener's Pangaea. One thing was for certain: no two representations of the world looked the same. Thinking about it now, I recall having seen the *Terrarum Orbis*, the "mundane egg," and Ptolemy's odd-shaped chunk of earth from his *Geographica*. There was Mercator's famous grid, of course, and something looking for all the world like a top, ready to be spun by the first toddler who happened by. There was the surface of the earth looking like it had been peeled from the globe, unevenly but mostly in one piece, in what I know now is a "homolosine equal-area projection." There were pages from textbooks discussing projections and showing parts of the globe, our globe, inside cones, cylinders, and rectangles that then got flattened into maps. And everywhere there were grids, oblong or ovoid, latitudes and longitudes slashing across pages. Continents were pulled or stretched or compacted between ice-blue ocean waters. Not far from where I stood was a world map just emerged from its brown-paper postal wrappings which Mr. Granger had taken odd care to tape next to it. The return address, I noticed, was in Germany. I also saw that the package had been addressed to Darby Millar with a postmark from just several years earlier, which, I guessed, meant that Mr. Granger had tacked up this vision of the world without ever having seen it. No doubt Miss Millar had described it to him and I wondered what words she had found to use. It was odd enough. It reminded me of a copy of a painting that used to be in the rectory which Father Wilhelm had told me was of Saint Jerome by a guy called *El Greco*, or "the Greek." I remembered thinking what a strange, pathetic figure he had painted Saint Jerome to be with his elongated face and flowing beard and those spidery fingers. On this particular map, the continents stretched down along the latitudes like they were right out of an *El Greco* painting. The pinched cheeks of Saint Jerome were the narrow width of nations. I stared at the map. The great continent of North America seemed small and almost cowering next to the never-ending lengths of South America and Africa or the massive spread of Asia. The vast wilderness of Canada and the Northwestern Territories was squished against the upper part of the map like smoke that had risen in a room and found itself trapped against the ceiling. On that map, the world looked nothing like I had ever seen until then. What was I supposed to believe it looked like in reality?

 I ran around the room, looking from map to map, comparing them. As I did, my stomach rose into my throat. The grids of different projections swam before my eyes. Longitude and latitude criss-crossed and intersected then turned into the squiggly lines of a television test pattern. The equator rolled like a wave across the earth. Continents grew and then shrunk. Michigan rivaled the size of Western Europe on one map, then on another it shrank back, indistinguishable, into the northern United States. Sometimes the Great Lakes were not even drawn in, and, on other maps, Lake Superior and Lake Michigan seemed to have been added as an afterthought, looking like feathers sticking out from a hat. But my most shattering understanding was yet to come. As I looked from representation to representation, I realized that in most cases, Puerto Rico was entirely absent. On those few modern projections where I found my beloved *Borínquen*, it was just a speck – a spot of ink escaped from the point of a pen or stains on a poor copy. I no longer knew where to look, didn't want to have to look anywhere. My eyes ached in their sockets. If I were only as blind as Mr. Granger, I thought.

Then, on the work table, I noticed it. The piece of black, molded plastic lying like tranquil waters in the turbulence of lines and shapes around me. I didn't care what Mr. Granger thought if he woke and found me. I strode to the table and pulled out the swivel chair. Once seated, I closed my eyes and let my shaking hands wander over the mold, caressing every mound and searching every crevice. Its smoothness quieted me. Its coolness calmed the heat trying to erupt from the back of my throat. Its voluptuousness aroused me. It was delicious. I reveled in it, eyes closed. And when I finally opened them again, I found I had the strength to get up and leave.

I pushed the chair back against the table and walked to turn off the lights, intending to go out. I had forgotten about the poster hanging just above the door. It was what had struck me on the head as I walked in. It was another reproduction of a map of the world, an old one, I have found out recently, dating from about 1590. The map itself was located in the facial shield of something that looked almost like the helmet of an old diving costume except that small, curved wings protruded from each side. Each wing ended in a tiny globe-like decoration. The map bore various inscriptions in Latin, two of which must have been important to Mr. Granger. On the bottom of the map, near the South Pole or what would be the chin of the diver, was an expression that had been encircled a number of times with an ink pen. I figured if Mr. Granger had done that, he had done so years ago before he lost his sight, otherwise, how could he have so perfectly circled it? So it couldn't have been intended entirely for me, even if on that particular day, I was sure that it was.

The inscription read, *"Stultorum infinitus est numerus. Salomon."* I stood staring at it for a minute, trying to remember as much as I could from my Latin classes with Father Wilhelm. The irony of it struck me that, if I had spent more time studying the contents of my Latin notebook rather than copying the map of Puerto Rico onto the back of it, I might have been able to understand the inscription right off. The name, Salomon, meant that the phrase probably came from the Bible. The thought crossed my mind that I could try to look it up in the King James Version we had at home. Unfortunately, I had to admit to myself that as little time as I had spent with the Bible in my hands, it might be quicker for me to learn Latin. In any case, three of the four words were relatively easy to figure out. *Infinitus* meant infinite, unlimited. *Est* was the verb "is." *Numerus*, of course, meant numerous. But *stultorum* didn't ring any bells. Then I had an idea. The dictionary! Of course! I found Mr. Granger's *Shorter's Encyclopedic Dictionary* on a stack of newspapers next to the work table. On a hunch, I flipped directly to the 'stul' section figuring that, one way or another, I would find a word whose origin was related to *stultorum*. I had to give Mr. Granger credit. I'd never look at a dictionary the same way again. Stultification. Stultificatory. Stultify. I slid my finger to the right. From the middle 18th century. From the late Latin verb, *stul-*

tificare or the Latin noun *stultus* meaning "foolish, fool." The first definition was a legal one. "Allege or prove to be insane or of unsound mind, especially in order to evade some responsibility." I left the open dictionary on the stack of papers, and walked back to look at the poster. Something about foolishness. But what?

The other inscription was written across the top in larger, block letters. It read, NOSCE TE IPSVM. This one had been translated for me, I guessed, by Mr. Granger, but this time more recently, maybe even just the night before after he had tacked up the map. I figured that much because the last two letters, "l" and "f," were written on the wall, as though someone hadn't realized they had run off the poster. The rest of the letters of his translation didn't line up exactly the way they might have had a seeing person written them, either. But what he had written was clear enough. *Know thyself.*

Churning inside, confused anew and, for some reason, boiling with rage, I stormed out of the cramped basement. Blind to what I was doing, I smacked my head on the upper stairwell and knocked myself cold. I don't know how long I lied there like that, but that bump on the head only served to make me fighting mad once I regained consciousness. I understood then a little why Pa had pitched fast balls and Ma had beaten rugs bare. Maybe even, finally, why Treat had run off.

I drove straight to the county library. Darby Millar was standing near the circulation desk, surveying the empty room. She greeted me as sweetly as always, looking prim in a straight skirt and pale blue cardigan. I felt like strangling her.

"Hello, Bass," she said.

"Why did you lie to me?" I demanded.

She slowly removed her half-glasses and let them dangle from their granny chain onto her chest. She looked at me a long minute. "Lie to you, Bass? About what?"

I wanted to scream, "About everything. About knowledge. About the world. About Mr. Granger."

"About my ma," I said.

She was clearly taken aback. "Why, I've never said anything against your mother."

"You said she couldn't translate Mr. Wegener's book."

"That was true."

"Like she wasn't smart enough or something."

"I never said *that*, young man. As I recall, I said the book was too terribly technical – "

"For a poor little Belgian *farm* girl!"

"Never!"

"Your friend couldn't translate it, either."

"My friend *refused* to translate it. But, that's another story."

"You were just jealous of my ma. Mr. Granger called her – " Dang, I couldn't remember exactly what he had said. "Beautiful."

The word hit her like a slap in the face.

"And you lied to me about Mr. Granger, too," I continued.

She shook her head slowly, "No, I don't believe I ever did."

"Then you lied about how you *feel* about him."

"How I *felt* about him, maybe," she said. "And sometimes, if I let myself, how I still feel about him. When he shows those flashes of humor or brilliance that I knew in him when he was a young man." Her words seemed to fall into a heap at her feet. She stood looking down at them.

I felt my anger drain out of me. This was new in me, this desire to hurt and the clear knowledge that I could do so.

"I'm sorry, Miss Millar," I said.

She found my face then with her eyes. "That's okay, Sebastian. We all need to go a little crazy sometimes. Blame somebody for something. I've done it myself. Life can get so confusing."

"I guess I'm really mad at Mr. Granger." I thought of the maps tacked around his apartment. He had put them there to make fun of me, to make fun of my desire to go to Puerto Rico to become a brave lord. He had so much as called me a fool.

She smiled. "Nick been after you?"

"Yes, ma'am."

"Try to take the good sides of him. They're there."

"Did you want to marry him?"

She touched the nape of her neck. "Once. A long time ago."

"What happened?"

She looked at me a moment as if she were deciding whether or not she could tell me.

"He and my father had a fight. A very big fight. Nicolas said he couldn't accept my father's narrow vision of the world. You know how he can be. If you say something is black, he'll say it's white. If you say it's square, he'll swear it's round. Just to be contrary. Then he doesn't understand why people turn against him. And he certainly wasn't going to win my father over by belittling everything the man stood for, everything he had worked so hard for. After that fight, Father refused to grant my hand. And dedicated himself to doing all that he could to ruin Nick's professional reputation."

"You could have run away with Mr. Granger if you really loved him. Gone off somewhere. Gotten married," I said. That's what my ma would have done, I bet.

"Where?"

"I don't know. The world's a big place," I said. So people kept on telling me.

"*My* world was here. It still is. Nick has never accepted that."

"Why is that do you think?"

She shook her head. "I don't know, Sebastian. Maybe because he had to leave home early. Lost his brother to the First

World War, then got called back briefly into active duty to train young military cartographers during the Second World War. People killing other people because of a flag. Set him off against flag-waving, against people defending identities, national or otherwise. He could never understand the feelings my father had for this town."

"Because Mr. Granger wasn't from here?"

"Maybe because he wasn't from here. Maybe because he didn't feel like he could ever belong here, or anywhere, for that matter. Maybe he'd just seen too many things. Plus, Nick has never been in particularly good health. He's always had problems with his legs. He never could have farmed for example. He just simply wasn't strong enough. I think that made him feel odd, here, in this community."

"Why didn't he move away? I mean farther away than just Painted Creek."

"He was doing some teaching there. Besides," Miss Millar grimaced, "he didn't have anywhere else to go."

"Why, he could have gone anywhere in the world!" I countered.

"Nick's a bit soured on the world, if you haven't noticed. Has been for a long time."

"Then why did he do the *Atlas*?" Seemed like an odd thing to do for someone soured on the world.

"He did the *Atlas* because he didn't know how to do anything else and he needed to make a living. It's ironic, though, because, ultimately, the *Atlas* was what ended his career. And our story."

"Why was that?"

She slipped her glasses back onto the edge of her nose. "I get the feeling you don't know that *Atlas* as well as I thought you did. Why don't you go get it?"

I shuffled off to the Reference section. I'd never be able to admit to her that the only part of the *Atlas* I had ever really looked at was the map of Puerto Rico.

"Here," she said, opening it randomly. "Here, look at this map of Port– "

My heart skipped a beat.

" –ugal. I already mentioned Nick's, let's call them 'experiments,' with color. Look closely."

"Yes, ma'am."

"Don't you notice anything?"

I didn't want to admit it, but I didn't see anything that seemed too out of the ordinary. But, then again, what did I know?

"For one thing," Miss Millar continued, "the colors go completely against convention."

Other than the map of Puerto Rico in *Granger's World Atlas*, I hadn't really *studied* any national map before. And the familiar U.S. map always showed the 50 States in a bunch of different colors. The only world map I more or less knew was the Mercator projection from my school textbooks, but I had always seen it in black and white or gray. And I probably looked at it the way most kids my age did: long enough to recognize a greater world that I had been simply taking on faith existed and looked like that.

"Look. Land is red, streets are yellow, rivers are brown. Look. The forests are orange."

"What are they supposed to be?"

"Good heavens Why, green! Like leaves!"

"Maybe he made the map in the fall," I suggested sheepishly.

Miss Millar laughed. "Maybe. *That* would be like him, wouldn't it?"

I nodded.

"That's just one example. There are plenty of others," she

said. A strand of whitish yellow hair fell across her face and she took the time to guide it back behind her ear before continuing. "He made up his own set of symbols or used symbols from European cartography which don't generally have the same meaning to an American map user. He swayed away from standard size and script in lettering, or worse, inverted them. And – well, you don't really see it in this atlas – decided which landmarks were important and which weren't, especially on street maps. You'll never find a church indicated on one of his street maps, for example, although he would have happily put every green grocer and shoeshine boy on them!"

"But I thought your pa wanted him to 'reinvent' cartography," I said, although I knew I was taking a risk. "Seems to me like that's what he was doing."

"By 'reinventing cartography,' Father didn't mean flying in the face of good sense or tried and true methods. Nick did all of that just to shake people up. He says as much in the introduction to the *Atlas*," she added, turning to the front of the book. "Everything is explained here – the use of color, symbols, everything. But most people don't read the introduction to an atlas or even bother to refer to the map's key. Some reactions to color are very intuitive, like the example of green for forests, and, without hardly knowing it, we've been trained to understand certain things from certain symbols. When people realized that Nick had turned things upside down on them, the reaction was very hostile – both from the general public and the professional community. And my father was just beside himself with rage."

"Because Mr. Granger had humiliated him?" I remembered that Mr. Granger had called Millarsburg "an insignificant little divot."

"Partly. His collaboration with Nick was certainly embarrassing. But it also cost him a lot of money. Father was financing the cost of the atlas and, as you might guess, color plates are *very* expensive. Once he realized what Nick had done, Father hit the roof."

"How did Mr. Granger react?"

"He was totally surprised by the whole thing. I think he honestly thought he was doing people a good turn by putting them on their guard against, well – taking maps at face value. Plus, he kept on saying how he had explained everything at the beginning of the book. That's what 'reinventing cartography' meant for him. It meant sensitizing readers to the fact that we only see what cartographers want us to see. That they make choices for us."

"Do you think he was wrong?"

"Oh, I think he was just a little ahead of his time. Some exciting things are starting to happen in cartography. For example, there's this German fellow who has done a very provocative map of the world."

"The one that's taped up in Mr. Granger's apartment?"

"He's taped it up in his apartment?" she asked, looking pleased.

"Well, with about a million others he wanted me to see."

"Oh," Miss Millar replied.

"Why did he send it to you? The German guy, I mean."

"Despite the controversy Nick's atlas started, it did identify Father as someone interested in cartography. He made a lot of contacts that way. One of my early ideas for the library was to have a map and chart room, something that might eventually become known, our own bit of fame right here in Millarsburg! So I started corresponding with people around the world, asking them to send me any copies they might be able to spare of interesting or important maps. The 'millions of maps' you saw are ones that I have collected in that way. I finally gave them to Nick some years back when Father passed away. But, apparently, I've remained on some mailing lists. Someone suggested to this fellow that he send a version of his map to me after having heard him describe it at a meeting of the Hungarian Academy of Science a few years back."

"What does Mr. Granger think of it?"

"He didn't say?"

"No, ma'am."

"Well, he dismissed it out of hand, of course. Without ever having seen it."

"You described it to him?"

"As best I could," she said. "It *is* rather unusual."

"Why didn't he like it?"

"It wasn't that he didn't like it, necessarily. He said it'd already been done before. I suspect that's not the real reason, however."

"Was there another one like it before?"

"Possibly. I think just about everything has already been done in cartography. But times have changed and so have issues. And Nick is put off by the 'message' behind this map."

"What kind of message?"

"My! You do ask a lot of questions. Suffice it to say that this map is starting to garner support in certain circles not very often frequented by Nicolas Granger!" She snorted.

"Do you still love him?"

Darby Millar turned away.

"Isn't that why you want someone to take him to Washington?"

"I feel partly responsible for what happened, that's true. I had to choose at the time between him and Father. I chose Father." She swung back around to face me. "Nick was an unknown quantity. I didn't know if I could trust him. He's never forgiven me for that, either. I'd like to see it made up to him."

I turned to go.

"And you're right, Sebastian." Miss Millar called over to me. "I *was* terribly jealous of your mother. She was lovely. Your father obviously adored her. My own mother died when I was very young, younger than you were when you lost your mother. I became more of my father's partner than his daughter, psychologically I mean. He used me to bounce his ideas off of, to tell me about his dreams for this town. At the time, it made me feel very important. But by the time I met Nick, I was starting to feel like I had gone from daughter to intellectual partner without ever having lived through the part most women dream of – which was motherhood. I was desperate to have a child."

She turned. "Nick was dead set against having a family. Don't ask him why. He'll give a thousand reasons and none of which, I suspect, are the truth: that having a child brings you face-to-face with all of your own inadequacies. Nick's pride was the only thing he had left to him. And I had hurt him very deeply. So, yes, I do want him to go to Washington. Yes, I do want him to get some recognition – finally. Yes, I do watch after him, try to take care of him as much as he'll allow me. That's all we have left."

For some reason, I didn't tell Miss Millar about my intention to take Nicolas Granger to Washington. "What do you think that black thing is, Miss Millar?"

She found her laugh again. "Who knows? Some kind of map, surely. A map for the blind, I would wager."

"A map of the world?"

"To my knowledge, Nicolas has never done a world map. Even for the *Atlas*."

"Yes, he has," I countered.

"Oh, *that*. A freehand drawing. Inspired by that dreadful book."

"The Wegener book! But you gave it to him. You were reading it to him!"

She waved a hand. "If it makes him happy. I personally prefer to have nothing to do with that kind of thinking. Nor did my friend, for that matter."

"Maybe it's part of a globe," I suggested, returning the conversation to the black piece.

"I'm wondering if it might not be some kind of topographical map. A prototype, maybe. That's why he's keeping so quiet about it. And that's why it's so important for him to take it to Washington!"

CHAPTER SEVEN

In the end, I think my decision to leave was finally fueled in part by the deep loneliness I felt, and, in part, by the strange certainty that in Puerto Rico I would magically be transformed into a Taíno, a brave, but gentle lord. I would be admired and respected by all, and, yes – even loved. I drove one last time over to the patch of bare ground where I had first heard the sounds of the *cuatro*, the double-stringed, hourglass-shaped guitar that Celia's brother had played. I felt his stirring cry reverberate in my chest. *Ay-le-lo-lay, lolaylelolelolela.* I heard Celia's mother clanging like a one-man band as she came marching out of the trailer with metal serving spoons in her pocket and steaming platters of food in her hands. The new tastes banged their way into my consciousness. The names of the dishes rattled my tongue: *habichuelas, lomo asado, arroz.* From time to time, Enrique's booming laughter struck the air like percussion.

I let my eyes roam over the vacant lot. Finally, I could accept the stories I'd heard and had found so impossible to believe until then: Civil War battlefields that still echoed blasts of cannon fire and the moans of the wounded; prairies resonant with the pounding of horse hooves as Indian braves rushed off to battle.

If pressed, though, I would have to admit that my vision that day didn't represent things entirely as they had been two summers before. Most importantly, Treat and Erik were both absent. Treat – my hero, my friend, and my constant tormentor – was not there to ridicule or tease me or worry me into trouble. Erik, though kinder in his ways, was not there to confuse me with a romanticism that I was just learning to experience. This time, too, I danced with Celia. Loose and confident, I swung her over the uneven ground, turning her, catching her, holding her. And not stumbling once. Her ma looked on, nodding, so pleased was she to see her princess daughter in the arms of such a confident, dashing suitor – a real man. *Ay-le-lo-lay, lolaylelolelolela. Yo soy puertorriqueño.*

On the way home from the campsite, I stopped back at Mr. Granger's place. I caught him just coming in his back door. Clumps of grass were sticking to the knees of his dark corduroy pants. For the first time since I'd known him, I seemed to have caught him off guard. I noticed the pile of stones was missing again.

"What d'you want?" he growled.

I straightened up and took in a deep breath. "I'll take you to Washington, Mr. Granger."

"Fine."

He bent half over and brushed at the legs of his pants. The hands on the ends of his short arms reached to just above the kneecaps. The grass clung stubbornly to the cloth.

"Here, let me help you with that," I offered, walking towards him.

He swatted at me. "Off with you. We're wastin' time. Let's get going."

"Get going?"

He stuck his chin out at me. "Didn't you just tell me that you were taking me to Washington?"

"Well, yeah. But I didn't mean – "

"When?"

"– right this instant!"

"When are you taking me, then?"

"Well, once we're ready."

"I'm ready."

"I'm not," I said.

"Oh," he said, shuffling past me to his cot. "Never mind, then."

"But I thought – "

"Stop thinking so much."

"I thought maybe on Saturday – "

"When's that?"

"In two days."

He clambered into his bed. "Might be dead by then."

"Friday then," I countered. I hated it when he made references like that.

He pulled his blanket over him. "Same difference."

"When, then?"

"If not now?" he mumbled.

"If not now," I answered.

"Tomorrow."

"I can't be ready by tomorrow morning."

"Afternoon, then. Evening. Even better. Better to travel later. Still too blasted hot. Now get out of here and let me sleep."

Luckily for me, Erik was at the Sinclair station seeing to Granny Stein's Plymouth. I told him that I was planning on leaving a lot sooner than expected – like the next day. To my surprise, he actually tried to talk me out of it, but when I insisted, he asked The Boys to take care of my car before his and give it a good looking over. We sat sipping bottles of RC Cola on a couple of folding chairs in front of the station.

"Bass, are you sure you know what you're doing?"

"You're the one who told me not to stay around here for the rest of my life!"

"I didn't necessarily mean you had to leave right away!"

"I might not get another chance like this."

"You're only sixteen."

"Almost seventeen."

Treat left when he was my age, I thought.

"All right. Almost seventeen. You've got plenty of time," he said. "Does your pa know about this?"

"Yeah."

"And he agrees?"

"Sure. Why wouldn't he?"

"Did you tell him everything? The whole truth?"

I sucked on the thick glass rim of my bottle. "Not exactly."

"Bass!"

"I'll be all right. I'm not a baby anymore."

"I know you're not. I just don't want you to go off and do something stupid."

"*You're* going away."

"That's different, and you know it. Besides, I'm almost nineteen. And what about school?"

There was no way I was going back to Millarsburg High School, I thought to myself. "I can go back once I get settled in Puerto Rico."

Erik shook his head. "There are such things as procedures,

Bass. Forms. You'll need to transfer your records and you won't be able to do that without your pa's approval."

"I'll cross that bridge when I get to it," I said, waving my hand *à la* Mr. Granger.

"Yeah, just don't fall into the water," he answered.

We sat silently for a minute.

"You got enough money?"

"Yeah, yeah. Don't worry," I said with a forced nonchalance.

"How much?"

"None of your business."

"How much?"

"Like I said, none of your business."

"*Shit,*" he said, shaking his head. He reached into his pocket with his good hand and pulled out a crumpled wad of bills.

"Here, take this. It's only about fifty bucks, but it's all I've got on me."

"I don't need your money," I said.

"Take it." He shoved his hand at me. "I said, 'take it,' Bass."

I reached over and took the money. "Thanks."

He got up and walked into the office. He came back out a few minutes later. This time he shoved a piece of paper at me.

"Here. It's Father Wilhelm's number. If you have any trouble and you don't want to call your pa, call him. He knows people all over the country. And he'll know where to reach me."

I actually got kind of choked up when, after The Boys had finished working on the Fairlane, I had to say goodbye to Erik. I even hugged him hard, like a brother, and didn't feel the slightest bit funny about it. He stabbed at a tear with a crooked finger.

"You can always change your mind, you know."

"So I can drive around in circles?" I asked.

"The world *is* round," he answered, smiling.

"And big," I countered.

He shook his head. "Be careful."

* * *

Leaving was looking to be a lot less romantic than I'd thought. On the evening before I left, we all ate dinner together out at the picnic table and then sat there, looking for UFOs and talking. Well, that's not entirely true. Pa ate quickly and excused himself, going into the house and, I guessed, shutting himself up in his study. But except for that, it was nearly like old times – except it wasn't, and everyone had changed. I studied the faces around me. Kate was turning out to be a pretty young lady. She was still sewing up a storm and, who knows, maybe someday she would even be famous. I worried that by then she would have forgotten me. Aunt Sally was looking more and more her age, but somehow she had become more attractive over the past couple of years, like she was settling into herself. When I looked over at Uncle Will, I found him staring back at me.

"Have you decided about your trip?" he asked.

The macaroni and cheese we'd had for supper felt like a bowling ball in my belly.

"Actually, Mr. Granger wants to leave tomorrow."

"How exciting!" Kate said.

"Tomorrow!" Aunt Sally screamed. She placed her napkin on the table. "No, but honestly, Bass. This is totally unreasonable. Is this fellow a madman, or what?"

"Settle down, Sal," Uncle Will said, staring at her while she smoothed down her skirt, before turning his eyes on me. "What's the rush?"

"I guess his meeting got moved up or something," I answered. I was going to hell for sure.

"Thomas told me he was presenting something before Congress."

"I think so," I said, shrugging.

"To the best of my knowledge, son, Congress isn't in session, yet. Won't be until after Labor Day."

"I think he's just meeting with one person, and that person needs to see him early." That, for all I knew, might have been the truth. But it was a close call, anyway.

"I see." He looked over to Aunt Sally before looking back at me. "Did you leave a telephone number or something with your pa? You know how upset he is about this, don't you?"

I ignored that. "I don't know where we're staying, yet. I'll call Pa when we get there."

"Did you go by Triple A like he told you?"

"Yes, sir."

"You want me to go over the route with you?"

Ironically enough, I was no stranger to a map. "No, thanks. Pa and I did that already."

"Well," Uncle Will continued, "I guess there's not much left to say, then." He looked over to Aunt Sally. So did I. She was staring intently at her lap.

Packing my bag was a lot harder than I ever would have imagined, too. I wanted to take all of my summer clothes, since I was going away for the rest of my life and all, but I couldn't let Pa think that I was taking more than just a light travel bag, otherwise he was sure to get suspicious. He had been in to check on me a few times – see if I needed anything, he said. Finally, I decided that I'd pack a small bag and then get up in the middle of the night, grab the rest of my stuff and hide it in the back of the Fairlane. I knew I wasn't going to be able to sleep, anyway. Later that night, I lied in bed listening to the sounds of the house settle down around me. I was completely awake. I set my travel alarm for 4 o'clock, just in case, though, then stuffed it into my pillow case and shoved that between my legs. That way, it wouldn't wake Pa up when it went off.

Then I stretched out on my back and fantasized about Celia — about *me* and Celia. Me and Celia on the white, sandy beach. Me and Celia eating in a fancy restaurant. Me and Celia dancing a slow dance. Me and Celia getting married — which was totally crazy because she was probably already married to Treat. Although I was just fantasizing, the thought bothered me. Would I be as alone in Puerto Rico? I started wondering about my life there. Despite what I had said to Erik, I knew full well that I wouldn't be able to go back to school, at least not right away. I'd have to work. The problem was, I didn't really know how to do anything. Maybe I could fish for my living, like the *ancients* had. I knew how to handle a canoe pretty well. My pa had taught me the summer after I turned ten years old. That memory made me think of being a little kid again, protected by my folks. I got up and looked out the window. There was no moon, but the sky was strangely bright. I wondered if Mr. Granger was crawling on all fours in his backyard, an old dog digging up bones.

I decided to go to the cemetery. Somehow, I felt like I had to try to explain things to my ma, especially since I couldn't find a way to say them directly to my pa. I pulled the alarm clock out of my pillowcase and switched it off. Then I got up, and put on my jeans and a T-shirt. Then I jammed the rest of my stuff into a big Samsonite suitcase that used to belong to Ma. On my way out, I stopped in the kitchen and took a swig of orange juice straight from the bottle since I knew that there was no-one around to catch me at it. The refrigerator door creaked as I closed it, but the garage door slid easily on its greased wheels. I hopped into the Fairlane and was just about to switch the ignition on when I saw her. She was standing in their doorway, clutching her bathrobe around her as though it were the middle of winter and she were freezing. She hadn't taken the time to comb her hair, but it looked like she had run her hands through it without thinking, so that it stuck up and out on both sides. Her eyes showed brightly in the car lights like those of an animal you surprise by the side of the road. She pushed her slippered feet across the oil-stained cement and came to the driver's side of the car. She reached in and latched onto my left forearm. I looked down at her hand. I couldn't remember the last time Aunt Sally had touched me. Her grip was like a vice.

"Bass – where are you going?"

For once, my best answer was the truth. "To the cemetery."

"To the cemetery?" I felt her hot breath brush my cheek. "At *this* hour?"

"I can't sleep."

"Can't you go tomorrow?" she asked in a low voice.

"I'm leaving tomorrow." I thought about the extra clothing I had already stored on the floor in the back of the Fairlane.

"I won't ask if you want me to go with you. I'm sure this is something that you want to do by yourself."

I nodded.

"I'm not exactly the world's greatest sleeper any more, either." She squeezed my arm hard once before letting go. "If you feel like having a little snack when you get back, just come on over."

"Thanks."

As I drove off to the cemetery, I remember thinking how glad I was that I wasn't, in fact, running away that night. The thought of Aunt Sally sitting at a kitchen table set for breakfast for the two of us and waiting for me might have been too much to bear. It was better that I was going off as planned.

The outer gate to the cemetery was locked, so I had to climb over the wrought-iron fence. I thought that it was probably the first time someone had tried so hard to get into Millarsburg Memorial Park. Sheriff Walker told us once, though, how some young kids had gone in a couple of years before and had destroyed tombstones and stolen flowers and such and that's why the cemetery was locked in the first place. All I needed was for one of Sheriff Walker's men to find me there and throw me into the slammer before I had a chance to explain. I'd never get to Puerto Rico that way.

Ma's grave was in pretty sad shape again, so the first thing I did was clean it up. Then, I tried to explain to her what I was doing, going to Puerto Rico and all, but I didn't get the feeling she was really listening. She would have been especially angry about my dropping out of school – it was one of the first things she had mentioned after Treat had run off – and there was absolutely no excuse for not talking to Pa about what I wanted to do. It amounted to lying, something I had been doing non-stop for the past couple of days. As I was getting ready to leave the cemetery an hour or so later, I realized that if I lived in Puerto Rico for the rest of my life, I'd never be back to visit Ma's grave. It would be like losing her all over again. I found a Dixie cup in the trash by the groundskeeper's shed, went back to her grave, dug up a little bit of the earth with my fingers and put it in the waxed cup. It wasn't much, but it would have to do.

When I got back to the house, I found Aunt Sally sitting out at the picnic table, nursing a cup of coffee. There was juice set out for me and a couple of sweet rolls. I thought it was nice of her to make an effort like that, and so I took a sip of juice and bit into one of the rolls even though my throat was knotted with emotion and I felt the still undigested ball of macaroni and cheese in the pit of my stomach.

"I think Treat tried to call," she said quietly after a few minutes.

"What?" I cried. "When?"

She took a sip of coffee. "A couple of days ago. It sure sounded like him."

"What did he say?"

"Nothing. When I answered, he said, 'hello,' so I said 'hello,' and he said 'hello' again. Then hung up."

Poor Aunt Sally, I thought. A couple of anonymous "hello's" and she was imagining Treat home again.

"What makes you think it was him?"

"Like I said, it sounded like him. And it would make sense. You know, deciding to call and then maybe losing his nerve and hanging up. It's made me so hopeful though. Maybe he's decided to come home. In any case, I feel pretty sure now that he's alive."

She squeezed her eyes shut, but not before a tear managed to slip out of one corner and roll down her cheek. She dabbed it away quickly with her paper napkin.

"I'm sure he's alive."

"Bass," she turned to look at me. "Do you know where he is?"

I wondered how long she had been waiting to ask me that question. "No, ma'am. I sure don't." I looked back at her. Her skin looked pulled tight against the thin bones of her face.

"Not even an idea?" she asked.

Ay-le-lo-lay, lolaylelolelolela!

"No, ma'am."

* * *

I slept like a rock until late afternoon, fully-clothed and lying on top of my made-up bed. When I woke, I realized that I was meant to be leaving. I rolled over and pressed my cheek to my pillow. I remember very clearly staring at the pine wood of my night stand. I studied the way the grain moved away from the dark knots like light ripples on the water after a pebble is dropped into a pond. I was sure that I had never seen anything so beautiful in my whole life. And I had never even noticed it before. I took a minute and stared at the different objects in my room. A miniature milk-pail lampshade. A wooden bookshelf that Ma had stained antique blue to match my upright dresser. A braided blue and gray rug. I fingered the stitches in the patchwork quilt that I used as a bedspread. Each thing was more beautiful than the others. I'd never see them again.

I heard Kate come in from school. She and Aunt Sally exchanged a few hot words. I looked at my alarm clock. It was almost five-thirty. Kate was more than a little late. I figured that's what the rapid-fire exchange was all about. I needed to get up, too, I thought. Get myself going. Still, I clung to the bed a few more minutes.

"Bass?" my pa whispered through the door.

I tumbled out of bed and raced to open it.

"I thought you said you were leaving today, son."

"Mr. Granger prefers to travel at night," I answered. "Not so hot."

"Not much used to night driving, are you?" he asked.

I swallowed hard. I was already worried enough about it. "No, sir," I said.

"Well," he said, chewing at the inside of his lip, "less traffic that way, I guess. But promise me you'll rest when you get tired. No meeting in Washington is as important as your safety."

"Yes, sir."

"What time are you supposed to pick him up?"

I couldn't very well tell him the truth – that we hadn't arranged a time. Like Aunt Sally, he'd start wondering what kind of madman Mr. Granger was.

"Around six-fifteen, sir," I said. Lies slid off of my tongue more and more easily. Was that part of becoming a man?

"Well, then, you and I can have a bite to eat together." He looked up at me.

* * *

I could hardly get a thing down my throat. Pa said that it was probably a good idea not to eat too much before a long drive. A full stomach might make me sleepy. So he packed up a few sandwiches for me and threw in a couple of whole tomatoes from the garden and the rest of the cherry pie I had bought the day before at the IGA.

Then he took me in his arms and squeezed me so hard, I thought my bones would break. My heart was breaking and I know Pa's was too, and I could only imagine that he wasn't screaming at me and ordering me to get my backside back in the house and get ready for school the next day because we both knew that I'd go off with or without his blessing. He didn't walk me out to the car, but stayed in the house, closing the door between us quietly.

Surprisingly enough, Uncle Will, Aunt Sally and Kate were all gathered out by the Fairlane, and I couldn't tell if it was because they were getting used to people leaving – what with Treat running off and Ruth Anne going to Africa – and knew how to behave, or if it was because, despite everything, we had somehow grown closer over the past year with my ma gone and my pa just a shadow of himself. I'd also noticed recently how Uncle Will called me "son" a lot – even more than my pa, who almost always called me by my nickname. I hugged Aunt Sally, and Uncle Will solemnly shook my hand. Kate gave me a hug and kissed me on the cheek before going back into their house. She was wearing a Varsity football sweater from Black River – Tim Kirsten's, I guessed. That must have been what the commotion was about.

Just before I settled in behind the wheel, Aunt Sally rushed over to me. I was reminded of the night before. She stuck a neatly-folded twenty-dollar bill at me.

"It's not much," she said shyly, "but use it to buy yourself something nice." Then she kissed my forehead and hugged me tightly.

"Be careful, Bass. Come back to us in one piece," she added, then walked back to Uncle Will.

"We'll miss you, son," he called out.

"Have a great trip," Aunt Sally called out more brightly.

I sat there like a ninny. Finally, all of that lying had caught up to me. It occurred to me that I could do what I said I was going to – take Mr. Granger to Washington and bring him back. And come back with him. The problem was that it would allow me to be honest with everyone else, but lie to myself. Hadn't I given myself plenty of reasons to go through with my plan? Wasn't this what I wanted? Isn't that why I had posted a letter to Darby Millar on my way to the cemetery asking her to explain everything to my family? I settled in behind the wheel of the Fairlane, yanked off the break, and threw the car into reverse. Aunt Sally followed me down the driveway as I backed out, Uncle Will behind her. I risked a quick glance in the rearview mirror as I drove off to Mr. Granger's. They were at the end of the driveway. Aunt Sally had moved to Uncle Will's side. She had taken one of his hands in hers. With her other hand, she was waving.

* * *

I found him standing outside on the sidewalk in front of his apartment. Beside him on the ground was an old army-issue duffel bag and what looked like a pile of newspapers. Mr. Granger had his arms crossed over his chest and he was straddling a place where the cement was raised and broken by the unchecked roots of a nearby tree. He was wearing the same dark corduroy pants he had on the last time I saw him and a long-sleeved woolen gray shirt. I screeched to a halt in front of him and bailed out of the car.

"How did you know I was coming?" I asked.

"You said you were."

"I meant *now*, you know, at this hour." I was sure he knew what I had meant.

"Didn't," he answered.

"Well, how long have you been waiting out here?"

"Forgot to check my watch, urchin." He held up a bare wrist.

I ignored him. "A long time?" I thought his legs weren't so good. "Why didn't you wait for me in the apartment?"

"I'm ready," he said.

I bent over to pick up his bag and noticed that it was still open. I couldn't help but look inside. He had packed one change of underwear, a bar of Lava soap in a faded wrapper, the Wegener book, his worn blanket, and the box of saltines that I had bought for him the Saturday before. When I tried to close the bag, I found that the drawstring was missing.

"What's in the newspaper?" I asked. The papers were obviously protecting something. They were held together with masking tape, tacked here and there like bandages.

"In your opinion?"

The black sculpture, I thought. I slung the duffel over my shoulder and carefully picked up the bundle of newspapers. Mr. Granger fingered his way around the Fairlane and into the front seat, so I managed to get the back door open on my side, slide the bag onto the seat and wedge the bundle of newspapers sideways on the floor.

When I climbed into the front, Mr. Granger was curled to one side facing me with his eyes closed.

"Are you okay?" I asked.

"Let me be," he growled.

"Do you want your blanket?" Mr. Granger tilted his head at me. Caught red-handed. "I couldn't help but notice. Your bag was open and everything," I started to explain.

"No!"

"Isn't that why you brought it?"

His eyes sprung open. "What?"

"The blanket."

"What do you normally use a blanket for?" he asked.

"Well, for sleeping, but – "

I'd never stayed in a hotel before. I kind of had the idea they provided the bedding.

"Why do you ask me such asinine questions?"

"I thought in hotels they – "

"In hotels! Whoever gave you the idea we were going to be staying in some fancy hotel? You gonna pay for that?"

"No I just thought – "

"Well, think again. You're the one who's always waxing poetic about Mother Earth. Now you'll have the chance to feel her up close and personal – against your backside."

"You mean we're going to camp?"

"Call it what you will."

"I wish I had known," I said. "I would have brought some camping equipment." I had plenty of Boy Scout stuff.

"Don't go complicating things. A man needs to know how to travel light, otherwise he gets bogged down. All that baggage just slows a body down. Never dally upon this Earth, urchin. We'll all soon be underground!"

I looked down and noticed that I had dirt under the fingernails of my right hand. I picked them clean.

"Are we going to camp in Washington, too?" I asked. "I mean, you've got all these important meetings and stuff." As far as I knew, Washington didn't even *have* campgrounds.

He waved a hand at me. "Cross that bridge when we get to her. Are you going to get moving or are you going to sit there all night jawing at me?"

He grumbled, but I made him put on his seatbelt. Between the two of us, I figured, we had about as much recent experience traveling a long distance in a car as the Man-on-the-Moon, so I wasn't taking any chances. Then I gently pressed on the accelerator and steered away from the curb. Mr. Granger rested his head on the back of the seat and closed his eyes. By the time we hit the corner of Elm and Baron, I wondered if he were asleep. The old cashew seller was packing up his wares for the day. Through my open window I could smell the acrid smoke from the fire burning out in his makeshift roaster. I heard a mother call her kids home. Somewhere nearby an ice-cream vendor chimed one of his final summer rounds. The world around me was winding down for a peaceful evening. And I was taking off on what was maybe the most foolhardy adventure ever. I think if I had been streaming through space in a rocket ship with only the night stars to guide me, I wouldn't have felt more overwhelmed by what I was doing. Nor, despite the presence next to me, more alone.

I headed out towards the highway, following the route that the man at Triple A had given me. We weren't twenty minutes out of Painted Creek when I heard Mr. Granger make a sound like a belch. I looked over. It seemed like his stomach was coming up on him. He made a face and then shot upright.

"Pull over! Quick!"

As I pulled onto the shoulder of the road, he groped for the door handle. As soon as I could do so safely, I reached across him and flung his door open. He tilted over and retched onto the side of the road. When he had finished, he wiped his mouth with the back of his free hand.

"I need to get out," he said. His upper body was slung across the space between the seat and the door handle. He was trapped by his safety belt.

"Hang on," I shouted. I glided the car up about a foot so that he wouldn't step out into his own vomit, then I clicked the silver buckle on his seatbelt. "There you go."

He grunted and struggled out of the Ford.

I scooted out across the front seat. "Are you all right, Mr. Granger?"

He groped for his stomach.

"Get me the saltines, would you?"

I scrambled back into the car, found the box of saltines, and went back to Mr. Granger. He was seated on the ground, both legs spread out in boned arcs in front of him.

"Are you not feeling well?" I asked, handing him an open package.

He swiped at his face, pushing his bushy eyebrows into the hollows of his eyes. "I should have figured this would happen." He forced a laugh.

It took me a minute to realize what he was saying.

"You mean you're carsick?" I asked, incredulous.

"No, urchin. I'm pregnant. Just didn't know how to tell you." He fell onto his back. "Confound it."

I couldn't believe it. The world's greatest living cartographer was carsick. The man whose work had inspired me to want to explore the world and sail the high seas had motion sickness.

He stuck his chin up in the air. "What are you starin' at? Never seen someone get carsick before? Never been carsick yourself, I'll bet."

"Yes, I have." I remembered the trip to Ocqueoc. "They say it's better when you're the one driving."

"Driving. Hah! That's a good one!" He slapped the ground with an open hand. "How about, 'better when you can see'?"

"You mean – "

"Tell me, what's there behind us?" He pointed his arm up over his head.

I started to say "nothing," then remembered the conversation we'd had about blank spaces on a map – "silences," he had called them. Maybe there were silent places on the real Earth, too.

"An open field," I answered.

"Is there a fence between here and the field?"

"No."

"Good." He sat up. "Close your eyes – keep 'em closed – and go run around that field for the next twenty minutes. I'll wait here."

"Mr. Granger?"

"Go ahead. See how it feels."

Like almost all kids, Treat and I used to stand in one or the other's front yard, close our eyes and spin around until we became so disoriented, we'd fall over laughing. After the ground stopped gyrating behind our eyelids, we'd dare each other to do it again.

My gut quaked once and then calmed. "I think I know how it feels," I said.

He tilted his head, but accepted my answer.

"How did you go blind, Mr. Granger?"

"From staring at the sun, urchin. Like the ancient mariners," he added. "Most of 'em went blind, at least in one eye. From taking reckonings at sea. Trying to figure out where the heck they were." He held up an imaginary sighting stick. "Lots of famous explorers and discoverers went blind. Look at Galileo. Spent years with his eye glued to a telescope following Jupiter's moons. Know what he was doing?"

"No."

"Looking for a way to measure longitude. Trying to help those poor seafarers to determine their position. What'd he get for his trouble?" Mr. Granger raised both hands, palms facing upward before letting them fall into his lap. "Old and blind and probably crazy."

"But you didn't go blind from your job, did you?" I challenged.

"No, just went crazy. In fact, they thought I was crazy before I really was."

I looked at him to see how serious he was being. He pressed his palms to the sides of his head, and rocked back and forth.

"Headaches. Mad headaches. Then I started seeing less and less. But that was all right with me. I'd seen enough."

"Enough of the world?" I asked.

"Which one?" he answered.

I remembered all of the projections he had taped to the walls of his studio.

"The real one."

"Which one is that?"

"I was hoping that was what you'd tell me."

"None of the above, then. The one you carry around in your head. He patted the ground near him, "The square foot you're connected to at any point in time. The rest is just *purty* pictures. Like the *Madonna and Child*. A striking image of something we have to take on faith." He let his back touch the ground. "Look here, urchin."

When he heard me move nearer to him, he said, "Sit

down." Instead, I dropped to my knees. "What's out there, beyond that field you were just telling me about?"

I looked out past the open field. "More fields. Farmland. A few houses and barns."

"For as far as the eye can see?"

"For as far as the eye can see," I answered.

"Where is the sun?"

"I'm facing it." The orange ball hovered above the horizon.

"Look carefully at the line where the Earth meets the sky."

I did. And truly saw for the first time the curvature of our planet, the arching platform that I was kneeling on. I described what I saw.

"Now, you've understood everything," he said, turning onto his left side and pillowing his head with his arm.

I didn't understand anything. "That the Earth isn't flat?"

He waved a hand at me. "No, urchin! Besides, there's nothing to prove people ever really thought it was. The sun is a sphere. The moon is a sphere. Why shouldn't the Earth be? Two hundred and fifty years before Christ, the Greeks already understood that just by looking up into the dome of the sky. Eratosthenes even used spherical geometry to calculate the Earth's circumference, so he had to understand that the Earth wasn't flat."

I looked up at the first star as the arms of the night sky wrapped around me.

"Then why is that always the legend?"

"Legends are part of cartography, urchin." He grinned.

I pictured a stylized, miniature airplane or the hatched lines that mark a disputed boundary.

"I meant – "

"So did I. Why should maps be different than anything else? Why do folks always figure they aren't influenced by the same forces or suffer from the same prejudices that other things suffer from?"

"Because they show the Earth – and the Earth is real."

"They *represent* the Earth. They can never show it as it really is. It's one of cartography's many riddles. Get used to it. The more we try to represent reality, the further away we get from it."

"Even with pictures?"

"Even with pictures. Photographs provide a cone-shaped view of an area. The further you get away from the center of the picture, the more things get distorted. I told you once that it takes distance to make a map. That's true. But the greater the distance, the more area you want to show on a map, the greater the distortion. Those are the facts, urchin. Stop fighting 'em."

"Then how can you ever show the whole world? I mean – all of the continents."

"On paper? Can't really."

"What about a globe?"

"Can you see everything when you look at a globe?"

"No," I conceded. Even the picture they sent back from space only showed half of the world. "Only some of it."

"That's all you can over hope to see clearly. In reality or on paper. Don't ever try to see more. You can't. It'll drive you crazy."

I sat back on my heels.

"On Mr. Wegener's map you could see all of the continents."

"That's true, urchin. That's what I liked about it. It totally shook folks up. After all those centuries of science and exploration and folks creating a new image of the world by conquering the unknown, here comes a guy with a map right out of the dark ages. An island surrounded by water. Hah!"

"An island? Sounds like paradise to me," I said, thinking of Puerto Rico.

"Islands have represented both paradise and purgatory. On medieval maps, paradise was located on an island off of the coast of China. In the totally opposite direction, the Canary Islands were considered the place where pagan souls roamed around aimlessly and forever. Pagan souls like mine. Hah!" he laughed. "No surprise, then, that's where the first prime meridian was drawn. Time, urchin. Time is what has always mattered."

"Why in the Canary Islands?" I asked. I'd never heard of them.

"They marked the limits of the known world. People have always been afraid of the unknown. If you ask me, that's why your man Wegener's ideas bothered folks. He had the nerve to suggest that there was something *under* the water, *under* the surface of the Earth – something we couldn't see – that was acting on our lives, and not in a terribly spiritual way either! Something unseen and unknown that had split the continents apart. Your man was ahead of his time. Someday people are going to realize that the things that need to be mapped are the things we *can't* see. The mountains are higher and valleys deeper under the seas than above them. If we could draw off the oceans – then that would be something. It would seem like a whole different planet. Folks wouldn't recognize it. Wouldn't that be fine!"

Mr. Granger stood up suddenly. Crumbs from the crackers he had eaten fell like gold dust from his rough shirt.

"Time's a wastin', urchin. Let's be off."

I was pinned to the ground. "It's not fair," I said.

"Life's not fair," he said, walking off in the direction of the car. Then he stopped and tilted his head. "*What's* not fair?"

The words slipped out of a wound in my chest. "You don't

want other people to see places in the world because you can't see them anymore."

Mr. Granger came back towards me, fingering my words as though they were links in a chain. His legs worked like a wind-up toy. He reached out a hand that landed on my forehead. He held it cupped there.

"Places don't matter, urchin. Not as much as folks would like to think they do. Only time matters." He lifted his hand from my forehead and traced an arc in the sky. "Without it, we'd be lost at sea." He let his hand drop. "Speaking of which. I'm not getting any younger."

"All right, Mr. Granger. Let's go."

The night sky gave me the impression that we were not touching the ground. As hard as I tried to imagine the four, flattened surfaces where rubber met road, I couldn't. I stared ahead as luminescent white lines got sucked up into the hood of the car and then re-appeared broken in my rearview mirror. Mr. Granger sat quietly next to me. Maybe he dozed. In any case, he made only one sound all night – an explosive burst of laughter. At the same time, he had reached instinctively for the belt loop that normally held the aluminum cane. He seemed disappointed to realize that he had forgotten it. I had announced that we had just crossed the State line into Ohio. As we did, despite myself, I leaned towards my half-opened window curious to know, after all, if boundaries existed only in our minds or if they were, in fact, mapped onto the ground. As I looked down, I unintentionally tugged on the steering wheel, jerking the car sideways. That's when Mr. Granger had laughed. Somehow, I was sure he had understood exactly what had happened. I shifted us back into place. He settled back down to sleep.

I didn't put on the radio thinking that it might disturb him. In the silence, my thoughts wandered loosely in my skull. I knew that if I didn't concentrate on something, I risked falling asleep. I tried to remember the words to songs I knew or even to recite poems, but I couldn't think of any. I wasn't like Antoninus, Spartacus' friend, who recited a poem about his homeland that so moved Spartacus, it made the gladiator ashamed of not being a learned man. There were so many things that he needed to understand. *Why did stars fall from the sky and not birds? Where did the sun go at night? Where does the wind come from?*

The air smelled of rain. I prayed that it would hold off. I was worried enough about driving such a long distance for the first time and at night, without having the extra burden of rain on my windshield and water under my tires. The night pressed against my eyelids. Whenever I felt as though it would overtake me, I looked over at Mr. Granger curled sideways in his seat. Could it be that he really trusted me to get us to our destination? I couldn't betray him. I put all of my energy into focusing on the road.

A thousand and one demons came to trouble me that night. The ball of my right foot – inside my sock inside my gym shoe – itched. My arms tingled. My backside had gone numb. My left eye twitched. I felt a sudden, inexplicable need to straighten my left leg. I was thirsty, hungry, sleepy and had a constant urge to go to the bathroom. I wished Mr. Granger wanted to talk. The motor raged like a storm in my empty ears. My heart leapt each time a car or truck came at us from the other direction. Once I flashed my lights just to have a response, some human response. The car's headlights blinded me and then disappeared quickly into the darkness. Its rear lights glowed fainter and fainter like two embers growing cold. The faces of all of the people I knew and loved – my parents, Aunt Sally and Uncle Will, Treat, Kate, Ruth Ann, Erik, even Sheriff Walker and Darby Miller – spun like moons around me. And Celia, of course. There was always Celia.

Celia and Puerto Rico had become forever linked in my mind. As the numbers on the lighted odometer ticked off like the seconds on a clock, I tried to imagine that I was driving on the island of *Borínquen*. I figured the main road would probably be bordered by palm trees, and maybe even ran along the ocean. I'd never seen real palm trees before, much less the ocean so it was pretty hard to imagine. And maybe the road signs were all in Spanish so I wouldn't know which direction to take. I'd be lost all of the time. Lucky thing for me Puerto Rico was an island. At some point, I'd simply run out of road before getting too far off track. Of course, I'd be driving some other kind of car. I wouldn't be able to take the old Fairlane with me. I thought how great it'd be if I could sell it before I left the mainland. Not that I knew how to go about selling a car that, in fact, wasn't even mine to sell. I sure needed the money, though. Otherwise, how was I going to live? In fact, I was starting to think that maybe one of the best things I could do as soon as I got to Puerto Rico would be to buy an airplane ticket back home. Just in case. And while I still had some cash. What would I do when I ran out? Maybe I'd have to live on the street like kids I'd seen in special reports on the *Evening News*. Those reports had shown little kids in ragged clothes scrounging in piles of garbage, fighting each other, sleeping in doorways. It was pitiful. Their noses seemed to be dripping all the time. And what if I got sick? Who was going to take care of me? I hoped I would be able to find Treat. He was my only hope. Unless, of course, I found Celia.

I pretty much spent the whole night driving and worrying like that. At times the fear was so real, I felt its icy hands at my throat. The only thing that saved me each time I felt that way was to look over at Mr. Granger resting peacefully next to me. He was real and familiar. If I had wanted to, I could have reached out and touched him. And hadn't I just crossed a state line for the first time in my life? Each border I crossed would take me closer to that person I knew I could be. Stronger. Braver. More alive.

That doesn't mean I was sorry to see the sun rise. The new light comforted my thoughts, and cleared my head. I started to look around me again. And realized I was lost. I don't know how I had managed it. At some point during the night, I was supposed to have made a change from a highway going south to one heading east. I had missed the junction. We were still heading south. I didn't think Mr. Granger had realized it and I toyed with the idea of not telling him. He had slept most of the way, anyway. I figured that was how he kept himself from getting too carsick. Or maybe he just slept a lot. I didn't check the map for fear that he would hear me unfolding it. I figured I'd just keep on going until I found a way to get back on the right track. It seemed to me that I remembered Mr. Granger telling me stories of sea captains running their ships aground in much the same way. Holding a steady direction, despite all evidence to the contrary. I wouldn't run out of wind, but I was running out of gas. And was going to have to do something about that soon.

By the time I noticed the Shell sign off in the distance, we were pretty much running only on my hopes. Then I got turned around in a residential area trying to head myself toward the towering sign which was tauntingly close as the crow flies but nearly impossible to find by the road. I stopped at a red light, thinking maybe I should get out and ask someone for directions, otherwise, I was going to be pushing the Fairlane to the station and I'd hardly be able to keep that from Mr. Granger.

There was a light on at the house on the corner to my left. From where I sat, I had a pretty good line of vision right into the kitchen. A woman was standing up, still dressed in her bathrobe and with curlers sticking out of her hair. The warm smell of toast filled my nostrils and I felt the cold slap of orange juice on my tongue. The woman didn't move and seemed lost in thought. Maybe she was waiting for her coffee to drip, standing there thinking about the day ahead of her. Maybe she was getting up to prepare breakfast for her husband and children before sending them off to work and to school. Or maybe she was even getting ready for work herself. I wondered if she were happy – if she had a job that she liked and a husband who loved her, kids who obeyed. I wondered what she was thinking about. Maybe it was hard for her to live at a crossroads. Maybe she even looked out of her window each morning as she sipped her coffee and wished that she, too, were going somewhere. Maybe she would even turn and look out at me and imagine – well, imagine just the kind of adventure I was having. Little did she know that at that moment, I would have traded places with her in a minute. I turned left when the light changed, because it took me past her house. The road also led me to the service station.

It felt good to get out of the car, to stand up and walk. Mr. Granger even got out and had me direct him to the toilets. I didn't have to help him, though, and I was grateful about that. Along with Erik, that would have been the second man I'd helped in a month to relieve himself and I figured that would have been some kind of weirdo record. While he was in there, I made sure to ask the attendant how to get back on the road to Washington. I'd gone at least 100 miles out of my way. Then I bought two bottles of RC Cola and a couple of candy bars, paid for the fill-up, then took care of some personal business myself. The attendant didn't know of any campgrounds in the area, but said that once we were on the east-bound highway, we could always pull into a rest stop and catch a few winks in the car. That was fine by me since sleeping in the car was what I was planning on doing anyway. I still had a little bit of driving ahead of me since I didn't want to stop before I was sure I was heading towards Washington. I was of no mind to miss that junction again.

I ran into Mr. Granger on the way back from the john. He followed me along almost dutifully, accepting an RC Cola, but refusing the candy bar saying the only thing he would eat between where we were and Washington would be saltines.

"Where are we, anyway, urchin?"

"Ohio."

"We're not in Pennsylvania yet?"

"Not yet," I answered.

He spun around, searching the screens behind his eyes.

"Not kidnapping me, are you? I'm not worth much."

I laughed. "No, Mr. Granger. I got a little lost."

He stuck his chin out at me. "Well, as long as we're not in New Orleans or some such place," he said, stumbling a few steps away from me. "Then again, never been to New Orleans. Which way is the confounded car, urchin?"

I got us both settled into the Fairlane. Another hour or so of driving and I'd be able to sleep. I felt a little relieved. Mr. Granger hadn't gotten too upset by my getting lost. Getting to Washington was just going to take us a little longer than planned, that was all. I was actually kind of pleased with myself. I'd driven all night and we were still in one piece. Maybe that morning as I pulled off the road to sleep, Darby Millar would open the letter I had mailed to her. I wondered if she would call my pa and how he would act when he got the news. Maybe I would call him from Puerto Rico to tell him that

I was all right. Not that I wanted him to try to find me, but that I was all right.

By the time I had driven a while on the highway and then found a place to pull over and sleep, Mr. Granger was wide awake. We were the Canaries and that island off of the coast of China: paradise and purgatory, polar opposites in a limited world. I cleared our things out of the back seat so that I could stretch out back there. I put our bags in the trunk with my big suitcase and, at Mr. Granger's request, carried the black piece to a picnic table in the shade in the rest area, and helped him to unwrap it. He still refused to eat, so while he ran his hands over the sculpture, I dug into the paper sack Pa had packed for me. The sandwiches were so good, they were poison. I was sure I would never taste anything as good again. I'd already forgotten the dreams I'd had of a life eating *arroz y habichuelas*.

I slept fitfully at first. I hadn't been able to pull the car up into the shade because of stone curbs placed around the parking lot. The sun beat mercilessly through the back window. I was hot. I couldn't get comfortable. The seat sloped back and tilted me into its crevice. I was too tall to stretch out completely, so I had to stick my feet through an open window which meant I was basically forced to lie on my back – my least favorite position. As the day went on and cooled some, I finally did fall asleep. And had a strange dream. I dreamt that I was a spaceman in the galaxy of Krypton, a spaceman like one Kal-El had dreamed of becoming. Once my space rocket had blasted off from Krypton's super gravity, I found myself hurtling towards "The Blue Planet," being reeled in by its atmosphere like a fish on a line. Frightened that my space rocket was going to crash into what looked like a watery planet and that I would drown, I gravely pushed the button that operated the "ejection" seat and was thrust from the craft. As I watched it crash into the blue globe below me, I breathed a sigh of relief. But my relief was short-lived. I was alone and floating in an unknown galaxy. My last thought was that maybe no one would ever find me.

I awoke with a start. The quick realization of my true situation wasn't much comfort, either. I couldn't help but think that the dream was some kind of omen. I wondered if I were doing the right thing. In any case, I had slept a lot longer than I thought. The sky was a smoky, orange haze. I was hungry again. I carried what was left of my picnic – a couple of pieces of cherry pie – over to the picnic table. Mr. Granger was seated there exactly as I had left him, hunched over the black piece.

"Well, well. If it ain't 'Rip Van Winkle,'" he said.

"Morning. Er – Evening. Whatever." I said, stumbling onto the bench next to him and inserting a leg under the table.

"Want some pie?"

"Gad, no. Trying to kill me?"

I shrugged. "No. Just trying to be nice."

Mr. Granger tilted his head. "I know that, urchin. I'll take some saltines when you get a chance."

I slid out from the table, got the saltines from his bag in the trunk and took them back to him.

"Thanks."

"Have you been sitting here the whole time I slept?" As soon as I asked the question, I was sorry. Mr. Granger stopped chewing long enough to stick his chin out at me. "Never mind," I said, quickly. "Don't answer that." We both laughed.

"How much longer until we get to Washington, urchin?"

"If we drive all night, I figure we ought to be there by morning," I answered.

"Sure you're on the right road this time?" he chided.

"Yeah. I checked. It should take us straight into D.C.," I assured him. "When is your meeting?"

"When I get there."

"Even on a Saturday morning?" I didn't bother to remind him that it was also Labor Day weekend. Everything would be closed, people were off from work.

"Got the fellow's phone number," he said, patting his shirt pocket.

I resisted the urge to reach into his pocket and check. If he were being dishonest, so was I. I guess that's why I'm the only one to blame for what happened. Mr. Granger went back to his work. I stared at the black, molded plastic. Darby Millar had guessed that it was a map, a prototype of some sort. While watching Mr. Granger run his hands over its valleys and slide them into its depressions, I had a sudden revelation into what it might be: a section of the Earth as he had been wanting people to see it – the Earth stripped of its clothing of oceans, its mask of seas. Mr. Granger had made a model of the plates that we had by then come to know existed – *under* the oceans – an acknowledged existence that had come too late to prevent Alfred Wegener from becoming the laughingstock of the scientific community with his theory of continental drift. Those working but unseen forces that had shaped our lives and determined our identities. That would explain why Mr. Granger had brought along the book. And why the model was black. Something that normally couldn't be seen didn't *need* color. It didn't need place names or route markers or state lines. It was the anti-thesis of everything cartography represented. Didn't Mr. Granger tell me once that he wanted to be the "anti-Christ of cartography"?

I swallowed the last bit of sandy pie crust and found myself wishing I had bought another bottle of RC Cola. I could have used something to drink – even a warm soda. I didn't know how Mr. Granger was dealing with all of those saltines, but they didn't seem to be bothering him. Anyone else would have choked on them by now. In fact, nothing seemed to be bothering him, he was so focused on his sculpture. For once, he didn't even seem to be in any particular hurry to get on the road. I figured it was my chance to ask him about the black piece. He had told me he would explain it to me when he was ready – *but there's nothing guaranteeing you'll understand*, he had said. I had learned and understood a lot of things since then. I felt like I was ready to know. Maybe he was ready to tell me. I was going to find out sooner or later, anyway. We'd probably be in Washington the next day.

"What is that, Mr. Granger?"

He tilted his head. "What?"

I laughed. *None is so blind as he who will not see.* "That. That thing you're touching. You said you would tell me. I'm ready to know."

"Then come here," he said. I slid up next to him. "Give me your hands." As I did, he placed them flatly on the sculpture and rested his own hands on their backs, layering my fingers with his. In the dusky light of the early evening, they looked like two white spiders coupling in a shadowy recess. He moved our hands together over the sculpture. I had never admitted to him that I had already touched it that day he had plastered his walls with map projections and lie sleeping on his cot. At its contact, I had the same, slightly sexual thrill. Something bid me to close my eyes. I felt a rush of pleasure then release. I saw myself as a bird soaring above the Earth. There was nothing of the terrifying flight of my dream; instead, there was an exhilarating feeling of movement, of freedom.

"This is great," I said, surprising myself.

"Oh?" Mr. Granger asked. "Tell me."

I knew he would probably end up making fun of me, but I couldn't resist trying to describe the emotions touching that black sculpture brought out in me. There was something so simple, so pure about it. Because it was all black and unscarred by markings of any kind, there was no image to confuse my mind – just this tactile sense of terrain at my fingertips. At the same time, there was a heady sense of flight, of being above things looking down.

"I feel like I'm flying," I said, turning to look at Mr. Granger. "Isn't that what you feel when you touch it?"

The old man wagged his head.

"Because of your motion sickness?" I'd forgotten about that.

"No, it's not that."

"What then?"

"Because it's my work."

"And there's no thrill in that?"

"Not the same."

"Why not?"

Mr. Granger held me in a non-blinking gaze.

"Because I know the work intimately. There's no romantic distance. And because I know the reality."

"Which is?"

"That it is a map – "

I closed my eyes at his words and felt my stomach rush as though I had just become airborne again. I imagined myself flying over that slightly mountainous block of obsidian as though it were the lava-rich crest of pressured earth.

"– of my backyard."

I opened my eyes.

"What?"

"Look, here," said Mr. Granger putting pressure on my right index finger. "This," he slid my finger into a groove, "is where there's an old drainage system and the ground has started to sink in around it. And this," he slid my hand over a slight mound, "is where I buried my old dog, Max."

I yanked my hands away, horrified.

"What's the matter, urchin? You said you wanted to know what it is. I'm telling you."

Maybe Aunt Sally was right after all. He was some kind of a madman. Here I was driving him to Washington, D.C. to show a *map of his backyard* to someone in Congress. We were sure to get thrown out on our ears. If they didn't throw us into the nuthouse. To think that I had left school for this. Erik was right. The world is round. And I kept ending up where I had started. Puerto Rico was the furthest place from my mind in that moment. I had more pressing concerns. I sat there stunned for a long time, not knowing which way to turn.

"I told you, you wouldn't understand."

What was to understand? Man had walked on the moon. We had discovered new depths to the sea. Medicine was charting unknown reaches inside our own bodies. And Mr. Granger's vision of "re-inventing" cartography was this: a hands-on map of his own backyard. A monument to his dead dog, Max. I stumbled away from him, saying I had to go to the bathroom. The cherry sweetness in my mouth tasted sickeningly like cough syrup. I wanted to vomit, but couldn't. The taste that seeped into my mouth slowly soured. Inside the rustic outhouse, I sat on the toilet and held my head in my hands. The place reeked of sewage and buzzed with flies. I didn't care. I cried – long, gasping sobs. I knew that I could never leave him in Washington. In fact, it would be cruel even to take him there. I was sure that no one was waiting for him, that he had no appointment. I'd known it all along, but had refused to acknowledge it. The irony of my behavior didn't escape me. I had handled this situation in much the same way I had always looked at maps: not daring to see the artifice behind the intention. What was I supposed to do? I couldn't very well abandon him on the side of the road, hoping that some strange wind, some angelic force would guide him safely home. In my mind's eye, I saw him as he was when I had gone to pick him up – standing on the sidewalk, his arms crossed over his chest, with the duffle bag and the black sculpture wrapped carefully in newspaper next to him on the broken cement. I should have left him there. I should have driven past him without even slowing down. He would have eventually been forced to return to that hovel of his that he had wallpapered with images he could no longer see. I would be breaking my promise to him, but maybe saving the two of us. Here I was responsible for his life when I hardly knew how to care for my own.

I heard Mr. Granger call out my name. I needed to get up. As awful as I felt at that moment, I still had to admit to myself that sitting in an outhouse sobbing wasn't going to help me any. I dried my eyes and went out to join him. Somehow, I managed to help him wrap up the sculpture; then I carried it back to the car. As I was doing so, the thought crossed my mind that maybe if I let it slip – or better, threw it hard to the ground – I would manage to break it into a million pieces. Then Mr. Granger would have no more reason to go to Washington. He'd be mad as a hornet, but my problem would be solved. The only reason I didn't throw the plastic piece to the ground was the quick and sad understanding that my problem wasn't the sculpture, but the man. Somehow, I was going to have to separate myself from him. If I ever wanted to reach Puerto Rico – and I did suddenly then more than ever – I was going to have to get him on a bus back to Painted Creek.

Despite myself, I slid the sculpture into the back seat and helped Mr. Granger into the front. I pulled out onto the highway and drove like a robot for the next several hours – eyes straight ahead and my mind a total blank. I realized somehow then what a rolling weapon of destruction a car is. Despite my somnambulistic night driving, I hadn't – miraculously enough – forced anyone from the road or provoked any major mishap to another vehicle. Traffic was relatively light. As far as our safety was concerned, well – I wasn't so sure I cared about that anymore. As we drove on and on, deeper into the night, I became more and more certain that the only solution that remained was to break the black sculpture. Only in that way would Mr. Granger ever agree to return home. Besides, I wasn't planning on giving him any choice.

We had passed the turn-off for Pittsburgh a long time back. None of the names of the other Pennsylvania towns on the passing signs sounded even vaguely familiar. I figured that in order to find a Greyhound bus station, I'd probably need a pretty big town. I'd get him on a bus going back towards Detroit. The problem would be to get him from Detroit to Painted Creek. His nephew wasn't around to pick him up, and Darby Millar didn't have a car. I could call Father Wilhelm, but I almost hated to use the call. I'd probably be needing his help myself later. With a bit of luck, Erik would still be around. He owed me a favor as far as I could tell, anyway. I'd call him and ask him to drive down to Detroit and pick up Mr. Granger.

That decided, I drove on. With nothing to measure them against, both time and miles flew by. Truth be told, I was probably going way over the speed limit. And, Lord knows, my thoughts were racing even faster than the Fairlane. When I finally read the time on a lighted sign announcing a service station, it was already five o'clock in the morning. I told Mr. Granger that I needed a break and pulled off into the nearest rest stop. He wanted to stay in the car, but I made him get out saying that I wanted to touch the black piece one more time before we got to Washington. That I wanted to understand. I carried the sculpture to a nearby picnic table and unwrapped it. The pre-dawn air had an eerie stillness to it. Mr. Granger hurried me along, saying the time for understanding had come miles ago. I didn't tell him how right he was. As I was carrying the sculpture back to the car, I let it fall. It hit the ground with a dull thud. Mr. Granger didn't flinch.

"C'mon," he said, irritated.

"Oh, Mr. Granger!" I cried. "I dropped your map!"

"I heard," he growled. "No biggie. Almost impossible to break. Unless you take a hammer to it, of course. Or put a ton of pressure on it. Made it that way on purpose. Now, let's get going."

I picked the sculpture up from the ground and took it to the car. I tossed it into the back seat and slammed the door. So much for Plan A. *"Damn it!"* I thought to myself.

"Gad, urchin. Need to be makin' such a racket? Enough to wake the living dead!"

My anger soon gave way to desolation. Mr. Granger had become an albatross around my neck. The rest of the trip would be sheer penance. The car crept slowly down the narrow corridor of the on-ramp towards the highway. I had become so numb I couldn't even feel the accelerator beneath my foot. I directed us out onto the highway without looking left or right, ahead or back. In fact, I think I was looking down at my hands on the wheel to see, in fact, if I were really holding it. The deep sound of a truck horn pierced the silence of the dawn. In my tortured mind, it sounded like an ocean-going freighter leaving safe harbor. Or a fog horn blasting through the mist. I heard it as if I were under water; it sounded slower and somehow more distant than it actually was. When I finally lifted my head, a blinding flash of light shot out from the rearview mirror. The horn bellowed again like the dying moan of a sacrificial cow. I heard the screech of brakes as the 18-wheel trailer truck tried to slow to avoid us. I gripped the wheel and pulled hard right. Starboard, captain. Then the lights went out.

* * *

I came to wondering if I had died and gone to heaven, which was surprising after all of the lies I had told recently. I was devastated. I was too young to die. I hadn't even had time to live. It took me a minute to realize that I was still alive, so then I wondered if the beams of light shooting up and over my head were the *aurora borealis*, but I didn't know if they could be seen in Pennsylvania. What were they?

The question shook me from my stupor. They were the lights of emergency vehicles. I looked over at Mr. Granger. He was sitting, still strapped in his seat, his head tilted to one side the way he had been for most of the trip. His eyes were closed and he didn't move. I softly called his name. No response. I looked out in a trance over the hood of the car. The headlights were buried into the ground. Tufts of grass stuck out from where the metal had buckled. I felt a presence behind me. I turned to look and saw that the back seat had been pushed forward and tilted up, and that, in fact, the entire rear end was up and over our heads. We were sandwiched between two layers of metal. Near my head hung a shredded strip of old newspaper. The black sculpture was wedged between floor and ceiling, now a mere foot and a half from each other. It was cracked cleanly in two.

* * *

Nick Granger died – several years later, that is. We both made it out of the accident only badly shaken up and with lots of bumps and bruises, but alive. The firemen who pulled us from the car had said it was thanks to the fact that we were wearing our seat belts. The Fairlane had borne the brunt of the impact. I had turned off the road and directly into a drainage canal that ran alongside. As the front end nose-dived, the back end smacked the hard, upper rim of the canal and creased the car in two. When Pa and I went by DiVolterra's after I got out of the hospital to salvage whatever we could from the trunk, I had to admit that it looked pretty spectacular. A big steel *taco*.

Mr. Granger was a big hit at the hospital. Nobody could believe that a man his age had made it through an accident like that virtually unscathed. The nurses waited on him hand and foot and he flirted shamelessly. He had insisted that we share a room. I was feeling pretty bad about the sculpture and all. And I told him so. He said not to worry about it, that he still had the mold he had cast it from at home. He could make another one. Besides, he had added, he had an open invitation from the manager of the art gallery to show it any time he wanted.

"*Art* gallery?" I asked.

"Yeah. Art gallery."

"I thought it was a map."

"It is, of sorts. Tongue-in-cheek. It's meant to be a kind of pun."

"I thought you were taking it to *National Geographic* or someplace. The Smithsonian."

Nick Granger tilted his head. "What do you think, urchin? I'm crazy?"

After we got back home, I went to see Mr. Granger every day, even on the weekends. He promised to teach me as much about cartography, sculpture – and life – as he possibly could. And he kept his promise. It didn't take me long to realize that I wasn't very good at sculpture, but I loved feeling the clay in my hands. At Pa's urging, I enrolled in an evening course in pottery at the college. As my potter's wheel spun around and around, I created worlds, then destroyed them then built them up again. It was very satisfying. I went back to school at Millarsburg

High School and never said a word to anyone about my trip. I decided to study hard, and completely ignore everyone else around me – everyone, that is, except for Lisa. She was a dark-haired, doe-eyed girl who had recently moved to Millarsburg. Her father, Mr. Martinelli, had opened up a deli in town. She worked behind the counter after school. That's where I usually went before going off to see Mr. Granger. Sometimes she came out from behind the counter and sat with me at the small, wrought-iron table in the front of the store while I finished my hot chocolate and *cannoli* – but only if her pa wasn't watching.

I didn't go back to the library much after the accident and, the few times I did, Miss Millar never said anything about my letter. I began to wonder if she had ever received it. If she hadn't, I had no idea where it could have gone off to. And if she had, she had never said a word about it to anyone that I could tell. It was just as well. Everyone had other things on their minds.

Not but a few hours after my departure that Thursday evening, Treat had shown up. Aunt Sally said she found him standing like a ghost at her back door. He had grown thin and looked haggard beyond his years. Uncle Will told me that Treat had agreed to see a doctor for a physical, but refused any kind of psychological help though the best description of the way he looked would have been "shell-shocked." He hardly spoke a word for almost six months, so it took us that long to find out a little bit about his tale. He never fully admitted to where he had gone nor why. But his health was so run down by the time he came back to us that he received a medical dispensation from the Army. Uncle Will wondered aloud more than a few times if he hadn't already served – sneaked off and joined up – given the way he looked.

It was just as I was getting ready to enter college in Painted Creek and Lisa and I were a pretty steady thing, that I got up the nerve to ask Treat about Celia. He acted as though he hardly remembered her. When I insisted, he suggested that I write to Erik. He and Celia's brother, Carlos, had stayed in contact all of that time. I found out later from Erik that Carlos was gaining a fair renown as a musician. He played for one of the big-time *jíbara* orchestras in *Nueva York*. Celia's mother had finally left Enrique, who, it turns out, wasn't Celia's father after all, but an auto worker from Detroit whom her mother had dated briefly and had finally left because he beat her. Celia's real father had died of cancer when she was young. Celia was apparently so devastated by his death, that she had pledged to become a doctor when she grew up and conduct cancer research. That thin wisp of a woman who had so tantalized my thoughts for months was nothing of the gypsy waif I had tried to turn her into. Erik wrote to say that she had won a full scholarship to study at the University of Michigan. Erik, for his part, was working in a gay bookstore in San Francisco and, from his letters, seemed to have found a place where he belonged.

Treat started part-time at the University last fall, so he and I drive together, and it's almost like old times except that he's much quieter than he used to be. I figure he'll tell me what happened to him when he's ready – or never. That's all right by me. On the way to class, I purposely drive past Mr. Granger's old apartment and get a little pang each time I see that a light is on. Darby Millar paid for a burial plot for him in Millarsburg Memorial Cemetery. He and ol' Copernicus are probably both spinning in their graves. Mr. Granger's plot is not too far from my ma's, so when I go to take care of her grave, I tug a few weeds from around his as well. But not too many. I can almost hear him yelling, "That's enough, urchin!" I'm sure he wouldn't want it looking too tidy.

The summer after my eighteenth birthday, and just before I

started at the college, Ruth Anne and Jean-Christophe paid for me to visit them in Brussels, where they had gone for the birth of their daughter. They named her *Kiese*, which means "joy" in the Kikongo language. On the flight to Belgium, I read a strange story in *The International Herald Tribune* of the bizarre death of a young Nigerian. It seems he was so determined to go to Europe, despite having no money to pay for the ticket, that he hid himself in the landing gear of a plane headed for London. High above the sweltering Sahara, his body had fused into a frozen block of blood and bones that fell from the sky when the plane reached its destination. I decided that no one should ever want to go anywhere that badly.

That said, I'm still hoping someday to make it to Puerto Rico. If not to live, then at least to visit. Maybe I'll take Lisa one day for our honeymoon. But only after we both finish school. At present, I'm trying to figure out which way to direct my studies, now that I've got a year of college under my belt. Mr. Granger pretty much convinced me not to study cartography – or at least, not to specialize in it. He said I'd only end up being a bad sculptor. I'm starting to lean towards geology. Plate tectonics has become a serious field of study and Alfred Wegener is finally getting the recognition he deserved. He was the one who got me started on this odyssey, after all. Sometimes I take out his book and open it to his picture.

He knew I'd never become a cartographer.

That's what he was grinning about.

ACKNOWLEDGMENTS

Although Bass' journey begins in the late 1960s and takes place over several years, the path this novel took from the first version (written by hand into a bound notebook) to this version spans over three decades and as many continents. As pleased as I am that it has finally found a safe harbor, it is possible that many of those who helped along the way have forgotten its existence. I hope I have forgotten no one in trying, these many years later, to thank them.

The first person to thank is Lisa Diane Kastner of Running Wild Press for being willing to publish what is, in fact, a simple story from a different era, but a story of self-discovery I hope still resonates with many.

Thanks also to Juanita Jauer Seichen for reading and correcting a very early version of the text and to Leslie Séveno for putting us in contact. My former colleague, Andrew Davies, read a later but no doubt equally horrible version with a great deal of attention and seriousness – for which I thank him. A tip of the (baseball) cap to my friend Joel Treese, a gentle soul who left us much too early. Cynthia Costas-Centivany was a willing public relations ambassador for the extraordinary island of Puerto Rico.

I am particularly indebted to Professor Mark Monmonier whose work, *How to Lie with Maps* (2nd edition, University of Chicago Press) and *Drawing the Line: Tales of Maps and Cartocontroversy* (Henry Holt and Company), so greatly impressed and influenced me I wrote to ask him if he would review the parts of the novel dealing with the history of maps – and he generously agreed.

While not an exhaustive list, several other titles consulted during the early gestation of the book helped to broaden my knowledge of the history of mapmaking including *The Image of the World: 20 Centuries of World Maps* by Peter Whitfield (Pomegranate Artbooks), *Longitude* (Walker and Company) by Dava Sobel, and Peter Gould and Antoine Bailly's book examining the work of Brian Harley, *Le pouvoir des cartes: Brian Harley et la cartographie* (Philippe de Lavergne, translator; Editions Economica). I first saw a copy of the "Know Thyself" map Nicolas Granger hangs in his apartment in Mireille Pastoureau's book, *Voies Océanes: de l'ancien aux nouveaux mondes* (Editions Hervas).

Continental drift theory and plate tectonics are, of course, the topic of Alfred Wegener's book, *The Origin of Continents and Oceans* (John Biram, translator; Dover Publications, Inc.). I also consulted *New Views on an Old Planet* (University of Cambridge) by Tjeerd H. Van Andel.

The dictionary Mr. Granger wants Bass to read from is based on *The Oxford Companion to the English Language* (Tom McArthur, editor. Oxford University Press, 1992).

ABOUT RUNNING WILD PRESS

Running Wild Press publishes stories that cross genres with great stories and writing. RIZE publishes great genre stories written by people of color and by authors who identify with other marginalized groups. Our team consists of:

Lisa Diane Kastner, Founder and Executive Editor
Cody Sisco, Acquisitions Editor, RIZE
Benjamin White, Acquisition Editor, Running Wild
Peter A. Wright, Acquisition Editor, Running Wild
Resa Alboher, Editor
Angela Andrews, Editor
Sandra Bush, Editor
Ashley Crantas, Editor
Rebecca Dimyan, Editor
Abigail Efird, Editor
Aimee Hardy, Editor
Henry L. Herz, Editor
Cecilia Kennedy, Editor
Barbara Lockwood, Editor

ABOUT RUNNING WILD PRESS

Scott Schultz, Editor
Rod Gilley, Editor

Evangeline Estropia, Product Manager
Kimberly Ligutan, Product Manager
Lara Macaione, Marketing Director
Joelle Mitchell, Licensing and Strategy Lead
Pulp Art Studios, Cover Design
Standout Books, Interior Design
Polgarus Studios, Interior Design

Learn more about us and our stories at www.runningwild-press.com

Loved these stories and want more? Follow us at runningwildpublishing.com, www.facebook.com/runningwild-press, on Twitter @lisadkastner @RunWildBooks